Shakespeare's Revenge

John O'Shea

iUniverse, Inc.
New York   Bloomington

Shakespeare's Revenge

Cover art: Willem Claesz, Vanitas Still Life, Royal Picture Gallery Mauritshuis, The Hague.

Cover design by Rachel Liu

Map of Maine courtesy of the U.S. Geological Survey.

iUniverse books may be ordered through booksellers or by contacting:

iUniverse
1663 Liberty Drive
Bloomington, IN 47403
www.iuniverse.com
1-800-Authors (1-800-288-4677)

Because of the dynamic nature of the Internet, any Web addresses or links contained in this book may have changed since publication and may no longer be valid. The views expressed in this work are solely those of the author and do not necessarily reflect the views of the publisher, and the publisher hereby disclaims any responsibility for them.

ISBN: 978-1-4502-3982-0 (sc)
ISBN: 978-1-4502-3984-4 (dj)
ISBN: 978-1-4502-3983-7 (ebk)

Printed in the United States of America

iUniverse rev. date: 9/14/2010

Acknowledgements

All authors, even the mighty bard himself, get by with a little help from friends. Thank you Tommy, Jimmy, Nicole and Mom for your reviews, and early encouragement. And Mom, thanks for the translations.

Timmy O'Shea, thanks for your suggestions.

Thank you Dave King and Claire Matze for your editing skills. Your suggestions made for some great improvements. Karen Vice, the march forward wouldn't have been as much fun without your guidance.

Rachel, thank you for thinking through the design and appearance.

Thank you family—Beth, Jack, Dillon, Kenzie, and Keely—for letting me huddle with the research and the laptop at all hours and locations. There's a little bit of each of you in here, mostly on the good guys' side.

Under the weather, I never got better, wrapped up in my disease...

Stare it Cold

The Black Crowes

Revenge should have no bounds.

Hamlet

Shakespeare

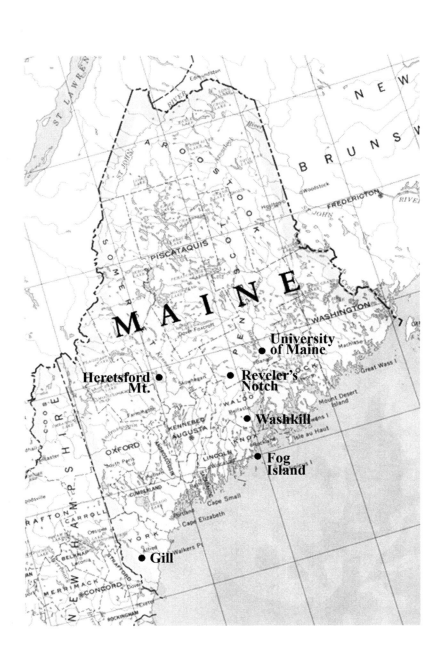

Prologue

Friday, September 6, 1628

Captain Dwyer manned the wheel as First Mate James Swanson staggered up to the deck, one hand holding his neck. The man's weight had deserted him. His beard had turned to a stringy filth. Just as Dwyer had hoped, the disease was taking control. Still, he had to admit, Swanson had proved resilient. Swanson's voice faded in and out as he struggled to speak. "Porter just jumped."

The news was no surprise to Dwyer—that man was a lunatic. "Sorry, James."

"Said he was going to burn the cats."

Dwyer tried to think of something sympathetic. "He was a digger. He dug holes his entire life. Holes that went nowhere. And he never wanted for more. Men like that are rarely in their right mind."

Swanson lunged to the ship's rail and started retching. Dwyer watched Swanson's back stiffen with each dry heave. The man's resistance embittered Dwyer. *Just jump, already ...*

Instead, Dwyer watched Swanson struggle for the next couple minutes. Dwyer touched his own neatly banded hair and was reassured by its firmness. Swanson seemed to gather himself, and then he tugged his telescope from the pouch tied to his belt. He put it to his eye and looked toward the horizon.

Dwyer snickered to himself. *That's right, no help in sight.* He had long envied that telescope with its two arching falcons etched in bronze on the sides—a handsome piece. Swanson had said it was a present from his wife's family. No matter, it would be Dwyer's soon. Swanson was too weak to keep his focus for long, and his hands collapsed to his sides. The telescope clocked the deck and rolled away from him.

A wind drove across the deck and stretched the sails. Dwyer felt it in the wheel. "Who can assist if we get stronger winds? Or if this grows—God forbid—into a storm?"

Swanson shook his head. "Holstom and Breckenridge have passed. We're the last who can stand."

Outstanding, Dwyer thought. *His lordship is a genius. One hundred percent effectiveness.*

"It makes no sense," Swanson said. "There were no signs of sickness on the way over, nor ashore for that matter. By design we avoided contact with anyone. How could—"

"James, don't torture yourself."

Dwyer saw Swanson's jaw tighten, as if he were readying for an argument. A sudden calm seemed to settle on his first mate and his shoulders relaxed. "Maybe you're right." Then Swanson slid down and sat against the ship's side.

Dwyer saw him eyeing the deck cannons piled next to the wheel. *What's he thinking—that I am aggregating fortifications to be able to defend the ship?* Dwyer followed Swanson's bloodshot eyes. The first mate looked across the deck to the empty ship's rail, where one of the guns was normally mounted and could be easily swung from side to side in the final stages of battle; accuracy at that point wasn't essential. Dwyer eyed the man cautiously.

"I'm curious," Swanson said. "Every time I begin to wonder where this sickness came from, you divert me."

Dwyer saw him struggle with each word. The man's throat was clearly burning.

"What—what aren't you telling me?"

Dwyer edged the wheel to keep the ship on course. He would've liked to have used Swanson's telescope. Mayne should be coming into view soon. With the scope's help, he would've been able to see it edging over the horizon.

"Why're you smiling?" Swanson asked.

Dwyer wasn't aware that he had been smiling. *Shit.* But did it really matter now? Swanson couldn't stand any longer, and he was the last with any strength, maybe the last with a heartbeat. Dwyer squeezed the wheel in victory. After five months of planning, Act One, as the old man called it, was complete. He remembered the night his lordship had knocked on his door. He had heard of the man, of course, but had never met him. He was shorter than Dwyer expected, but he was more compelling in conversation than even he would've thought. At first Dwyer was suspicious, but through the course of the bottle they shared together, Dwyer grew alive hearing the man's grand scheme for revenge. At the time, Dwyer still stewed with bitterness and anger. He had just returned from a voyage to Denmark and learned that his wife and child, while visiting her sister up north in Danbury, had been caught in a quarantine. In the end, they shriveled in desiccation along with the entire village.

His majesty refused to lift a finger to assist. As one of the last to enter the village, his wife Rita and son Charles surely could have been removed and evaluated. They were all he lived for, all he thought about during the long, cold nights in his quarters, rocking up and dropping down with each wave while chewing countless slabs of leather, night after bone-chilling night. Before the old man could finish telling him the details of his plan, Dwyer had sworn allegiance.

He looked over at Swanson. A tear of blood ran down the sick sailor's face, but he barely had the strength to wipe it away. "You've been a good mate, James," Dwyer said.

"What?"

"You served your country, your king, and Elizabeth before him well. Eleanor, Jeremy, and Mason will all be proud." *Too bad they won't know what hit them.*

Swanson's eyes dropped to the deck cannons and then shifted back to Dwyer. Even though Swanson's fatal condition made it irrelevant, Dwyer was thankful he had left half of the cannons on shore. He jumped into conversation, not wanting Swanson to focus on the deck guns. "I told you to decline this one."

"We—we've been through this ..." Swanson coughed up what seemed to Dwyer like a layer of the man's throat. "The old man offered gold, a lot."

"You did it to avoid Eleanor's wrath," Dwyer said. "I told you she would forgive you, but you wouldn't listen." Dwyer remembered the distraught, whiskey-soaked Swanson imploring him for a slot on the voyage. Swanson's wife had recently learned of his infidelity and had banished him from their home with a public rage. Every neighbor in a three-block radius could hear her scream, even the chickens and hogs in the streets scurried for shelter. Swanson came to Dwyer and said he needed time to let her cool. Dwyer and Swanson had been friends for years. They had crossed the latitudes together several times. Swanson implored him so savagely that for Dwyer to not bestow a favor might have drawn suspicion.

Swanson shook his head and wiped the ooze—his ooze—from his face. It turned Dwyer's stomach to look at him. "You've never seen her so mad ... you ... you ... *you* told *me?* Told me? Do you mean, *warned* me?" Swanson's face whitened. His hand fell to his gut.

"Conserve yourself, Jim."

Swanson squeezed his belly. Words came through his tightened teeth. "Why aren't you sick?"

"Jim, why don't you go lie down? We've got a few weeks left before we get back to London." *In your case, a few hours.*

"Why aren't you sick?" Swanson repeated, looking up and shielding his eyes from the sun with a hand. "We did everything together—dig, eat, sleep, drink. Wait, drink ..."

There it was. Dwyer glanced at Swanson and then back to the sea. He recalled the event from just over a week ago. It had gone just as they planned. While Swanson and the crew finished work on the second vault, his lordship closed the rum cases with his *solution*. Dwyer laughed. Even he had to admit the old man had a way with the language—always another meaning in the words. When the men returned that night from their final day's work, the old man surprised the crew with a gift—the rum.

"You didn't drink with us on shore eight days ago. Said you were shitting your brains through your arse."

"I was."

Swanson began to pull himself up the deck's sidewall. "You're ... you're lying."

"That will be enough."

Swanson squeezed his chest and coughed a fine spray of red onto the deck. "You and the old man ... you stayed up late. And he conveniently awaited our return on shore in the lighthouse we built for him. What—what were you doing?"

"Enough, Swanson!"

"You hate the throne! It curls you! But what?"

Dwyer didn't like the crease forming around Swanson's eyes. The sick man staggered free from the sidewall. He tried to lick his lips. *Good luck,* Dwyer mused, *you might as well try moistening tree bark.*

Swanson held himself firmly with his remaining strength as waves pushed the ship and its sails flapped. "You knew this would happen. That insane old man. We didn't just dig him a vault under a river, did we? He's not looking for a quiet retirement away from the mobs of London." Swanson coughed. "You ... you did this. You created this sickness."

"What's left of the rum, James?"

"These men have done nothing but serve loyally, goddamn you!"

"At ease, Swanson!"

"They have families!"

"In a year's time, none of that will matter."

With hands on knees, Swanson labored to breathe. Dwyer thought he looked as though an anvil weighed on his back.

Swanson raised himself to nearly full height and looked on Dwyer with disgust befitting someone diddling a four-year-old boy. "What do you mean, it won't matter? How did you ... did you avoid this sickness?"

"I can't explain it, Jim."

Swanson held himself upright with a line from the mainsheet. "What now? You're going to deliver a ship of disease to the wharf? Is that it?" Swanson tried to take another step, but his left leg buckled in front of him. He snagged a beam with both hands.

Dwyer wrinkled his nose as the breeze brought him Swanson's scent. "Stay where you are. We agreed. Keep your distance."

"Out with it, you cur!" Amid more coughing, Swanson sank to his knees. He choked on his cough, and globules of eggplant-colored muck splattered on the deck. He shook his head as if to clear the webbing from his mouth. "Out with it! I'm dead soon enough. Is this because of the judgment passed against him? He's a failed lord, a poet, a playwright—I don't give a goddamn—he thinks he was wronged so he destroys a ship?"

That line drew Dwyer's attention. When Swanson pulled himself up, the open sores on his hands left streaks of blood on the ship's sidewall. He had closed to within fifteen feet of the wheel.

Dwyer smirked. "A ship? Not rightly. He has his sights set a bit higher." Dwyer enjoyed seeing Swanson's face drop.

"What do you mean ... the king?"

"And then some." Oh, this felt good.

"What ... England?"

Dwyer couldn't keep himself from smiling.

"Don't you think they'll think it strange? A sole survivor on *The Broadside?*"

"Not when I tell them about the treasure I've found."

"Treasure?" Pronouncing the "T" made Swanson's nose bubble. It was leaking a blood-bile-rum-mix.

"I haven't decided yet. It could be a China passage, a city of gold, or the water of life. Whatever I choose, it'll be news fit for his majesty and the council."

"If England's your target, why are we headed back to Mayne?"

Dwyer smiled. "Need to tell my lord the experiment worked."

"You experimented on us. You infected us."

"Actually, it was his lordship."

"You're fooling yourself. He's no more a lord than you or I. They stripped him of that."

"We'll see about that."

"And the two of you will just sail this back across the ocean?"

Dwyer laughed. "Oh, I think *family* down in Virginia will lend us a hand."

"Bartholomew's men are smarter than that."

"In this case, blood runs thicker than brains. Our lord has fashioned a treat that the entire city will enjoy. It will be lovely when their royal selves are the first. He's such a genius with chemicals."

Swanson's eyes expanded. "My wife and son ... the whole city will perish?"

"It may not stop there." It was time to end this. Dwyer's hand flashed behind him and came around outstretched.

Swanson gasped. Dwyer held a pistol barrel eight paces from Swanson's face.

"You can't." Swanson coughed and gripped the beam so tightly his fingernails dug into the wood. "He had his chance. He had prestige. He had power. He had the fucking ear of the king! But he blew it! Why can't he just sit there with all of his *magnificent* works, all of his secrets and die … for real this time?"

Dwyer's shoulders hiccupped as he giggled.

Swanson's neck and face reddened. "We crossed the Atlantic for him! We built the fucking light station! The river was a killer—we lost James!"

"Don't forget the inscription you managed. To bury Caesar? Not quite." Dwyer's thumb brought the hammer back. Suddenly, like a change in the wind's direction, Swanson brightened, and his cracked lips and bile-lathered teeth managed a smile.

What's he doing? He's dead! Doesn't he get it? Swanson's repudiation siphoned the sweetness from the moment. In that instant, the disconnect sparked images in Dwyer's mind, his imaginings of the last moments of his beloved Rita and Charles, puss-soaked and suffering, curled in mud.

Swanson coughed. "Enjoy hell." Dwyer squeezed the trigger.

Klapcho!

Dwyer thought the musket ball sounded like a broom beating a rug when it slammed into Swanson's chest. Swanson toppled back and crashed onto his ass, his head clocking the mast. Dwyer sniffed the gun smoke—he loved the smell of sulfur. He heard Swanson gurgling, struggling to breathe. The fool looked as though he were trying to will his eyes open.

Dwyer turned to toss the gun onto the barrel behind him and glimpsed a flash, a hint of someone behind him. The flaming captain's lantern crashed down on him in a burst of glass, fire, and oil, and Dwyer felt an incredible spike of pain across his head. As he roiled in pain, he saw Midshipman Marcus Porter standing and dripping seawater behind him, coughing and holding a mangled lantern.

Dwyer stumbled sideways, blood running from the top of his head and flowing down over his ears. Lamp oil erupted in flame up and down his body. In the first instant, there were pockets of fire, but within a second the patches of flame joined together.

Porter's ragged shirt and pants also ignited. He flailed his arms to extinguish the blaze, but his motions only fueled the fire. The shaggy Porter giggled like the sick, aged seaman he was. "Ocean was too cold today." His rotted, toothpick teeth shook in his smile. Then his hair flashed into flame.

Dwyer back-pedaled and tucked his arms under one another. He spun desperately, clawing at everything, hoping for something to stop, to cool the heat! His final moments of sight were flashes of images—Swanson coughing blood over his chin, Porter's blackened, burning body bent forward over the wheel, the wheel and the deck around it flaming now, the deck cannons stacked solid, ignorant of the flames around them, and a hint of the shore in the distance, a tease—the ship would never make it. The searing pain was so intense, Dwyer dug his nails into himself to strip off his own flesh. His chest erupted, then his hair, his nose!

Swanson tried to stand, but he had lost power in his limbs. Better this way. The ship and its contagion would burn to the sea. He had no idea why Porter came back or how he managed to board the ship after jumping, but God bless him.

Swanson's head knocked against the deck. His lungs were too full to function. He saw the deck cannons staring back at him. *See you at the bottom, lads.*

Through slits, he watched Dwyer, or at least his flaming legs and boots, stagger and collide with the rail and then disappear in a flip overboard. With his last tick of consciousness, Swanson heard a splash.

Chapter 1

The minivan's wheels were twenty feet from his back tire.

"Goddamn lunatic!" Tanner Cook muttered. His shins and forearms shook as his bike soared across the back road's surface.

The minivan closed the gap. Tanner curled his six-foot frame, his legs crunching through rotations on the pedals. The minivan's front bumper grinned, ready to crunch Tanner's rear tire.

"No!" Tanner jerked left, and the minivan cut through the image of where Tanner had been. Tanner lifted the entire bike—back and front—and sailed over a wide dip. The minivan dropped into the pit, scraped its front bumper, and spasmed up and down.

Tanner's ankles blurred around the pedals' center. As he approached a sharp turn, he heard the minivan's engine snarl in pursuit. He plowed forward at an all-out sprint—up off the seat, over the handle bars, and leaning full forward. When he hit the turn, he squeezed his rear brake and leaned into the left armpit of the turn. He exhaled and leaned lower and lower until he was inches from searing his left leg on the unpaved road. He had done this before, but not for ten years.

Nearly flat to the ground, he rubber-banded around the curve. A simple pebble under one of the tires at the wrong angle could topple him and scatter him across the road. The minivan sailed wide, and its wheels locked up, sliding it across the road. Tanner righted himself and jumped back up on the pedals, punishing them. He put distance between himself and the shaken minivan.

The house sat an eighth of a mile up on the right. Tanner's brakes hissed as he skidded to a stop in front of the house. A dust storm swirled around him and stuck to his lathered body. He dismounted and let his bike down gently, the way a lead dancer might dip his partner. The tall, dry grass swallowed the bike. He unstrapped his helmet and put his gloves into it. He knew the goofball would be along shortly.

Across the wide lawn of tall, uncut grass stood an ancient colonial. It leaned hard to its right as if it were nursing an old bullet wound. The Maine September air smelled clean. He wiped his brow and took in the house.

The owner here had died tragically in the woods upstate, his body discovered fully clothed in the basin of a river. The autopsy revealed he had drowned. Without a will, the house had been turned over to the state to dispense with as part of its unclaimed property program. Tanner's role was to ready the property for public auction since neither the town nor the county viewed this out-of-the-way lot a potential strategic asset. During his preparations, Tanner was also supposed to see if any connections to relatives were left undiscovered by the county's brief search process. Perhaps there was something telling in the house, or maybe a neighbor was aware of distant relations. Judging by the decrepit shape of this home, he had his work cut out for him. There was something odd about this house, even beyond its tilt.

From behind him, Tanner heard the growl of the minivan. It pulled to the side of the road in front of Tanner's bike. A round man stepped from the driver's side. He was Tanner's long-time friend, Rack Manning.

"It's a shit hole," Rack said. His blubbery arm shielded the last of the day's sun from his eyes.

"How about a little appreciation for the speed, my man," Tanner said.

An attractive young woman popped out of the van's passenger side.

"Hi," she said. "Awesome speed back there."

"Hi," Tanner said. It was all he could think to say. Her smile illuminated her face. She was tan and seemed full of energy.

She waved as she approached. "Kyle Murray."

"I'm Tanner."

Rack came around the minivan. "Kyle and I met last night. Just after you went to bed, Grandma."

"Ahh," Tanner said.

"Kyle is new in town, from California. She wanted to tag along today and see what a real-life estate coroner does for a living."

Tanner enjoyed the opportunity the introduction gave him to view Kyle. He couldn't find a flaw—athletic body, no fat, a beautiful face, and a healthy tan. *She's definitely not from around here.* "Welcome."

"Thanks."

Tanner turned to Rack. "Coroner, huh?"

"Dude, you clean out homes of dead people."

"I work for the state—more like a paralegal with a broom. I get a call as soon as the corner's office can't locate any next of kin."

Kyle nodded and dipped her chin in the direction of the house. "How long has he been … you know …?"

"Coming up on four weeks. He drowned hiking in the woods upstate. System can work pretty quickly sometimes. The state traced him through the library card in his wallet. Public notice was listed in the newspapers two weeks ago. I got the call two days ago. Sorry you had to drive with Rackles, here. What was it for you guys, an hour and a half before you caught me?"

"Exactly." Rack produced a can of Miller Lite beer from his shirt pocket. "How's the kicker?"

3

Tanner looked down at his right leg and flexed it. His thigh felt as if someone was tenderizing him with an ice pick, but he didn't want to appear weak. "It's fine. So, why'd you want to come all the way out here?"

Rack glanced over at Kyle. "Can't a friend check in on his buddy? Haven't seen you pedaling, in, what, five weeks now?"

"Six, I think." Tanner turned toward the old house.

"You think we might see you training soon?"

Tanner turned sharply back toward Rack and gave him a death glare. When he saw Kyle and her high-energy grin, he relented.

Rack gestured toward the house, clearly trying to transfer the conversation in another direction. "I can't believe you got stuck with this outhouse."

Tanner started high-stepping through the forest of grass. "Let's see what we've got."

"I'm probably picking up a good dozen chiggers in here," Rack said as he waded to the house. He cracked the beer. "My horticulturist says they usually travel in packs of ten."

"Then carry me." Kyle hopped up on Rack's back.

"Jeez." Careful not to spill his beer, he caught her legs and bent forward to support her weight.

Tanner watched the antics over his shoulder. *Where does she get her energy? Does she* know *who she's dealing with?* Tanner's foot *klunked* against something in the tall grass. "Shit!" He reached for his stinging toe.

"Big-ass chigger?" Rack asked and laughed. His rider giggled too. Even Tanner cracked a smile.

"No." He lifted the rusty skull of a mailbox. It was attached to a rotted wooden pole.

"Hats off to the postman who can find that sucker," Rack said. With Kyle still on his back, he marched past Tanner.

Tanner pulled a handful of envelopes out of the box. "Your hair, nails, and bills all continue to grow after death." He stuffed the letters into his pocket. "Wait up!"

"Remember the place in Manorsville I told you about?" Tanner asked. He stepped ahead of Rack and Kyle as they neared the porch. He thought the house looked dehydrated with the rotten peels of paint chips curling down its sides. "Let me go first."

"Manorsville?" Kyle asked.

Rack approached with Kyle on his back. "His foot went through a rotted floorboard."

On the front stoop, Tanner eased increasing amounts of pressure on the first step, like a four-year-old testing a diving board for the first time. He covered the remaining steps just as gingerly. He fished a key out of his knapsack. A thin string connected the key to a punctured paper tab with the word, "Dreavor" scribbled on it. Frank Dreavor was the name of the deceased owner. Tanner had picked up the key in Portland the day before. As Tanner turned it in the lock, the key clicked clockwise to 4 PM.

Even out in this secluded area of the county, Tanner thought folks six miles back in Kargil could hear the door's squeal as he swung it open. Were those the original hinges? Had they ever been oiled?

"So are you just responsible for cleaning these houses?" Kyle asked.

Tanner tugged a digital camera from his knapsack and snapped a picture of the front hall. "And for finding any relatives not known to the state."

"Smells like socks," Rack said and then slugged his beer. "Old socks."

"You can make the distinction?" Tanner asked.

Kyle laughed with her chin on Rack's shoulder.

Tanner walked down a short front hall to the kitchen. "Electric company said there hasn't been live voltage inside for twelve years."

Rack followed with Kyle on his back. "How do you live without electricity for twelve minutes, let alone twelve years? How would you get ice?"

Kyle popped off Rack's back, her flip-flops slapping on the warped wooden kitchen floor. "Or run the hair dryer?"

"I guess you'd have to learn to drink everything neat, and towel dry." Tanner snapped a picture of the kitchen.

Rack ran a hand over the curved, metallic fridge door and whistled. "Man, I actually think this looks kinda cool. What do you think, 1950? Can you imagine what the original owners' faces would look like if they saw today's models—you know, an ice dispenser or flat screen TV on the door?"

A lone dish, spoon, butter knife, and fork stood in a drying rack, looking like storybook rejects. Above the sink, a grimy window opened on the backyard and the woods beyond. Tanner opened all four slim kitchen drawers, each empty. "He had one spoon, knife, and fork?"

Rack hopped up on a counter and gulped his beer. "Easy to keep track of, nothing piles up."

"Classy," Kyle said.

Tanner smiled and looked at her, quickly. Her jeans had to have been custom made for her legs … like moonlight on water, they were the perfect highlight. He opened an upper cupboard—it housed five Campbell's Tomato Soup cans.

Tanner put a hand around the refrigerator door handle. "Okay, brace yourself. Remember what I told you about that house in Falmouth."

"Gnarly?" Kyle asked.

Tanner smiled at her. "Rancid would've been an upgrade."

Rack put the open crack of his beer can under his nostrils. "Ready."

Kyle cupped her nose.

Tanner tugged the refrigerator door, and it opened with a *mumph*. Inside, the refrigerator was dry and empty. "At least it doesn't need to be cleaned out," Tanner said.

"Guess this guy knew he wouldn't be home for a while," Rack said. He put his can on the counter, and it *denked*, empty. He tugged a new one out of his left shirt pocket.

"I wonder if he ever used the fridge," Tanner said. "The eccentrics keep it interesting."

"I'm going to see if the plumbing works." Kyle disappeared into the powder room off the hallway they had entered.

Tanner saw Rack look over at him with a devilish smile. Rack leaned close and whispered, "Don't talk about your biking, your scholarships, cum laude, nothing! Got it? She's mine. You left early! Early bird, baby."

"You don't mean *early bird*?"

"Shut it."

"She was there last night?" Tanner asked.

"She knocked into me just after you left."

"She went home with *you*?"

"I picked her up at her place a few hours ago."

Tanner smiled. "So she knew she was going to be here today with me."

Rack crushed his empty beer can. "I'm warning you."

"Relax, I've got work—"

At the sound of a dying flush, Tanner glanced over his shoulder to see Kyle slip out of the powder room. "Works," she said, smiling at the two of them.

"Excellent." Rack slid past her into the bathroom.

Tanner stepped into the adjoining room, a dining room. He saw the circle of the sun shrinking into the treetops behind the house. He ran a finger through a layer of dust on the table in the center of the room. He snapped a photo.

"How much do you get per house?" Kyle asked.

These Californians are direct. Tanner didn't mind. "Two hundred and fifty bucks," Tanner said from behind his camera. How obvious would it be if he spun around and took her picture?

"How many do you do in a week?"

"Depends on the complications. Sometimes finding a next of kin is as easy as looking in the phone book." He photographed the aged mustard curtains that dripped across the rear windows of the house. Unconnected shards of twine sketched the bare remains of rattan chairs in the sitting room. Tanner walked out onto the porch and looked around, up, and down.

"Rack told me about your brother," she said. "I know that's why you like to move fast."

"I guess." *Very direct*, he thought. Again, he didn't mind. Somehow it felt good to have her know, and to be reminded.

Tanner photographed the empty porch, but the image was overlaid with another of his twenty-six-year-old brother Jimmy sitting on an iron bench, smiling and staring at a jungle gym while fellow inmates zombie-wandered around the playground. All of them were like Jimmy, severely mentally challenged in one way or another. Tanner's heart began sinking in on itself as the details of the scene began to fill in: a Thorazine-derivative soaking through Jimmy's bloodstream, and one $7.50-per-hour attendant for the sixteen of them, doodling on her *Maine Tribune* front page with one hand while supporting her cheek with her other as she spoke on a cell phone to one of a dozen of her friends at similar observational jobs. It was one of the finest institutions of its kind that the state, let alone Tanner, could provide. And it was closing four days from now as the state consolidated its homes for the handicapped. Jimmy would be moved two hours away, north of where Tanner lived. Since their mom's death seven years ago, Jimmy was all Tanner had for family. One day Tanner hoped to be able to provide a private home for Jimmy, one that was closer. But that would take money Tanner didn't have just now.

Rack emerged from the bathroom and called to Tanner and Kyle out on the porch. "What do you think the upstairs is like?"

The comment shook Tanner from his thoughts. "I don't know. Probably glamorous. Let's check it out."

They regrouped on the house's only stairwell.

"Go slow on these suckers." Rack narrowed his shoulders and started up. The stairs groaned individually. "Thomas Jefferson didn't build this place with me in mind."

"Don't be too sure," Tanner said and laughed. Smiling, Kyle tiptoed up the stairs in Rack's wake.

The light in the house had slowly faded to gray. At the upstairs landing, Tanner took the Maglite from his knapsack and followed its beam. He used the flashlight's head to edge open the door on the left, revealing a bed caught in full stretch, with rumpled sheets and comforter. The bureau stood with its drawers open. Clothes spilled over the edges, and some items lay on the floor. Tanner poked his nose in the open closet. There were a few hanging flannel shirts and as many rusted wire hangers scattered on the floor.

"He is either a super slob ..." Kyle said.

Rack arched his eyebrows. "Slob? Isn't that being a little—"

"Or he left in a hurry," she finished. "Or maybe vandals?"

Tanner shrugged his shoulders. "Probably. All it takes is one mention in the paper." He led the way across the hall to the other empty bedroom, which stood vacant—no bed, no bureau, no lamp, just a galaxy of dust motes floating in the last of the afternoon's sun coming through the window.

Tanner captured the emptiness with his camera.

"T, you have to clean this up?" Rack asked.

"Yeah, later."

Rack smiled. "Later. Good." He shook his beer can between thumb and index finger. "I'm hungry and low, you want one?" He started backing out of the bedroom.

"I'll take a Green Delite," Kyle said.

"Green Delite?" Tanner asked, a bit absent-mindedly, as he continued to take in the room.

Rack shook his head in disgust. "Some healthy wheatgrass soup. California, remember?"

Kyle held her index finger and thumb an inch apart in Rack's face as he passed her and headed toward the stairs. "Slightly more healthy for you than Miller Lite. Just a touch."

Tanner turned in place. Something bothered him about the room.

"We'll come with you," Kyle said.

Tanner followed Kyle, who followed Rack toward the narrow stairway.

"You know," Kyle said, "even before the mess or vandals, this place is … lacking."

"Yeah, how's that?" Again, Tanner spoke as if hardly present. He checked over his shoulder back up the stairway. What was it?

"You think anyone could live like this?" Kyle asked.

"Like how?"

"No photographs, no memories, no hobbies, no … no dreams."

"Minimalist," Tanner said. "Some people like it."

"Fine for some people, but a seventy-year-old?" Kyle asked.

"Seventy-two."

When they stepped outside, Tanner felt early fall's evening chill beginning to settle on the land. "Would it surprise you if I said many of the houses I work on are similar?"

"Yeah, actually. I'd like to think that we are all a little bit different."

Tanner spun as if someone had punched him on the shoulder. That was it. He ran back into the house.

"Wait up," Kyle called after him.

Tanner walked from the kitchen across the house to the sun porch. He concentrated on his steps, mouthing numbers. At the far porch wall, he stopped, turned, and looked up. He went back upstairs.

"What are you doing?" Kyle asked him, following in his footsteps.

Once atop the stairway, Tanner inspected the floor, the hall walls, the ceiling.

He was right. Something was missing.

"What is it?" Kyle asked behind him

"Downstairs measures about ninety feet," he said. "From the outside, the house rises straight, not much indentation. Yet up here," he spun in a circle, still eyeing the walls, "up here, we're about a dozen feet too narrow."

He walked into the first bedroom, which faced the front yard. His flashlight flicked back and forth. "One bedroom, about twelve feet by twenty, and another half that …" Then Tanner went to the rear bedroom. He felt the right wall and then rapped with his knuckles. The knock was swallowed by the hardness. He tugged the closet door open, and his flashlight's nose poked through the flannel shirts. Each wire hanger squeaked as he slid it across the rack. He tapped the back wall, revealing a deeper sound.

"What do you hear?" Kyle asked as Tanner slipped into the closet and pushed on the wall first with his fingertips and then with his shoulder. Suddenly, the rear wall swung in to a room.

A window at the far end of the room permitted the final purple hue of the setting sun. Tanner's flashlight provided added illumination, and it caught stalagmites on the floor. No, not stalagmites, stacks of books. Tanner's heart raced. "Now, what do we have here?"

Kyle slipped under the closet bar and into the room.

Tanner rotated his camera and clicked a picture. The flash made him blink. He crouched low and put his light on the first stack of books.

"*King Lear … Twelfth Night …* Shakespeare." He directed the light to the next stack. "*Romeo and Juliet, Richard I.* And those." Tanner's pace quickened as his focus moved from stack to stack. His curiosity rose. He mumbled as he waded further into the room. "Not exactly what you'd expect up here."

Trailing him, Kyle spoke over her shoulder. "This what you meant when you said most of your projects were similar?"

Tanner turned to smile and show her he appreciated her jibe, but his flashlight caught something on the wall—lots of things. "Jesus." Tanner held the light steady. Dark streaks scarred the bare pine walls as if the walls were bleeding.

"Pen streaks?" Kyle said from close behind him.

"Homework can do that to you," Rack said.

Tanner glanced over to see him standing at the closet entryway.

Tanner continued to explore the room. *The Merchant of Venice, Sonnets, As You Like It.* Shakespeare's titles went on and on. There were several bookshelves on the walls, each filled with Shakespeare. He felt Kyle looking over his shoulder. "Lots of repeats," she said.

"How many different ways can you read *Hamlet?*" Tanner asked.

"That's what I told Professor Milken," Rack said from behind them. "But you had to show up with your paper, on time and in one of your faggot-ass plastic protectors."

Tanner laughed. Looking above him, he saw the ceiling was covered with maps held in place with nails. Tanner felt a dose of claustrophobia from the way the ceiling appeared lower. Nova Scotia, Italy, Spain, Ireland, Provence, London.

Tanner nodded to a collection of dried teabags stuck to the wall, obviously having been hurled into place.

"Lots of anger or frustration." Tanner flashed his light across the room. An oak desk rested under the room's only window. "I guess our vandals didn't find this room."

"What makes you so sure? The books probably scared them off," Rack said.

"Frightening, aren't they?" Tanner said.

Rack narrowed the distance to Tanner, who felt his friend's cold stare. Tanner remembered Rack's warning not to show him up in front of Kyle.

"Ahh, light, please." Kyle requested.

Tanner obliged with the flashlight.

With her toe, Kyle pushed aside a crushed mouse inside a wooden mousetrap.

"Guess he didn't want anyone nibbling on his books," Tanner said.

"Dude, that reminds me, I haven't eaten since noon," Rack said.

"*That* reminds you!" Kyle said.

"I think he's still working off the image of the empty refrigerator," Tanner added.

Rack shoved Tanner in the shoulder, nearly plowing him into a box of squat candles.

Tanner caught himself on the desk. Two large hurricane lamps book-ended the top of the desk. Each lamp contained a melted candle. A few lonely items sat between the candles: a box of matches from Shop Rite, a mason jar full of BIC pens, the tops all mangled with bite marks, and a Radio Shack calculator with the numbers on its buttons nearly worn clear. The desk itself had chips missing from its top; at the crevices of the chips were lead marks or red ink spills. Tanner poked with the flashlight at a small pillow with browned drool spots that sat atop the desk next to the pen jar. Tanner touched his toe to a trash can overflowing with crumpled extracts from a legal pad. Lumps of dried out, used teabags slumped in and around the trash can as well. He concluded that the room held the ingredients—especially considering the caffeine and pillows—for late-night "study sessions."

Kyle unfolded one of the balled pages from the trash can. "Looks like algebra, I think."

Rack unfolded one for himself. "Yep. Although, I can't tell what he was solving for."

Kyle smiled and looked over at him. "Look at you, math detective."

"I think Rack was the only one at the university to minor in his major," Tanner said.

Behind Kyle's back, in the trace of light, Tanner saw Rack give him a look intended to stop a heart from beating.

Tanner watched Kyle inspect a stack of books.

"Well," Rack said loud enough to draw attention to himself, "I'll let you count up the *Macbeth*'s and meet you down at the car. I'm beginning to feel the hunger. In this town, we might be forced to trap and shoot our own."

"Right." Tanner sunk down to search through another stack. "Give me a couple of minutes and I'll be down."

"My Juliet, you coming?"

"I'll be right behind you," she said.

Rack's foot crunched shards of a BIC pen. Reflexively, he snapped his foot up and knocked over a stack of books, whose members toppled another stack, colliding with still another.

"Oh, man, am I done with this," he said and stormed into the closet.

Tanner shook his head and smiled. He looked over at the kneeling Kyle. The curve of her thigh was perfect. Tanner heard the staircase moan under Rack's weight.

Tanner checked the desk drawers: empty. Through the window at the head of the desk, Tanner looked out over the rear property. The backyard contained a small pond, which backed up to the woods. Tall pines and maples, some birch—all Maine natives. Tanner knew from the property documents that the forest was protected and extended for nearly six miles, all county land. He could hear the evening crickets tuning up.

"What a strange portrait, huh?" Kyle asked. "Campbell's Tomato Soup and Shakespeare."

"I know." Tanner smiled. "Why couldn't he have been into rum and porn?"

She laughed.

"So, how did you and Rack meet?" Tanner poked through a milk crate of loose papers next to the desk, one of a dozen or so similar crates scattered throughout the room.

"Nothing too unusual. I was with a couple of friends at The Overlook last night. He was there, soaring through the crowd, probably a few deep, and he collided with me."

"Bowling for bimbos" is what Rack called that maneuver, Tanner knew only too well. While Rack's side of the story was different, sometimes after his ninth beer, Tanner knew even Rack couldn't tell whom he was knocking into.

"We finished out the night talking and drinking. He mentioned that he would be helping you clear out a house today as part of an estate appraisal, and I thought that sounded fun."

"You don't work?"

"I'm working at Hanely & Henderson, an accounting firm downtown. They're moving offices today. Gave everyone the day off."

With his flashlight Tanner turned to leave, but his foot knocked over a stack of Dreavor's books and that started another literary domino reaction.

Kyle laughed. "Et tu?"

Tanner reached down for the nearest toppled victim: *Othello*. He thumbed the pages. There was writing on the pages ... every page.

That's strange.

There were sentences in freehand, calculations, algebraic equations, and geometric shapes, all in red ink. Curious, Tanner put *Othello* down and picked up the next nearest book, *Macbeth*. The writing spread across its pages like a disease. The next, *Love's Labour's Lost*, had the same infection up and down the yellowed pages.

"What is it?" Kyle stepped close enough to read over Tanner's shoulder. He felt her breath on his neck. His blood warmed, and his pulse quickened.

"Take a look." He handed her the book and took the opportunity to look at her up close. *What does California drinking water do to make someone's eyes so blue?*

As she flipped pages, he moved to the opposite side of the room. He tugged a book from the middle of a stack, disregarding the ripple of toppled volumes he set in motion. *A Midsummer Night's Dream*. The writing was there, in the very same red ink.

Christ.

He looked around the room again and calculated that there were well over two hundred volumes. He sank down next to the nearest stack. *Twelfth Night* was littered with the mathematic notations.

Rack called from the bottom of the stairs. "Hey, how about it, Romeo? Cheeseburger?"

Tanner called over his shoulder, "Yep, in a minute."

"So, what's all this?" Kyle asked.

"Beats me. Seems like someone was trying to make more of the words than just the words themselves."

"Like code?"

"I guess."

"What are you thinking?" she said and stood.

Say something smart. "I don't know." *Smarter, idiot.* "Let's see. He could be searching for the true author of Shakespeare."

"Other than Shakespeare?"

"Yep. There's this belief that Shakespeare wasn't the true author of his plays and poems because he came from such simple beginnings and many of the plays revolved around royalty and stuff he couldn't have known about, like law and the politics of other nations."

"I sort of remember something like that. You think this stuff is related?"

"I don't know. Maybe. It must have taken years to come up with all of this."

"At least years," Kyle said. "I wonder if he did this all from inside this … this place."

"Spooky, huh?"

"What will you do with it? What becomes of all of these?"

"Well, same as anything attached to an intestate estate. It's auctioned off."

"You think the guy whose house this was uncovered anything?"

"Well, nothing *that* remarkable. We would've heard about it, I'm sure."

"Judging by the rest of the house, he certainly didn't have a website."

"No, just plain old webs."

Kyle smiled and shook her head. "Hungry?"

Tanner didn't want to stop talking with her in the empty room and with Rack out of sight. But Rack was his friend. He sprayed his flashlight in a path toward the closet door. "After you." He held the light steady and watched as she navigated the battlefield of books. He followed and then stopped short at the door. A single volume lay across the top shelf. Tanner picked it up. *The Complete Works of William Shakespeare.* He flipped through it and to his surprise found clean, unannotated pages. He kept it and turned for a last look at the room. And then he dipped back through the closet door.

Chapter 2

They drove in the minivan through the absolute black for another fifteen minutes, chatting and listening to satellite radio. Tanner had secured his bike to minivan's rear bike rack.

"Is that light ahead?" Rack asked. "Dare I say we are nearing civilization?"

Kyle leaned forward. "It's town. Gosh, could you imagine living out here in such a deserted area your whole life?"

"Nice quaint church, right up there on the road, huh?" Tanner observed.

"A pharmacy, a five-and-dime store, and a food mart." Kyle observed.

"The typical Main Street, right? And here's what we're looking for." Tanner turned the minivan into the driveway below a tall, neon-lit sign.

"Betty's: Home of the Deluxe Burger," Rack read in mock reverence. "Now we're talking! Can you expense this?"

"What am I now, an investment banker?" Tanner asked, pulling into a spot between a Chevy pickup and a Subaru.

Rack unclipped his seat belt. "Hey, this is business."

Tanner turned to Kyle and smiled. "He's not always like this."

"Better?"

"Worse." Tanner turned toward Rack. "I'm employed by taxpayers of the great state of Maine, which means, one way or another, you're gonna pay for your own Deluxe Burger." They walked to the front door.

"The first one, I can handle," Rack said. "The second is on you."

Tanner held the door for Rack and Kyle; he enjoyed a clear view of her rear. Betty's Diner was a collection of vinyl-covered booths and a long counter with spinning stools, populated by flannel shirt fans, men and women. Tanner smelled a delightful blend of cheddar and smoky grease. He slid into a booth across the table from Kyle and Rack, who sat side by side.

A wobbling black woman approached their booth with a smile. She was heavyset, and Tanner thought she was losing a battle with facial hair. "Hi, I'm Betty. Can I get you something to drink?" She handed out three one-page laminated menus and then flipped open a wrinkled order pad.

Rack licked his lips. "Do you have any specials tonight, Betty?"

"Just the sunset," she said.

"The sunset?" Kyle asked.

Betty smiled. "It's always special."

"Maybe we'll need just another minute," Tanner said.

"No problem," Betty said.

"I, on the other hand, would love a couple of Schaefers," Rack said.

Betty jotted down his order and moved to serve another table.

After she was gone, Tanner leaned forward. "Schaefers?"

Rack wiggled his eyebrows. "Two beers or not two beers."

"Cute," Kyle said.

Tanner thumbed the pages of *The Complete Works*. "I wonder how many years Dreavor was working up there."

"Who knows, could've been dozens," Rack said. "How old was the guy?"

"Seventy-two."

"He could've been at it for fifty years. No one twenty-five or younger gives a shit about Shakespeare."

"Spoken like a true math major," Kyle said.

Tanner laughed. "Where did you go?" he asked Kyle.

"Stanford. Economics and Pre-med. How about you?"

He almost didn't hear her through the eye lock he had on her face. Her teeth were perfect. "Oh, I was UMaine, History."

"Lots of history jobs out there," Rack said.

"Is that right?" Tanner had expected Rack to go after him. He didn't mind.

"Yeah, I saw in the help wanteds that Pratt & Whitney was looking for ten people to help with the Renaissance."

Kyle buried her face in her arms. Rack cracked up.

"I'll check into it," Tanner said, smiling.

Betty returned, fingertips under a tray bearing the Schaefer's and ice waters. "You folks ready to order?"

Rack handed Betty his menu. "Three cheeseburgers, one large fry, and two more Schaefers."

Betty smiled. "Do you all want salads with your—"

"Betty, Betty, that was my order."

Betty paused and lifted her eyes off her notepad. "You, son, are welcome anytime."

Rack beamed with pride and winked at Kyle. "I get a lot of that."

Kyle returned her menu to Betty. "Salad with oil and vinegar for me."

"That all?"

Kyle nodded.

Rack interjected, "She's from California."

Betty nodded solemnly, humoring Rack. Kyle rolled her eyes and smiled.

"I'll have a cheeseburger, medium, no onions. Thanks," Tanner said.

"You two good with drinks?"

Tanner and Kyle assented, and Betty turned away.

Tanner pulled his wallet out of his back pocket and called to Betty. "Hey, can I ask you a question?" He picked an item out of his wallet.

The waitress paused on her way toward a nearby table. "Yeah?"

"Have you ever seen this man?" Tanner held up a photo of Frank Dreavor in the morgue, lying on a slab with his eyes closed. A gray sheet ran up to his chest, but one could detect there was a bit of power surrounding his neck and shoulders. His hair was white, as were his eyebrows. In fact, his skin had a mashed-potato pallor. His face was thin, his jaw line and nose prominent, and the skin covering his teeth appeared unusually thin.

She stepped forward, focused on the photo for a couple of seconds, and then looked up at Tanner. "That a dead man?"

"Uh, yeah."

"You a cop?"

Tanner shook his head. "No. That man's name was Frank Dreavor. He lived over near Wyatt Road. He didn't have a will, and I've been assigned by the state to make sure his property is properly disposed of. We can't locate any relatives. I thought you might be able to help."

Betty nodded. "He rich?"

Tanner shook his head. "I'm afraid not."

"Sorry," Betty said with a shrug. "Hmm." Her face squeezed together. "Did he ever cut grass?"

Tanner's face brightened. "Yeah, yeah actually. I mean, he was a municipal worker for the town. Guess he probably cut a lawn or two."

"Well, I don't know, but you should ask Tommy Norton. He runs the show, the town workers. He comes in here some weekends. You can find him at the dump most days. I'll go put your order in."

After she had moved on to the next table, Rack groaned. "What'd you have to do that for?"

"It might make my job a lot easier."

"Didn't the police report already tell you he has no relatives? That he was a municipal worker for twenty-something years? Why do you have to go pull the *Law & Order* routine?"

"First of all, after you're gone, I'm the one who'll be wading through the chigger infestation, making sure everything is geared up for auction."

"So?"

"So, if there is any way to lessen the burden by asking a waitress a harmless question, I'm asking."

"Seems like an innocent question to me," Kyle said. "The government doesn't always know everything."

Tanner wanted to take her hand in his own.

"You know, come to think of it," Rack said as he swallowed a mouthful of Schaefer, "there must be a badge for this kind of thing."

Tanner began to page through *The Complete Works*, and a small piece of paper dropped in his lap.

"What's that?" Kyle asked.

Tanner read out loud. "It's a ticket receipt. Fog Island Ferry."

Rack gargled Schaefer and said in a German accent, "Verry interestink."

"Where's Fog Island?" Kyle asked.

"It's up the coast," Tanner said. "Still part of Maine, but about a two-hour drive."

"I never knew how many islands Maine had until I flew in the other day," Kyle said. "What's it, like five thousand or something?"

Tanner nodded.

"How do you know Fog Island?" she asked.

Tanner glanced at Rack, whose eyes were wide and looking right back at him. Tanner got the message: this wasn't the time to bring up—and have to explain and demonstrate—his unusual memory. "Well, some of them have more memorable names than others."

"So, your hermit did get away every now and then," Rack said.

"Makes you wonder why he chose Fog Island," Kyle said. "I mean, maybe it was to see a relative or someone who knew him well?"

Tanner smiled at her attempt to help reason down a path that might help him. "Maybe." He dipped his attention back inside *The Complete Works*.

"I wonder why this book doesn't have markings throughout. All the others did."

"Maybe he kept one clean," Kyle offered.

Rack finished a swallow. "Maybe he got old and tired and realized he was wasting his life away. That's when he decided to take a vacation."

"You know that we're dealing with a search for clues within the text of Shakespeare."

"Clues for what?" Rack asked.

"Most likely who the true author is."

"Author of what, Shakespeare?"

"Yeah," Tanner said, still paging. "There is this whole field of study around who Shakespeare was."

"Besides being William Shakespeare?"

"No. I mean, yes. No one denies that William Shakespeare existed, but plenty of people believe that Shakespeare couldn't have written all the plays and poems attributed to him."

"Why?"

"Largely because he came from such simple beginnings. He didn't have much schooling or hang with royalty, and his writings are inundated with it all."

"How simple?"

"Son of a horseshoe man or something like that."

"Blacksmith?"

"I think."

"Well, I still can't see why someone would spend their entire life holed up in a shack trying to find the answer to that one. Who gives a shit?"

"As if there could be no historic riddle so important that anyone would devote their life to answering it?" Tanner asked. "Like discovering the *Titanic* or the location of Blackbeard's treasure?"

Rack swallowed two cheeks full of Schaefer and shook his head. "Different. This is marginal on a good day. Who cares who wrote the stuff? We've got it, and you can't walk a day in the summer without running into some outdoor festival performing one of them. Doesn't seem to stop anyone from using it."

"Think about what you just said. You can't walk a day without someone performing one of his plays. Think about that. Four hundred years old, and his every word is revered. You think four hundred years from now anyone will give a shit about Spielberg's movies? Hemingway? Another four hundred years from now they'll still be performing Shakespeare everywhere."

"You don't know that, T."

"I'd be willing to bet the farm."

"You haven't got a farm. Your dead friend didn't have a farm."

"He wasn't my dead friend. You're the only friend that matters to me, Rackles."

Kyle laughed at the phony sentiment. Behind his own smile, Tanner racked his brain for more humor, anything to keep Kyle smiling.

"So, what's the date of that ticket?" Kyle asked.

Tanner flipped it over.

"Hmm. That's funny," he said as he read. "It was five weeks ago."

Rack put an empty glass down. "I'm missing it. Was that the silly season?"

"No, that was a few days before his death."

Rack wiggled his fingers. "Ooo, spooky."

24

Kyle smiled.

Then a thought occurred to Tanner. "So, tell me, Racky, why did you want to see me so bad?" Tanner asked.

Rack swallowed and looked at his bottle.

Tanner lifted his eyes from *The Complete Works*.

"I—I—I am, I've been … working with Marty Hile." Rack slammed a mouthful of beer.

Tanner felt his heart collide with his liver. *Not Hile …* He was Tanner's top competitor in too many things. Tanner froze, hoping deep within his musculature that Rack would crack into a conniving smile and weave the announcement into a joke.

Nothing came.

"He's been raging. Trek's sponsorship let him focus on training."

Tanner tried to think about how to respond, but his mind was a car wreck of thoughts. Not long ago, a bike frame company had sponsored him, a sponsorship that enabled him to train in three extended sessions per day. The frame company, Founda, provided him with a modest income that gave him tremendous flexibility. All of that disappeared when Tanner crashed in a race in Spain six months ago. In the crash, he tore his thigh open—to the bone—and his rehab still wasn't complete yet. Rack had grown frustrated with Tanner over the past couple of months, not believing Tanner had been serious enough about his rehab. Tanner stole a glance at Kyle. She was watching him for his reaction. He felt ashamed, and he didn't even know her. Hell, Rack didn't even know her. "How long?" Tanner said at last. He still hadn't blinked.

"For about two weeks now."

"I mean *continue*. How long are you going to continue with him?"

"I—I told him I'd be happy to continue until he was … wanted to move on." Rack sipped the second bottle.

Tanner turned toward the rest of the diner. "You didn't think I was coming back?"

"No, no, I wouldn't say that. It's just that you didn't seem like you wanted to get better."

"What?"

"My guess is that you could've been 85 percent by now, but you keep inspecting old people's homes."

"You looked pretty good earlier," Kyle offered as a shock absorber.

Tanner flew past the comment. His voice rose with every word. "So, you go behind my back and work with ... with Marty? Marty Hile?" Several customers nearby lowered their silverware and turned.

"T, take it easy. What else could I do? Sit around and wait for you to get serious about training again? I asked and I asked. You refused to get another evaluation to see what was happening with the scar tissue. My dad's happy to front me rent, but only so long as I show him some work effort."

"*Jeesus*, Marty Hile?"

Kyle tried again to slow things down. "Is he on parole or something?"

"Don't act so surprised," Rack said to Tanner. "He was closest behind you in De Georgia and Colorado Springs. If you were me, who would you choose?"

Tanner pushed himself up from the table and scooped up the copy of Shakespeare. "I need to get back to work."

"Don't be like that."

"Nice to meet you," he said toward Kyle. She smiled brightly, beautiful ... *Maybe I should calm down*, he thought.

Rack put a thumb over his shoulder, toward the kitchen. "Don't you want to stay for something? There's nothing back at that house."

Rack's comment slapped him back to the moment. "There's soup. I'll see ya." Tanner stormed through the diner and out the door to the minivan. His mind was buzzing with a dozen questions fighting for priority. He slugged his knapsack over his shoulder and unclipped his bike from the minivan's rear rack.

"Wait, T." Rack ran up next to him.

"I'm glad we had this discussion." He clipped his helmet around his chin. "For the longest time I've felt my life being controlled by you. You and Jimmy. When do I get to live, huh? What the fuck am I doing with the two of you around my neck? I'm through, get it? Jimmy will be taken care of. Maybe not great, but it's enough."

"T, don't say that. He's your brother."

"He probably can't tell the difference anyway."

"T, calm down. You don't mean that. Come inside."

"And you can go fuck yourself. How about that? You and your fucking girlfriend. I've got a life to live." Tanner looked at the diner driveway and the main road beyond.

Rack seized Tanner's short sleeve. "I came out here to try to avoid you running off in a huff."

"Hope you don't think you wasted your time."

Tanner thrust the bike out and skip-leaped aboard. He cranked the pedals forward and bent into the turn that took him back down Main Street, back the way they had come.

Chapter 3

Cocksucker. Marty Hile. How could Rack side with him? Of course Hile was inking great times, it wasn't like he had another care in the world. Life is simple when you're wealthy. First, Hile stole Tanner's girlfriend. Who takes someone on a date to Switzerland to ski? Now Hile was stealing his manager?

Tanner pumped his legs, favoring the right one. He biked more slowly than he would have liked to allow for road conditions that reminded him of Northern Europe. There, harsh winters had wreaked havoc on poor concrete mixes and even poorer road repair budgets. On this empty country road there were no traffic sounds, no airplanes, no children chasing fireflies—nothing on this fall evening. Despite the thousands of miles Tanner had put on his bike over the years, he always felt spooked by the nighttime silence of secluded areas like this with nothing but the kiss of his tires on the pavement and the chirring of tree frogs. At least he had the moonlight to assist his single headlight.

It was here that Frank Dreavor had managed to seclude himself, he thought. If all the world was a stage, Dreavor had spent his time deep inside the dressing room closet.

Suddenly, a mighty horse of a moose stood in the road. Tanner white-knuckled his hand brakes. His tires cried, and his heart stuttered. The moose turned its head toward Tanner. Its upper teeth nearly rotated all the way around its lower jaw as it chewed. Tanner's front tire skidded to within ten feet of the moose's belly. Tanner let out the breath he had trapped inside. The moose didn't move, so Tanner steered around it. He could smell the moose's meaty scent. Tanner knew that each year in Maine, moose participated in three thousand traffic accidents. Tanner had been lucky. He cranked past and didn't look back.

Tanner pedaled back to speed, and his right thigh burned as if a squirrel were clawing around under the scar. All at once, his best friend and partner was leaving him, and his brother was being moved to an institution farther away. There was nothing Tanner could do about it. Tanner had no funds, no savings, and no family to call on. He felt a vice clamping on his heart. And what about that girl, Kyle? Easy. He'd never see her again.

"Fuck!" he screamed into the night. The only means he had to earn more money was to plow ahead and get this house cleaned out and ready for auction.

In minutes, Tanner turned down Dreavor's road, Wyatt Road. The ground became much rockier as the pavement ended. Without moonlight or streetlights, the house sat like a dark rock among the heavy grass and crowd of trees.

Tanner dismounted at the toppled mailbox. He could see the trail he and Rack had made to the front door earlier that day. The house seemed lonely—no neighboring houses, no residents. Tanner was pretty sure even the fireflies stayed in the surrounding woods.

Tanner hefted his bike onto his shoulder and waded through the grass toward the front door. He thought about how at night houses always offered more smells and were quieter and much darker. Yet, this one was mute and smelled like dead mice. The screech of the front door pierced the silence. Thank God not many things in the universe cried like that.

Without electricity, Tanner could navigate only by the moonbeams that penetrated the shreds of window shades. He didn't want to sit on the rotted loveseat on the porch or stare at the rounded refrigerator. The hidden attic intrigued him. Tanner felt he knew less about Dreavor than anyone on whose estate he had worked. Yet he also felt there was more to this situation than any estate where he had worked. Once through the front door, he went straight to the stairs and ascended them quickly.

What were you looking for—

An orange light blinked through the bedroom closet door.

Did I light—no, wait, did Kyle light the candles?

He stepped through the flannel shirts and emerged into the study. He saw that the two hurricane lamps were lit. The window was open. Otherwise, the room hadn't changed. Many Shakespeare works still stood in stacks, and many were sprawled across the floor. He felt a light wind from the open window, and the ceiling's maps rustled. Even the pillow with dribble—

From the corner of his eye, an image sprang from behind the door to the closet. Before Tanner could turn around, a mass of power rammed him in the lower back and thrust him forward. His hip stung where he crashed it into the desk. In the collision, the mason jar of pens shattered against the wall, the calculator flew off, and the hurricane lamps toppled, one shattering on the floor and the other caught by the waste basket.

Tanner pushed himself off the floor and saw the shirts in the closet swinging back and forth. The room was empty. He rubbed his aching hip. What the hell had just happened? Was that a joke? Kid vandals returning? Something worse? How many were there?

Behind him, he heard the waste basket erupt in flame with the sound of a bedsheet being shaken out. Flames lathered the desk and scurried across the naked floorboards. Tanner ran to the closet. He stepped through and then poked his head out into the bedroom. Could they be coming back? He edged his eyes into the hall. Nothing.

He scuttled down the stairway. The front door completed its swing back toward the house. Just as he put a hand on the door, he heard a crackling sound from above. The fire… The house was too old to let a fire grow out of control! He turned around, ran back up the stairs, and crossed to the rear bedroom.

When he parted the hanging flannel shirts, he saw the study was a mouth of flame, swallowing the maps on the ceiling and chomping toward him. Loose book pages hopped on the waves of heat.

Tanner felt unarmed against it. He scrambled downstairs to find a hose. When he burst through the front door, he heard an engine growl. Across the front yard of the property, where it ran down toward the beginnings of the forest that surrounded Dreavor's house, Tanner saw headlights flip on. It was a large vehicle from the sound of it. Squinting through the darkness, he saw that someone had just leaped into the rear passenger door. The front tires lurched forward, driven by an angry foot on the gas. The headlights bore down on Tanner.

There was the sound of a window shattering upstairs, followed by the heavy crunch of some structural collapse. Whether it was someone else upstairs or just the fire raging, Tanner concluded that the house offered no safety. His bike waited for him against the stoop. In two quick strides, Tanner leaped on and pedaled into the front lawn's tall grass.

He checked over his shoulder. The car revved, its tires spit dirt, and it jumped in his direction. Tanner drove his pedals. He had a hundred-yard head start. The car ground louder, closer. Would they ram him?

Tanner's right leg howled inside, but he drove through the pain. He leaped his bike up—both wheels—for a moment, and then he landed and crunched the pedals. Behind him, Tanner heard the sounds of metal crackling, thumping, clogging, and cracking. Tanner looked behind him to see the headlights jerk to the right. The car, an SUV, had caught Dreavor's hidden mailbox, the same mailbox Tanner had leapt over seconds before. As he would in any race, Tanner pushed forward to expand the distance from his pursuer.

He rounded the bend where Dreavor's road wrapped around the tall forest. Momentarily out of view, Tanner skidded, dismounted, threw his bike up over a thicket, and plunged headfirst after it.

It seemed like seconds before Tanner hit the ground, or at least before some part of him collided with the ground. The black world shushed and cracked in loops around him. Like an upturned turtle, Tanner rolled to a stop on his back, gasping to put breath back in his lungs. Above, or maybe it was to the side, the car sped past in a black blur. He listened as the noises of the car faded in the distance. Then he managed his first sip of air.

He waited. The crickets *sissed*. He lay on his back, not moving a muscle, simply listening for a few minutes for any sound of the car, the truck, whatever it was. Hearing only the crickets, his hands groped for his bike, patting dry pines, vines, and prickers. *Poison ivy would be icing on this.*

The ground grumbled—he felt it in his hands and knees. He craned his neck to see a distant fireball partially visible through the trees. A devil's jaw of flames consumed Dreavor's house.

Chapter 4

As if the burned house wasn't bad enough, Tanner watched the fire trucks' wheels scar the lawn. Two engines stood within range while four volunteer firemen doused the embers with their hoses. Tanner coughed from the smoke grit. He stood next to one of two police cars also positioned toward the crusty remains of Dreavor's house. The police in this small town doubled as firemen when needed. The cruisers' sirens flashed blue and red across the property. Tanner thought the lights needlessly called attention to the burning wreck. The police officer in charge had taken a position next to Tanner.

The policeman, Lieutenant Jerome Clay, stood in a soiled T-shirt with his fireman's pants suspendered up and dripping. "You took your flashlights with you—you're sure?"

"Yeah, it made getting to the car easier," Tanner said.

Earlier, from his hiding place in the brush, Tanner had dialed 911 on his cell phone and summoned the police and fire department. Shortly after, he had thought about trying to raise Rack on his cell phone but concluded it was useless. Even when they were on the best of terms, Rack didn't tend to answer his phone when he was with a lady. On top of that, Rack's chances with women never involved someone of Kyle's caliber. Given that he was still so pissed at Rack, Tanner had decided to not even bother calling him.

"No word yet from the staties on your SUV," Clay said. "By the time you reached us, they could've gone anywhere, including the highway."

Tanner nodded. His head spun at a flash of light to his right. An officer was crouched and bent toward the ground, taking photographs.

"Wish I got a better look."

"It was dark. Not much you could do. Be thankful you got outta there."

"It's a shame," Tanner said. "He had all these books with so much work poured into them."

"I would've never known Dreavor could read."

"Did you see him much?" Tanner asked.

"You know, he sat on that John Deere of his and cut most patches the town had any responsibility for. The courthouse, our station, the fire station, the two parks, the high school. I never remembered seeing him other than on the backside of that mower." Clay folded his arms. "He always had a ... a flat face, you know? Always staring at the ground in front of him."

Tanner nodded and rubbed his hip where he had collided either with the desk or the ground.

"He putted around town on his bike," Clay said. "Always on that bike of his. I thought he was retarded."

Tanner looked over at his stallion leaning against a tree trunk across the road. When he turned back, Clay was looking at him. Their gazes knocked into one another. "Not like your bike, of course," Clay said. "His was more Wicked Witch of the West, old fashioned-ish."

Blackness filled Tanner's eyes. He thought about his brother and the hundreds of times he had tried to teach Jimmy how to ride a bike, all without success.

"What became of his body?" Clay asked.

Tanner came back to the present. "I understand it was cremated. I guess they do that up in Washington County."

"Yeah," Clay said, now leaning on the hood of his cruiser and staring into the flames. Because Dreavor's house was so removed from town proper, the public water system had never been extended out to his road. "That truck's gonna run out soon. I guess none of this will help with the auction process."

Tanner shook his head. "You ever see inside?"

"No, you know, I didn't." Clay's beady brown eyes drew a touch smaller. "You ever bid on the property from one of your cases?"

Suspicion. Tanner noticed it; his skin grew moist. "Me? No, no, I haven't got the money. I just clean them out."

Clay kept staring at Tanner. "So, where are you staying?"

"I live up in Gill. I think I'll head back."

Clay eyed Tanner's bike. "On that? At this time of night?"

"Oh, I can manage. There are back roads."

"Back roads aren't any safer in the dark," Clay said. Tanner heard Clay's voice take on a subtle skepticism.

"I've got years of experience." Tanner saddled himself on his bike. "You've got my cell number."

"Don't you have any friends you can call to come get you? You've been through a bit of a tumble tonight. I can give you a lift to Fryeburg's hospital—it's not far. We should get you checked out."

After the six months Tanner had just spent trying to recover from his thigh injury, he would have preferred to throw himself down a dozen brush hills rather than spend another night in a hospital. He pointed his bike down the road, away from the singed wreck. "No, thanks. I know where to find you."

Clay waved Tanner to stop. "Hold on, hold on. Take a breather. I need your help on a couple more things." Tanner turned toward Clay. "You see, we've got Frankie Dreavor dead, alone, in the woods, with no witnesses."

35

"Coroner said he asphyxiated, drowned. Police report said it was a hiking accident."

"But, you see, now I've got at least a couple of people breaking and entering this dead man's house, at one point inside this man's secret attic. One of these guys assaults you, causes the house to burn to the ground, jumps in a late-model SUV, and tries to run you down while fleeing the scene."

Tanner didn't like the sound of Clay's summary.

"We've had to scramble the town's fireboys, spent two tanks, and now you just want to bicycle away into the night, with a major storm coming?"

"Look, Sheriff, I—"

"I'm not a sheriff."

Tanner paused, and his heart hiccupped.

"Now, let's go through this again," Clay said. "And maybe we can shake loose some sense of this."

"Let's not forget I was almost run down here."

"I want to know why in the hell someone would want to break into Frank Dreavor's house, a quiet, seventy-two-year-old man of limited means?"

"I don't know, Sher—er—officer."

"Let's figure it out together. What exactly was in that attic? What was so valuable?"

Tanner shrugged. Clay stared at him from across the car roof and then cocked his head without expression. Tanner felt as though there was a fishing line down his throat, drawing thoughts out of him.

"I-I-I guess if Dreavor was trying to find a mystery hidden within the texts of Shakespeare, and if he *actually did*, then that would be worth a lot."

"A lot?"

"Well, I'm not an expert, really. I mean, I don't know, I'm just guessing."

"Guess more specifically. For me. Please."

Tanner gripped his bike's seat and handlebar tighter. He thought about great, expensive works of art recently auctioned off. Wasn't there a Renoir that went for twenty million dollars? "Millions, tens of millions, more specifically." Tanner read the surprise in Clay's widened eyes.

"*My guess* is that that kind of money would make most people do some very extraordinary things," Clay commented. "What do you think?"

Tanner felt off balance. The police officer in charge of taking pictures snapped another photo of the tire tracks. Tanner blinked. "Officer," he said, "of course you're right. But I have no idea what Mr. Dreavor was trying to do. Maybe he was trying to uncover something about Shakespeare, but, from what I saw of his home, he didn't strike me as likely to solve anything like that."

"Mmhm," Clay nodded. "I agree. I was always surprised Frankie's mower didn't run out of gas more often." Clay checked his notes. "Tell me again, where did you say your friends ... Rack Manning and Kyle Murray go?"

"As far as I know, they went to Rack's apartment or maybe the Overlook."

"His apartment at 38 Cherry Road?"

"Yes."

"And this Kyle girl?"

"Like I said, I just met her. She said she works for Hanely & Henderson, some accounting firm downtown."

"How would you describe her?"

"Smart, attractive, five foot nine, blue eyes, blondish hair, one-fifteen."

"So you found her attractive?"

"I didn't have to find her—she came with Rack," Tanner said evenly.

Clay's eyebrows narrowed.

Tanner winced. Even he had to admit the remark was wiseass.

"And you're going to ride all the way back to your place on this?"

"It's not far. My average training run is four hours."

"Not at night."

"I've got a light. Besides, I'll stick to the back roads."

"When we're done here I can get you a cab."

"No, thanks. I'd prefer to clear my head."

"I'm a police officer, remember. To protect and serve. Keeping you off the back roads on a bike at night is part of the protect part. And maybe a service to others."

Tanner felt the body blow of Clay's words. Clay spoke into his walkie-talkie and gave the order to wind down the hoses. "I don't want these guys overextending with a nor'easter coming. We're gonna be busy over the next few days." He slipped off his suspenders. "I'm heading north. I'll give you a lift in the right direction."

"Really, don't worry—"

"I'm not worried," Clay said. "Put your bike in the trunk. We have a massive storm coming. I can't let you take off on a bike."

Tanner hadn't been forced to do anything for years, maybe since high school. He hadn't liked it then, either. Clay opened the trunk and put in his folded rubber pants, coat, and helmet. Tanner reluctantly put his bike on top. Clay rigged his phone headset on his ear and waved for Tanner to get in.

Tanner double-checked the backseat. *Glad that nobody's back there, especially me.* After they pulled out, Clay was immediately on his phone. Tanner listened for the next ten minutes as Clay checked with various departments around the town, other police officers, the sewer department, sanitation, and transportation. "No, no. Just tell Mark he'll need to ask the crews to stay ready until the storm passes."

"When's the storm supposed to hit?" Tanner asked when Clay paused between calls, his thumb hovering over the numbers.

"Tomorrow night. We're not going to get a direct hit, but close."

"So, it would've been fine to ride tonight."

"You never know whether you can trust the weatherman, right?"

"I suppose."

Tanner watched the road. The headlights illuminated a cone in front of them. Given the twists in the road, the view kept changing like channels on a TV. His intuition said that Clay didn't trust him.

"I'm going to head up to my sister's house two towns north. Want a lift that far?"

Tanner thought about it. He would have been heading up there anyway. "Checking on your sister?"

"She's dead," Clay said. "Father and two sons. Brother-in-law is not too altogether there, so I stop by every week or so."

So much information made Tanner uncomfortable. "That's nice of you. I wish we'd had that when my mom was way off course."

"So, do you think Frankie was on to something?"

Tanner shrugged his shoulders. The blipping lights across Clay's radio and scanner caught his eye. "He certainly put the work in. You should've seen those books."

"Dreavor and millions of dollars? Words I never thought I would hear in the same sentence."

"Well, I've no idea if he ever got anywhere." Tanner was trying to figure out how all of the equipment attached to the dash worked. What was the release mechanism for the shotgun? "I'm not even sure what exactly he was searching for."

"What happens next, then? Let's say the house wasn't a pile of ashes. You mentioned an auction. Did Dreavor have lots of other stuff?"

"Not much. Two thousand forty-six dollars in a bank account. No wedding ring, no crucifix, a Timex. And that's it."

"About what I would have thought." Clay's phone buzzed. "Clay."

Tanner wondered about Dreavor. The picture began crystallizing of a loner, a loser, unloved, and possibly mentally slow. Seventy-two years old. His chapters had been written. *How the hell did he find himself on this Shakespeare path?*

The deep, high woods passed by as the car drove. Tanner wondered what he would do once he arrived at Clay's sister's house. Clay finished a conversation with some electrician somewhere, threatening to prohibit the man's access to the Bull Hollow if the town's main stoplight was out for as long as it was last storm.

"You know, I think I remember reading about you," Clay said as he put the phone back in his pocket.

"Really?"

"You were pretty fast, right? Competed around the globe?"

"Yep."

Clay scratched his skull. "But you got hurt or something."

"Took a handle bar through my thigh over in Spain. Still working my way back."

"Right, right, now I remember."

They were quiet for a couple of minutes.

Clay broke the silence. "You work for the state to make ends meet?"

"Gotta pay the bills somehow." Tanner could see the profile Clay was trying to sketch. Once again, Tanner didn't like being the subject. *He couldn't know anything about Spain, could he?*

"What's the prognosis?" Clay drove with one hand on the wheel and the other on his fold-down armrest.

"For me? Doctors aren't sure. My muscle was nearly spliced in half. They challenge me to defy the precedent."

"Wonderful." Clay smirked. "Didn't you have a brother you used to look after or something like that?"

How the hell did ... Oh, shit, I've been played.

"You weren't talking to utility and authority members, were you? You were getting a download on me. You know all of these answers already, don't you?"

"Now, don't you think that's a bit paranoid, Tanner? You shouldn't be paranoid, now. I mean, unless you should be."

"Might be a reaction to being jumped at night on a secluded property."

"You still supporting your brother? Up at Freeman Institute?"

The magazine piece had mentioned Jimmy. "Yep, that's right."

"You didn't have any health insurance, huh?"

"Not enough."

"So I see why you'd need the cash flow, then."

"Why I need the *job*, right?"

"Of course. How much longer will you search for one of Dreavor's relatives?"

"Oh, uh, probably another week. There are certain protocols that are mandatory, like interviews with a few neighbors, co-workers. You have anyone you think I should talk to?"

"Well, let's see. There's Willie McHugh down at the town dump and Marty Randolph at Muni."

"McHugh and Randolph, got it."

"We should be done with the fire investigation within a week."

"A week?" Tanner looked over at Clay.

"Sure, we have protocols of our own and questions we need to ask of folks. SUV tracks weren't the only tires in the road in front of Dreavor's."

Tanner needed a moment to think that through. "Minivan, you mean? Those would be Rack's. I told—"

"Those and others," Clay said.

"What do you mean, in addition to the SUV?"

"I can't really talk about it, but yes."

To Tanner, it seemed as though the car flipped. Was Clay playing with him? Tanner couldn't figure out what he was really doing in that police cruiser. *He couldn't know the truth about*

Spain, could he? Tanner felt a creepiness seeping in through the window's edge.

"Folks saw you in a loud argument with a round man in the parking lot of Betty's. Say you took off in a huff."

Tanner's mouth was paper dry. He could taste the ash from the air around the burnt house. "That-that was ju-just me and Rack arguing about him taking on another rider. It had nothing to do with the house—"

"He was leaving you for another biker?"

"Well, we haven't seen eye to eye since my accident, and—"

"How important is a coach at your level?"

"He's not so much a coach as a road manager. We were classmates at UM. He's reliable. You need that in biking."

Clay looked over at Tanner. Even in the darkness of the front seat, the glance made Tanner feel uncomfortable. "You know, I think I'll get out here."

"My sister's place is just up ahead."

"No, this is good." Tanner unbuckled his belt.

"Don't be ridiculous—"

Tanner reached for the passenger door handle and popped the lock.

"*Jesus!* Hold *on!*" Clay barked. He slammed the breaks and jerked the cruiser to the right. When the car bucked to a stop, Tanner snapped the door open and stepped out. Clay followed him out. "Wait a minute!"

"Can you pop the trunk?" Tanner asked, ignoring Clay's direction.

"Now, hold on!" Clay slapped the trunk top. "I don't know what got your knickers twisted, but I'm just talking here. If you were me, you would ask the same things. Dead man, strange cause. Assault in his home soon after, house burns."

Tanner looked at him across the car. "Can I go now? I'd like to beat the storm."

Clay smiled. Tanner knew it wasn't entirely a reaction to humor. "You have any idea where you are?"

"We're on Belly Road. It turns into Route 41 about six miles up. That becomes 80, and as you know, that's—"

"I know, got it."

Tanner thought Clay's face showed an appreciation for Tanner's resourcefulness. Then, he felt the trunk pop open. "You have my cell if you need me." He dipped into the trunk.

Clay crossed his arms. "This is going to sound cliché."

Tanner slung his backpack onto his back. Then, in one swift motion, he hefted his bike and pointed it down Belly Road. "You're telling me not to go far."

"No, I'm telling you to watch your back."

Chapter 5

Jake Randal scrolled down through his blackberry. He sat behind the wheel with the engine off. Leaves skittered around the car. Mark Miller sat next to him. "What's it say?"

"Says to take the boy."

Miller turned to look across the street. The three-story brick building sat on a plot of land just barely big enough to host it. Most of the residents' lights were out. He sighed. "We're talking about the mental equivalent of melted margarine, here," Miller said.

"Says there are too many coincidences. The older one doesn't smell clean. You know as well as I do that there's a leak somewhere."

"Christ, leverage never ceases to get weird."

Randal took a manila envelope from atop the dashboard, and a scattering of pistachio shells sprinkled to the floor mat. He checked the gun in his shoulder holster, cracked open the car door, and turned to Miller. "Let the weird begin."

Miller opened his door. "I have no experience here," he said as he climbed out. "Can't they get violent?"

"The report says he's on meds. I think we'll be all right."

"But what if he has a seizure?" In his mind, Miller entertained negative scenarios of how this would go down. At all costs, he truly wanted to avoid encountering drool or soiled underpants.

Randal straightened his own tie. "Relax. He's retarded, not diabetic. Besides, your gun's loaded, isn't it?"

Chapter 6

The headlight on Tanner's bike pushed a faded cone of light no more than six feet in front of him. Over the past five hours, his eyes had grown tired from trying to see beyond the arc. It felt like someone was putting a Zippo to his thigh with every pump of the pedals. At times, he ducked back onto the fairly empty highway and plowed forward. He knew this was totally illegal, but he needed a break from the back roads and all of the trees that rose up like monster waves on either side of him.

An hour into the ride, he had begun to think less about the attic, the books, the fire, and Clay's reaction to his departure and more about where he was headed. At first he thought about simply heading home, but it seemed like such a dead end that he veered away. Then the idea hit him. The only tangible link to Dreavor's last days was the ferry ticket he found within the pages of Dreavor's book.

Why not?

He stayed close to the shoreline, and I-95 made it easier. As the sands in nighttime's hourglass began to run out, Tanner knew he was drawing near. He could smell the saltwater. Later he would call his manager, Jack Purcell, about the fire. That would be a fun conversation, and he didn't mind putting it off. Purcell was an older man, roughly sixty-seven. He had been running the state's intestate-recovery bureau for nearly twenty-seven years. He loved it, loved the mystery of what people left behind and the excitement of following those assets into the hands of a new owner.

Tanner coasted down the main road of Patterson, a small town on the shore of the Atlantic. The briny morning breath of the ocean hit him as soon as he rode over the crest of a hill. At that hour, there were few signs of life. He rode past the barber shop, the dirty windows of the Laundromat, and the Shanty Bar and Grill, where seagulls circled overhead, eyeing the rear dumpster overflowing with green trash bags from the previous day's customers.

At the end of the road sat Patterson's wharf, a small series of beaten, gray wood pylons set perpendicular to the ocean's edge. The wharf was protected by the mainland, which jutted out a quarter of a mile to both the north and south. The wharf may have been protected, but it wasn't insulated. On occasion in the past, storms had sneaked through and torn Patterson apart. Despite that, nothing had made it through in the past fifty years.

The fall temperature greeted Tanner. He always loved fall, the season with the most refreshing temperature for riding—it was like unending shade. He remembered biking as a kid on mornings like this, delivering the *Gazette*. He had built a tow and chariot for Jimmy, who would sit in the squeaky carriage with a smile—always that Basset Hound smile—shouting, "Faster!" whenever he got the urge. It sounded like "Fabter." Jimmy would lick his lips as they passed the Dunkin' Donuts, bless himself in front of the church—the gray stone Lutheran, not the white clapboard Methodist—moo at the old barn on Devonshire Road, and encourage Tanner up Morgan Hill. "C'mon, T, 'mon, T!" Neil Diamond's *Brother Love's Traveling Salvation Show* boomed from a small cassette recorder duct-taped to the chariot. Jimmy loved Neil. They would stop at the park a couple of blocks from home, in no hurry to subject Mom and Jimmy to each other any earlier in the day than was necessary.

Tanner would roll off his bike seat and lie flat on the ground. Jimmy would always sprint on over, smiling, and stand over Tanner. They both knew that Jimmy's Pampers would need to be changed. His pants frequently needed to be changed, even today, but now someone at Freeman's does it for him. God knows how often a twenty-six-year-old's Pampers need to be changed. When Tanner expressed concern, they told him they checked on him every four hours. Tanner wanted to have Jimmy live with him, but he couldn't afford the live-in help.

The clicks of Tanners wheels slowed as the ground leveled off and he neared the small dock. Chipped paint identified the words "Fog Island" on the aged wooden sign. Tanner watched a stout ferry chug into port, a faded blue Bronco 4x4 and a rusted Accord parked on its deck.

An older teenager leaped down from the breast bow, chewing a toothpick. He hooked a meaty rope around the short, fat pegs on the dock and lowered the ramp that extended from the ferry to the shore. A small, two-person hut watched over the entrance to the parking square, where an old minivan and a Toyota pickup idled.

Tanner stepped up to the shack and purchased a ticket from a fuzzy-faced teen in a Simpson's T-shirt. "They have a motel or something where you can stay the night?"

"I think so. Motel Gray or something."

"Is it open?"

"Don't know." The ticket taker jerked a thumb over his shoulder at the incoming ferry. "The boys on the boat will." Tanner plucked four singles from his wallet and picked up his paper ticket.

Minutes later, Tanner stood on the ferry's deck, paging through *The Collected Works* as black belches of smoke trailed behind. Secured in his knapsack, the book had survived the night's ordeal. The lines refreshed his memory—an eidetic memory. The words rekindled imagery of madness, true love, burdens of age, and lust, all portrayed in colorful language with multiple meanings.

He looked up from the pages to see the shoreline expand as they ventured toward Fog Island, just visible in the distance. He rested with his elbows over the railing, watching the ocean and the view. The railing vibrated up his arms in tune with the diesel's chug.

His knapsack buzzed loudly. He always set his cell phone to a loud ring so that when he was riding he wouldn't miss a call. He read the caller's name on the phone's cover before he opened it.

"What a surprise," Tanner said.

"I got cops calling me this early in the morning?" Rack asked.

Tanner knew Rack was pissed—pissed at having been woken up early more than anything else. "Was it a Lieutenant Clay?"

"What the fuck did you do to that house?"

"Nothing. Didn't the cops tell you?"

"Jesus, Tanner, now what? They going to can you?"

"I haven't talked to my manager yet."

Rack's tone eased a bit. "This connection is horrible, where are you?"

Tanner looked across the foggy horizon and turned to take in the rusty, stout ferry. Like a cheap special effect in an Ice Capades show, a dense fog was slowly, slowly starting to lift from the ocean's surface. "On my way to Fog Island."

Even with the rising static, Rack's voice boomed through the receiver. "Fog Is—Listen, genius, you're not Sherlock Holmes!"

"You think so?"

Then the connection failed. No reception. Tanner stared at the empty phone. Fog Island must be a little light on cell tower coverage. It was now close to 8:30 AM. He hoped a landline on the island would be able to connect him with Jack Purcell, his manager. Tanner shook his head. His conversation with Purcell would play out soon enough. Before him, a burger patty stretched across the horizon. As the diesel cranked, Fog Island loomed larger.

Had Dreavor choked on these same diesel fumes? Was there something remotely connected with Shakespeare and this lousy-looking rock? Was Dreavor in it for the money? Was there any real money to be had? Had the old man found something? And why was Tanner postponing life as the hell he knew it to chase some lunatic's last days?

Chapter 7

The ferry bucked when its bow crunched the cracked rubber of the aged tires nailed to the Fog Island dock. An ancient, rusty garbage truck sat waiting for the ferry to take it back to the mainland. Tanner wheeled his bike down the steel ramp. Everyone else on the ferry stayed aboard for its next stop at nearby Devish Fall.

Tanner couldn't detect any organization on this side of the channel. He passed between two huts. Each may have at one time been a vendor of tickets or arbiter of who was to go across in what order, but that was seasons ago, a time when those shacks had roofs, doors, and windows.

Tanner shielded his eyes against the hissing wind and the sand it roused off the shore. Fog Island was undeveloped. The only road looked as if someone had taken a knife and spread a slab of tar between the trees. Tanner rode forward. He saw a salt box house planted every so often in the grass, nothing with any New England charm. They looked like the epitome of the hard life that was survival in the early days of a coastal fishing village. Tanner coasted past the first couple of shacks, looking for signs of life. He glimpsed a laundry line flying pumpkin-colored pants and yellow underwear.

As he continued along the road, he wound his way between undisturbed patches of woodland. At the crest of another hill sat a large house. Tanner pulled up to the wraparound porch and stopped under a sign hanging above the front steps.

Gray Inn.

The inn rose three, maybe four stories, a height Tanner concluded was too tall for its own safety. Sections of the house clung to random stone chimneys like drunken sailors on lampposts. Two dented pickup trucks sat on the chewed yellow grass in front of the house. Tanner observed that tool boxes and rusted lobster traps were piled in the back of the first truck, and a collection of fishing poles, like splayed pick-up sticks, were thrown across the bed of the other.

A dog slept on the porch. As Tanner walked his bike closer, the weathered outer shingles on the sides of the inn amazed Tanner with their ability to stay vertical. The disjointed porch itself must have been quite uncomfortable for the ... mutt. Tanner was never very good at judging breeds of dog, but this one really looked like a dirty mutt.

A chilly wind slapped him in the rear and stirred the tangles on the mutt. The clouds had grown heavier since leaving the docks. The dog stood, stretched, looked over at Tanner as if to see he was still there, and then passed through a doggie door in the front door.

"I'm just supposed to follow you, is that it?" *Clever.* Tanner locked his bike to the porch, slung his knapsack over his shoulder, and entered the inn.

Tanner had begun to blink his eyes to adjust to the dim interior when tobacco smoke slammed into him. Because Tanner had spent so many waking hours slicing through crisp early morning air, he registered the smoke instantly. With his strong, clean lungs, he embraced it and continued into the house.

Tanner stepped into a mudroom, a narrow room with a series of hooks supporting thick rubber and leather coats. He continued into a short hallway with a series of framed photographs on the walls. He walked slowly to observe the photos, which were black and whites of fishermen, mostly, on dock or boarding their boats.

These were thick men with wet hair, scraggy beards, and black suspenders for full-body waders. Other photos included men and women on the beach enjoying a nice beach day, and there was a full porch of men in flannels, jeans, and boots resting on big wooden rockers, each holding a can of something. Voices murmured from deeper down the hallway—lots of voices.

The floor creaked under Tanner's steps. The voices grew louder. He had the feeling that he was walking into someone's home. The hallway opened up into a "great" room with a full horseshoe bar, a set of couches and La-Z-Boy seats, and a round dining table. A large, stone fireplace watched from the center of the room's far wall. A queen-sized bed could have sat on its irons. Tall bookshelves filled with old hardcovers ran from floor to ceiling and bracketed the fireplace.

Men stretched out in chairs and slumped at the bar. All were smoking cigarettes and gripping some drink in a beer bottle or a rocks glass. Their thick carrot fingers and meaty shoulders were the equipment of men who maneuvered nets in and out of the water for a career. Tanner felt a little dainty in his foul-weather nylon warm-ups and biking shoes. The only person of authority in the room seemed to be an old man behind the stone-based bar. Tanner drifted over.

"Hiya," the old man said. His left eyebrow was a train wreck of white hair and seemed permanently arched, leaving Tanner with the sense that the old man didn't believe a word he heard. He twisted a gray dishtowel inside a beer mug and smiled. "Welcome to our sceptered isle."

"Hiya. I'm Tanner Cook. I was just passing through. Saw the chimney smoke and decided to warm up."

The old man smiled, and his entire face squinted in a batch of wrinkles. This was a man who had spent time in the sun. "I'm Mack Horn. I'm the owner."

"Something smells delicious," Tanner said. Several of the men were eating big sandwiches—Tanner could smell the mayonnaise. Others were shoveling soup.

"We call it the Bunk: bacon under nice kelp."

"Bunk?"

"It's basically a BLT with some spices."

"I'll try it."

Mack called, "Jenny, one Bunk," over his shoulder. It was then that Tanner saw the serving window on the back wall, behind which was a kitchen. Mack looked back at Tanner. "My wife Jenny does the cookin', I mix the drinks. You want fries with that?"

"Sure."

"Full plate!"

From the back window, a small female voice acknowledged the order.

"What can I get you to drink?"

"Just seltzer, thanks."

"I got that." Mack scooped a glass through a bin of ice. "So you won't be staying?" Whether it was the house-fire chase, the bike ride through the night, or the rush of exploring the island, Tanner felt exhaustion creep under his skin. A pillow sounded good.

"Thinking about the night if you've got the room," Tanner said, nodding at the thick crowd.

"Oh, they mostly live on the island," Mack said. "*The Sentinel* landed this morning, back from a three-weeker. Boys are a bit hungry."

"I bet."

"You on vacation?" Mack asked. As they talked, one fisherman dropped a few pieces of paper on the bar with a word or two scribbled on them. Mack glanced at the paper and then set out to make a drink.

"Not really, just a weekend away."

"Where you from?"

"Gill. You get many tourists?"

"Not after August," Mack said. "This is the only place to catch a bite on the island. There's no shopping, no movies, no sights—not much here."

"Except the fish."

Mack tilted his head as he poured a black Guinness. "Even then, you need to head out a ways."

"Okay."

"Get ya another drink? A real drink?"

Tanner's watch said 11:30 AM. "Definitely later. If you can believe it, I rode all night." As the words came out of his mouth, Tanner felt Mack's eyebrow cocking at him. And why not? Who rides straight through the night for no good reason?

"Some mutinous winds out there," Mack said.

"Yeah, makes riding a bit less enjoyable. I would love to crash for a couple of hours."

Mack nodded and set up a fresh Jack Daniels on the rocks. "Sure, when you're finished eating, we'll get you settled."

The mutt panted its way through the lounge. None of the patrons seemed to pay it any attention. Tanner didn't suppose the health department ever found its way out there. When Tanner checked over at Mack, he seemed to be expecting Tanner's inquiry.

"That's Lucius. He won't bother you. Great watchdog, though." Mack put a plate with a sandwich and fries in front of Tanner.

"I bet he likes Bunks."

Mack hiccupped a laugh. "Raised on 'em. They're in his bones."

The ten-foot-tall windows on the left side of the room looked out on a stretch of dunes capped with tall grass. The house was built on a higher plane of the island. Tanner could see the ocean in the distance. The sky had grown rougher, the blue beaten back by smoky clouds.

"You ever have trouble with storms?" Tanner asked.

"Usually, but if you leave them alone, they'll generally leave you be." Mack shifted to Tanner's side of the bar to arrange

55

glasses and nodded at the remaining bits of sandwich. "What'd you think?"

"Oh, it's fantastic. Bunks is good."

"Now, don't go telling the world. If New Hampshire steals the idea, our tourist rush will be crushed."

Tanner laughed. "No worries, your recipe is safe with me." He thought he had earned a shot. He removed his small notebook from his knapsack and put a photo on the bar. "You remember ever seeing this guy?"

Mack drew his attention from pouring and squinted at the picture. He looked up at Tanner. "Don't think so. That guy dead?"

"Yes." Tanner thought the old man digested the corpse photo well.

"We don't get many dead guys in here. Although, sometimes it takes a while to tell." Mack cracked up at his own joke.

As a courtesy, Tanner laughed too. "Are there other places to rent a room on the island?"

Mack sobered quickly. "You a cop?"

"No, I'm working on his estate. We can't seem to locate any relatives, and before we auction his property to the public, we just want to make sure we turn over every stone. We thought maybe we might come across a relation if we followed his footsteps from the last few weeks of his life."

Mack continued drying glasses. "No, there are no other places to get a room on the island."

"Do folks put their houses up for rent for any—"

"You know, I do think I remember your guy now." Mack picked up another slip of paper.

Tanner nearly bit his tongue through the Bunk. He kept his eyes on Mack, expectant.

"He was a quiet guy. Stayed here about a week. Kept to himself, mostly. Wasn't long ago, maybe five weeks. Used to come down for eggs in the morning and then go out for the day, I'm not sure where, but he'd come home for dinner, early, and then retreat to his room, early."

Tanner's blood rushed and his breath shortened. He looked over at the crowd, all busy with their food, drink, smoke, and conversation. No one seemed aware of the amazing connection he had just made. No matter. Tanner returned his full attention to Mack.

Mack continued with his description. "Didn't eat much, neither. He read a lot, always carrying books. Didn't know anyone on the island from what I could tell. Sound like your guy?"

Tanner nodded with a mouthful of sandwich. While Mack exchanged a drink for another paper slip, Tanner hurried his chewing. He swallowed and asked, "You say he went out during the day, each entire day of the week that he was here?"

Mack nodded and called out, "Eddie, ready."

"Did he ever say where he went or what he was doing all day?"

Mack shook his head. "Naw, and I mean, there's not much to do here."

"Was it beach weather?"

"Yeah, maybe."

"From what I know about him, he didn't strike me as the beach towel and flip-flop type."

Mack shrugged. "I didn't pay that much attention." He dropped his attention to the next square of paper on the bar.

Tanner retreated to his fries, but his mind moved too fast to notice their taste.

"Kid, you want anything else?"

"Um, yeah. Did he come back sunburned?"

"It was weeks ago. Don't remember anything terribly interesting. Sorry, I can't help you much."

Mack pulled another slip of paper toward him and pulled his head back to be able to read it in focus.

"No, no this is very helpful." Tanner flipped his notebook page. "Any chance I could stay in the same room he did?"

Mack nodded and tipped a Beefeater bottle over a Collins glass.

"Tom?" Mack called to the crowd. Someone acknowledged. Then Mack turned toward Tanner. "Not much to it."

"I don't need much. I won't see much more than the bed."

"Mind sharing a common bathroom?"

"I'm used to it." Many of the low-rent places where Tanner stayed for races in Europe required the same.

Mack threw a thumb over his shoulder toward the kitchen. "Jenny and I could use the company. These lunks will be gone soon. Those that haven't left for the season have decided to sit this storm out on mainland."

Tanner wondered just what he was getting himself into. His only consolation, only real consolation, was that he had just learned that Dreavor had stayed here. And this old man took his time remembering it.

Chapter 8

The winds knocked against her car, a Taurus rental, and sand scattered across the windows. Tall reeds scratched at the doors as if trying to get in. Her binoculars sat on the dash. She eased her revolver from its holster and slid it under the front seat. Often when she sat, the gun's grip rubbed against her lower rib, and since she had been driving all day following her target, her side had begun to bruise. He was inside the inn and looked like he would be a while. She turned a page in *Romeo and Juliet*. Mr. Capulet raged about his daughter's infidelity to the family.

After a few minutes, she looked up from the book. Her eyes took a trip inside the car. The dash contained a wonderful stereo and a radio that operated with satellites in orbit. She hadn't turned it on—with the storm that would've been too much noise, no way to hear someone approaching. On the passenger seat was the rental agreement. She saw herself in the rearview. When did those wrinkles arrive? The miles behind those wrinkles didn't feel like her own—the years had been taken from her. Her life had been hijacked by the state. They kept her on the move in pursuits like this one. Never time or permission for love in her life, tragic or otherwise. She touched the wrinkled corner of her eye. Was this what the author meant by "scars that never felt a wound"?

Wind-driven sand *crickled* against the windows. Maybe there would be something to bargain with at the end of this trail. Maybe there was some way to play for a fresh and fuller life for her younger sister Daes and her family. With their freedom, they could enjoy themselves in peace on an island like this. In a split second, her heart sobered. Had too much time passed? Were thoughts like that pipe dreams? She turned her attention back to the inn.

Chapter 9

It was an old room, small, with everything constructed of wood many years ago. The mattress on the old four-poster bed had been compacted from years of use and damp, salty air. The bed springs squeaked with the slightest pressure.

Mack had described the house as early last century chic and then laughed like working sandpaper. He had slowly limped up the stairs to make sure Tanner found the right room and that he knew where the communal bathroom was. Mack and his wife lived in a bedroom off the kitchen. Tanner wondered how they were able to keep things together financially. Mack's health was obviously not good, and their main business was from the very cyclical world of fishing and the occasional wayward tourist. Where did one go for medical treatment around here? How could they afford it? Tanner compared that to his own situation. He lived with incessant medical bills, and now Jimmy's dialysis would begin soon.

There was one lamp in the room, and Tanner sat on the bed under its light. He tugged a piece of stationery out of his satchel and wagged it open. The envelope fell from his hand and disappeared between the bed and the wall. He had been carrying the letter around with him for more than a month. He needed that envelope. Since there was no headboard, he turned and put his face flush with the wall, looked down, and saw it ... and something else as well.

Wedged between the bed frame and the wall, about a foot from the ground, was an Eveready flashlight. He reached for it. He had to really stretch, but he snagged it and brought it up. As he sat back, water dripped from the head of the flashlight. Water had been trapped inside, even underneath the face. A piece of duct tape was wrapped around the handle with the words "Kargil Municipal" written on it.

Tanner felt as though he were levitating. His blood chilled. Kargil Municipal. Frank Dreavor lived in Kargil and worked for the town. Had he "borrowed" this flashlight? What did he do, take a bath with it? Why did he leave it behind? Had he forgotten it? He wouldn't have left it on purpose ... would he? Tanner flipped it on, and a faint ray shined on the bed, on his letter.

He picked up the paper. On Boston University letterhead, the first lines read:

> *Dear Mr. Cook,*
> *On behalf of the Selection Committee and our faculty we would like to invite you to matriculate with us next semester. As Chair of the Department of Archaeology it is my pleasure ...*

Archaeology. It was something he had wanted to do for as long as he could remember. It was late one night in February when, surfing the net as a distraction from the "Russia in the Twentieth Century" term paper he was working on, he found the BU site and filled out an application for their graduate program. Some might say archeology was an odd choice for someone who for the first seventeen years of his life never crossed any border other than those touching New Hampshire and Vermont. Often, he had wanted to keep pedaling, to stay on the highway, to plunge into the unknown, to see beyond. Archaeology—a chance to study the past and to trace the progress of civilizations.

What was he thinking? Study in Boston? Six hours away. Away from Jimmy. By moving to Boston, he wouldn't be able to see Jimmy, not with any real frequency. Jimmy's heart would break. Not to mention the costs; every minute in study was non-income producing. Tanner's expenses, if anything, were rising, not abating.

At that moment, his shoulders felt like they were twisting, like marbles had slipped under the skin of his neck. He jammed the letter back into its envelope and rammed the envelope back into his knapsack. That's why they called them dreams. He had intended to call Jimmy now that he was likely awake and into his morning routine. Screw that—Jimmy could wait. He snatched up his helmet and bolted out of the room.

Chapter 10

Tanner spent the day pedaling the circumference of the small island, six miles in all. On any other day, six miles would have been nothing, a morning's all-out sprint, but given Fog Island's never-cut sea grass, the spiking dunes, and soft sand patches, Tanner often found that he carried his bike rather than the other way around. He made two loops and found nothing that he thought might have even remotely interested Dreavor. His back dripped with sand and his sneakers squished when he trudged up the Gray Inn porch at about 5 PM.

Tanner had barely set one foot on the inn's front staircase when it struck him. One item, only one item on the island was not displayed in the photographs lining the inn's walls. Most every item, structure, location, or view could be found in one photograph or another. The docks, the ferry, the dunes, the beaches, the dock remnants, and the other houses or porches of the island were all there. And they were all fresh in his mind. In no photograph, however, did he see the lighthouse. Could that be a coincidence? Maybe. But if not, why omit the lighthouse? Tanner remembered it clearly from his run earlier in the day. Not a monstrous entity, but beautiful in its simplicity and noteworthy for its age—it was constructed of stone, and it stood alone on an even smaller stretch of dirt about seventy yards from shore.

Given his suspicious frame of mind, the only reason Tanner could think of to omit the lighthouse from the photograph wall was to prevent drawing attention to it. With that thought, he knew he needed to revisit the lighthouse. It was thin reasoning, but it was all he had.

The skies released everything on him as soon as he left the inn. The whitecapped ocean looked like a pack of snapping cobras when the lighthouse's trail flashed over its face. Tanner pushed his bike into the wind, right up to the edge of the dunes that separated the shore from the roaring ocean. The lighthouse stood alone on an even smaller island about one hundred yards from shore. Now, who was the genius who thought that one up?

Tanner could feel the rain drops through his rain suit. His pants flapped madly at his legs. Thank God it wasn't cold out. Despite the penetrating winds, he unzipped his jacket. He wanted answers.

Tanner had always been a good swimmer. It all started after his mother had run the house into debt. Tanner did everything he could to pitch in, his main job being a delivery boy for the local pharmacy. On his bike, he could cover ground quickly. Some of it was his raw speed on the bike, and some of it was his knowledge of which backyards led to which addresses and which wooded areas could be cut through.

On days when the first delivery of the day brought him anywhere near the vicinity of home, Tanner would pick up Jimmy. While Jimmy sat in his trailer and listened, Tanner would relate his entire school day. "Taxi Cab Geometry is a neat concept." Every now and then Jimmy barked a word that Tanner had just used. "Tabbi Tab!" On hot days, they would stop by Hile's Pond and swim. Of course, Jimmy couldn't swim all that well, so Tanner did double time. Necessity had once again made him stronger.

He swam toward the lighthouse in his rain pants and T-shirt, holding his headlamp, goggles, and shoes above water. The waves were like a croupier's rack, intermittently brushing him back.

When he reached the island, he slowly climbed the rocks on shore. As he began to weave his way up to the lighthouse, he admitted to himself that he was cold.

He climbed the last few rocks a bit faster in order to find some place he could tuck himself away from the wind. He couldn't hear his own exhausted breaths because of the runaway wind coming off the ocean. He put his hand up in front of his face to shield himself against the blistering rain, and then he looked back at Fog Island and saw that his bike was watching him from its point on the dune.

He shivered and bent forward into the wind as he circled the sixty-foot structure. This lighthouse was not large compared to some Tanner had seen. It stood roughly in the center of the island with about a fifty-yard radius to the ocean. Other than the spinning top light, the rest of the lighthouse was dark. Tanner figured the light must be automated with a failsafe or warning mechanism of some sort. Like most buildings on Fog Island, the lighthouse was made of stone. Over time, the stones on the side of the lighthouse facing the ocean had been shaved by blowing saltwater. Tall grass grew up near the door on the leeward side. Tanner looked up at the front door with its small window at eye-level. It stood atop a short staircase. The railings appeared to be of a more recent vintage than the rest of the house, as they were plain and did not demonstrate any craftsmanship. Storms had probably washed the originals out a long time ago.

He climbed the stairs with both hands on the rails. He stopped halfway and turned to look behind him. The rest of Fog Island lay downhill, but the clouds above obscured any moonlight. There were no streetlights. He saw a couple of Fog Island house lights way off in the distance, more like fireflies far out of reach. In the beam of his headlamp, the rain sliced from left to right in the steady wind. His sneakers clomped the rest of the way up the stairs. He wiped his goggles and his mouth clear, and then he reached for the doorknob.

The door was locked. He cupped his headlamp against the window and squinted through the deluge across his goggles to see if he could detect detail inside. A crack of thunder shook him out of his inspection.

Christ! What was he doing here? Why didn't he leave this alone?

He turned to head back to Gray's Inn for a shower in the communal bathroom, kidding himself that he didn't care if wrinkled Mack or his leathery, old wife were in there with him—the more body warmth the better. But a flash caught his eye—not lightning, more of a glint, a reflection, down below the stairs, where a normal house might have a cellar window.

Tanner swung down under the handrail. The base around the lighthouse was surrounded by tall weed grass, making a bit of a lean-to in the cubby of space where the lighthouse and stairs met. The decibels of the storm dropped a notch. Tanner parted the grass and came upon a fishing pole on its side. A bait bucket sat with water pouring over its lip. And that was it. Some local probably used it for his resting spot. Nothing more.

Tanner walked around to the windward side of the house. Stone disappeared into sand. Sand and seawater tore through the air on the wind. Shielding his eyes, he looked out on the ocean as best he could. He wondered what would happen to ships at sea without the beacon next to him. He imagined grown men, like the lunch customers of Gray Inn, being ground between the angry waves and the rocks below. His own shivering shook the images away. He wanted dry warmth. When he turned to head back to his bike, his foot crunched something. He bent to inspect under his shoe: shattered glass. Looking around and then up, he saw a broken window above him on the windward side, flapping in the gale. The natural stones that composed the lighthouse walls were imperfectly shaped. A bump here, an outcrop there. A man with flexibility and decent strength could …

Not worth it. I can come back in the morning if I really want to.

In minutes, he had scaled the wall all the way to the broken window. His thigh began to ache and cramp midway up, but it was just as fast to complete the climb as it would've been to work his way down. The trickiest part was simultaneously gripping the side of the lighthouse and removing his jacket so he could swat away the loose window shards. Climbing through the window, carefully avoiding the remaining teeth of glass, he maneuvered onto a wooden stairwell that wound up and around the inside of the tower.

It smelled like aged seaweed inside, but it was quieter. He was sure this place could heat up like an adobe oven under a summer sun. As Tanner latched the frame of the shattered window, he saw a vast ocean of snapping whitewater. He put his dripping jacket on so he could to descend the stairs with a hand on each railing.

The stairs creaked as if they were allergic to pressure. He stepped slowly and carefully given the slippery, old walkway. To Tanner's right, just over the handrail, the core of the lighthouse was a hollow shaft; he thought it was as creepy as the clock tower in *Vertigo*.

The ground floor held a kitchen with three inches of water on the floor, a wood-burning stove, and a sink. There was a loft with a space for what Tanner thought was a bed. A generator sat atop a stack of two-by-fours. Tanner spotted at least two drains in the sidewall, both apparently blocked. No item gave any hint of recent use. Tanner found the drawers and cabinets empty, and there was no trash barrel. He heard water streaming down throughout the dark lighthouse. He turned his headlamp to the ceiling and saw half a dozen lines of water dripping like vines in a jungle. A rusted tin roof kept the generator dry. A power cable came through the ground level and was attached to the generator. And that was it. If that were to be cut, what kind of backup systems or alerts were in place?

There was a door in addition to the one Tanner had peeked through earlier. Tanner turned the knob and it opened; a rush of the kitchen water spilled forward. Tanner's light spotted a set of descending stairs. Water smacked his heels and rippled over his feet. From the earthen walls, he knew that the cellar descended below sea level. Tanner crouched so he could fit down the stairwell.

The stairway was about ten steps down. The entire basement was only about twelve by twelve. The masonry down there was less weatherworn, but it was still ancient stonework. An odd wooden table held an old milk crate filled with packages of light bulbs, the sixty-watt kind. Water was up to his knees and rising. Tanner was about to return to the kitchen when his headlamp caught what he thought was a slug on the far wall. He drew closer and bent to inspect.

With a shivering finger, he traced a groove etched in the wall. Another next to it. A word was carved in the wall, like a date marker on a cornerstone. The letters disappeared beneath the water's edge. Who would bother etching words in this place?

The water was now hip high. The leaks were loud. Tanner directed his headlamp up the stairway: a steady spill of rainwater poured through the open door and down the stairs. He didn't need to do this. He could just go back to the inn. And then he put his head into the water.

He instantly vaulted up. *Christ! Fucking FrEEZing!* The icy shock forced breath out of his lungs. Tanner's eye sockets felt as if they had been left in an ice tray overnight. The headlamp's light cast a pale yellow. The water was now up to his waist.

What the hell am I doing!?

Then, he submerged again. He put his fingers in the indentations and traced their path. The darkness and the movement of the water made reading the words difficult, even with the pale yellow blip of his lamp. He got two letters on his first breath and then surfaced.

The water was above his belly button. The storm and leaks continued. He checked up the stairwell, comforting himself that he had a clear path to the open kitchen door. He could come back tomorrow. Have his Braille experiment then. No shame in that. Tanner inspected his quivering fingers, they were near Skyy Vodka-bottle blue. He knew well the signs of hypothermia. His winter biking training had taught him those symptoms long ago.

He plunged back into the water for another read. He had identified the first few words— "I come to bury ..."

On his sixth submersion, he was tracing the final words when he heard a thud, a sound so strong it carried underwater. By then, the water was collarbone high. He walked through the molasses-like resistance and felt as if his rain pants were lined with needles. He wrapped his arms around himself and started up the stairs—

The kitchen door was closed. It was open just a minute ago wasn't it? He tugged himself up the stairwell. The door wouldn't yield, and the knob wouldn't turn.

"Heyyy!" Tanner screamed. "Heyyy! Who's up there? I'm down here!"

He slumped down on the top step with his back against the kitchen door. The water lapped at his crotch. His dick and balls were tucked among themselves for shelter. He was amused at the thought, which meant his thinking was getting cloudy.

This is serious shit. Get up!

The stairway ceiling slanted down. When he stood, he braced himself between the narrow walls and hunched over to avoid clocking his head on the ceiling. He summoned his last drops of energy, propped one hand against each wall and swung his feet up and flat against the basement door. Water dripped and plopped in the stairwell below him. He curled himself as if he were crunching for a sit-up and then exploded his feet against the wooden door.

Choom!

The door croaked under his kick, but it remained intact. Tanner's breath came in shallow pants of steam. His feet splashed back into the stairwell and rested on the second step. The water was now near his sternum. Even if he didn't drown, hypothermia would gnaw on him soon.

He cocked himself again. The stupid motherfucker who shut that door had no idea what kind of power were in the legs of someone who could take a 45-degree, two-mile incline in under three minutes.

His legs shot forward. The basement door shattered in half, though the handle section remained locked in place. Tanner's right hand slipped and he lost his hold, splashing down into the icy water.

Chapter 11

After biking back to the inn, Tanner had taken a hot shower in the common bath next door to his room. Well, the shower wasn't quite hot, not even warm—it was more like ... cold. So, he changed into heavy cotton sweats and planted himself on the hearth in front of the fire, feeling it bake him, seeping into his muscles, and drawing them out. The fire held him with its dance. His mind was mud, and the swaying velvet butter and merlot flames beckoned him, drawing his attention, allowing him to set his brain afloat. In seconds, he stretched out on the firm hot mattress of the hearth. His eyes drifted up and down the bookcases as he read the various titles. Many classic works from authors from England. *Wait a minute ... something's not right.*

"That fireplace is the best in Maine," said a voice behind him. Tanner snapped up and spun toward the bar. Mack stood at the entrance to the room, leaning on the doorframe and keeping weight off his weak leg. "Didn't mean to startle you." He chuckled and limped into the room. Tanner watched him make his way over to the left wall's bookcase. His right foot dragged across the floor, always searching to catch up. "House is kind of quiet tonight. Jenny turns in early. She gets up before light to prepare breakfast. Drink?"

Mack pushed on the book bindings of a section of five or so hardcovers. The books swung inward and revealed a collection of dusty brown bottles on the reverse, hugged against the shelf by short iron bars.

"Nice," Tanner said. He wondered what other secrets Mack maintained.

Mack fished two glasses from behind the bottles. "What'd you see today?"

"A lot of beach. A lot of grass. Seems like there were a few different dock systems over time."

Mack uncorked a bottle. "Yep. A few."

"What happened—tides shift, old age?"

"No." Mack turned toward the fire. "Storms."

Tanner saw a flash from the skies ignite the raging ocean. Thunder shook the house, and the bottles tinkled against each other.

"It's a mean one tonight," Mack said. "Must've given you the needles out there."

"You mean the rain? Yeah. That's what you call it, huh?"

"That's what we call it."

The rocks glasses jittered as Mack made his way over to the couch that faced the fire. "You must be tired. I don't think you slept much today."

"Actually, no."

"Try this. It'll warm the storm out of ya."

Mack handed Tanner a glass of liquid mahogany. The fireplace roared as a downdraft lashed at the fire. Mack braced himself on the couch arm and folded in stages like an old measuring stick until his bottom rested on the leather. He sipped from his glass and, groaning with satisfaction, melted back into the couch.

Tanner looked at his glass and took a sip. Hot alcohol ran across his tongue and fell down his throat, leaving a sweet flavor in its wake. "Not bad."

"Hot and rebellious liquors, we like to say."

"Mmm." Tanner hurried a sip down so he could capitalize on a thought. "That reminds me. Why didn't you tell me the truth about Dreavor?"

The fire crackled, and sparks jumped from a wet patch in a log.

Mack stalled in mid sip. He looked over at Tanner. "What'd you just say?"

"Dreavor. You knew why he came here. You pretended otherwise." Tanner's heart thudded in his chest. The closest he had come to bluffing like this was ... never.

"What in the world makes you say that?"

"Your dog's name is Lucius. The most widely used name in Shakespeare's works."

Mack let out a crusty cough. He shrugged. "If you say so."

"You called liquor 'hot and rebellious.' Funny, that's how it was described in *As You Like It*."

Mack laughed in a shake of the head. "The rum works fast, eh?"

"What was Dreavor trying to do?"

"Vacation with seagulls, for all I know."

"Shakespeare's last play, *The Tempest*."

"Oh boy, wait, I know this. A tempest is a storm. And there's a storm going on. That's it, you got me."

"When I first saw you this morning, you called the winds 'mutinous.' A phrase from *The Tempest*." Tanner sipped his rum, hoping to settle his jittering hands. He couldn't believe Mack had let him stay after the accusations.

"Kid, you ought to write for a living. Normally, I'd say you can't make this shit up, but somehow you managed to. Relax, enjoy the fire and the rum. It's homemade."

"This room probably made a pretty good mini theater at one time, huh?"

"For Shakespearean performances? For the folks that live on this island? On second thought, maybe I should shut you off."

"What I haven't been able to put together was how Dreavor came to meet up with you. He was a loner, like a savant. He didn't read the newspaper. Didn't own a radio or TV, no computer, no internet. But he came seeking you, I think. What made him connect this place with his work?"

"Not that I don't think this is amusing on one level, but didn't you tell me you were looking for this guy's relatives? Are you going to accuse me of being his long-lost husband in a second?"

"No, I'm—"

"It's okay if you do, just keep it down, 'cause Jenny will positively kill me if she hears that shit."

With a *tink*, Tanner put his glass down on the stone hearth next to his sneakers. "I want to know what Dreavor was doing on this island."

"And vacation is out of the question? That's the problem with the modern day—you need a well-supported reason to do everything. You can't just sit and fish a day away anymore. It's such a loss of productivity. Global economy doesn't tolerate a day's jack-off."

"He wasn't vacationing."

"How can you be so sure?"

"Because I saw his workshop. Dreavor *was* his work. He wouldn't leave it to spend a week walking the beach. Why take a vacation in September? Why not the summer?"

"He cut lawns, right? Man works outside all day long, he has enough hot sun."

"Maybe, but he *was* his books, his notes, his calculations. He didn't seem like the beach, doesn't seem like it would've been for him." He wasn't making progress. Tanner retreated to his drink. *Think. Think.*

"Like I said, I never saw him during the day. After breakfast he was off and he returned later in the afternoon. On his last day, he let out of here so fast he barely had time to gather his things. Sorry to disappoint you, but we didn't go skinny dipping together for lunch."

75

Tanner decided to reach back and take another route. He shifted his eyes to the windows when a splay of rain smacked against them. It sounded as if a million horseflies were storming the inn. The horizon shattered with neon lightning. For a brief wink the thrashing ocean was lit.

"Anybody out there tonight?"

Mack sipped his drink. "Always seems to be. But I think most of the boys were on shore today. We'll hear in the morning."

"I'll be heading out in the morning."

"You giving up on your friend?"

"Dreavor? Not yet. But there are fewer and fewer breadcrumbs to follow each day."

"Maybe he was all alone in the world."

"You're probably right. I mean, as far as I could tell at his home, he had no photographs of relatives or anything. It seems so ... so disconnected, doesn't it?"

"You're asking the wrong guy. Take a look around, I love photographs."

"I know, I know. Except ..." Tanner sipped the dark liquor. It was a heavy, sweet liqueur. "I noticed you don't have a single shot of the lighthouse."

The cotton above Mack's eyes rose. "I don't?"

"Probably the oldest structure on this rock, and you don't have a single shot of it?"

"I'll be damned. Jeez, you're probably the first one to notice. I'll have to get one."

"You can have one of mine."

"What's that now?"

"I biked up there tonight."

"That's where you went? In this?" Mack threw a glance at the window. "Nor'easters like this have been known to sweep folks off the island and out to sea."

"I believe it. That ocean was no easy proposition."

Mack uncrossed his legs. "What'd you say?"

"I had a look inside tonight."

76

Mack sat forward. "The lighthouse? How did you get out there?"

"I swam."

Mack laughed and shook his head as if Tanner had claimed to be Santa Claus.

"It was locked up tight." Tanner read the disbelief in the old man's face. Tanner knew he was forcing clues together—Dreavor's visit, the wet flashlight, the absence of a lighthouse photograph— but the inscription in the lighthouse basement and the unlikely slamming of the basement door emboldened him to push his bluff with Mack. "One of the upper windows is shattered. A reasonably flexible person can make the climb. Or, on a more gentle night, anyone could jimmy the front door."

Mack seemed to summon his strength and eased himself up out of the couch's maw. "Tonight's a dangerous night to go poking around that old wreck." He stood and shuffle-limped to his hidden stash.

"Tell me about it. So, how did Dreavor get out there?"

"I didn't know that he did."

"Just before he left. You're saying he didn't mention it to you?"

Mack shrugged. "Like I said, we never discussed it."

"You know, it's funny, you've got some of the great British authors of the Renaissance on your shelves. Donne, Milton, Spenser. But no Shakespeare."

"He has a funny way of talking."

"It certainly takes a while to figure out." The rum haze infiltrated Tanner's sinuses. He closed his eyes and put his glass down on the hearth. The fire worked his back like a masseuse. "But no more than Donne."

Mack's head cocked from side to side as he opened his bookshelf bar. "Never liked him much either." He came back toward the couch with a reloaded glass. As he walked, he held it away from his body.

"The lighthouse had a faceplate that indicated construction in 1626."

"I had forgotten it was that old. What exactly did you do in there?"

"I walked around. Except in the basement. There, I more or less swam."

Mack stopped in his tracks. Rum spilled over the edge of his glass, and he shot Tanner a look. "Basement!"

The concern shook Tanner. Despite the roaring fire, his skin cooled.

"Know it?" Tanner asked.

"Part of the reason the place is no longer kept by a family is because the tide floods through the foundation. It's very dangerous. Didn't you see the signs?"

Tanner shook his head and started thinking. "On a night like this, it also floods from the top down."

"Th—that—that's why it's boarded closed."

"Doesn't help matters when you're locked inside."

"Locked?"

"Somehow the basement door locked, sealing me in."

"What?" Mack turned. Tanner watched the old man tighten and limp over to the fireplace. He looked out the window for a long moment. Tanner tensed. Mack stood to his right and said, barely loud enough to be heard over the fire, "Time for you to go." He took the poker out of the andirons. "Someone has been parked down the road a ways since you got here."

Tanner kept his eye on the poker. "Parked?"

Mack speared the flames and orange sparks exploded. "Get your things and meet me at the back door in two minutes."

"Hold on." Tanner flagged Mack with a hand. "I've been on the go since yesterday morning. Are you sure that someone didn't just park—"

"You don't live on this island as long as I have without being able to tell when something doesn't belong."

Tanner looked around the room.

Mack thrust the poker into its holder. "Boy, I can't protect you here. I wouldn't know how to lock this place up. I haven't in thirty years. Back door, two minutes." He turned toward the kitchen and left.

Chapter 12

Tanner's head punched the metal ceiling above the passenger seat. Mack tugged the wheel and straightened the old pickup, racing along one of the island's side roads. His good leg worked the gas and brake.

"You really think we need to go this fast?"

"Can't hurt."

"I don't see anyone behind us. I don't think anyone heard us—"

Mack never took his eyes off the road. "We'll be there in just a minute."

"Why—just tell me *why* we're doing this."

"Because I didn't lock you in that basement. I know everyone on this island. None of them would either. No one fucks with the lighthouse, okay?"

"Did you ever stop to think maybe it was the wind? We are in the middle of a storm."

"That's a heavy wood door."

"Was."

"Eh?"

Tanner tried to see past the reach of the headlights but couldn't. No way could he drive this thing at this speed. "Maybe it was a bunch of kids playing a prank."

"There are no kids on this island. You're the youngest on the rock."

What did you do with the kids, eat them?

"Look," Mack said, "I don't know what you did this afternoon or who you pissed off, but I can get you over to the mainland safely, and that's what I'm gonna do."

"You're convinced I'm in danger?"

"Forced drownings lead me down that path."

Tanner squeezed the seat. The road disappeared, dropped out. The truck fell and crunched against a new ground. Tanner felt his left knee knock his chin. Mack racked against the steering wheel. When he righted himself, he feverishly spun it back to its neutral position.

Tanner checked in the back, and his bike was still in the load. It had just flipped over ... at least once. "Mack, ease up. You can let me out right here! I don't share your little paranoia—"

"Relax, Molly. We're here."

The truck turned onto a thin path. They passed a collection of rotted fishing equipment, a pile of old netting, molded floats, and cracked poles. At the far end of the path was the beginning of a dock no wider than the pickup. As Mack put the truck in park, just before the headlights clicked off, Tanner could see the bow of a dated fishing boat alongside the end of the dock. Rain pelted Tanner when he stepped out of the truck.

"Grab your stuff," Mack yelled as he limped up the dock.

Ten minutes later they stood on either side of the flying bridge as the bumble bees of rain ticked across the windshield. Tanner shouted over the engine and the waves slapping the boat's bow, "So what am I supposed to do when I reach the other side?"

Mack was focused on the choppy waters. "You live over there, don't you?"

"Live? I live close to a two-hour *car* ride from Patterson."

"Oh."

"Yeah, oh. What the hell am I supposed to do in this junk?"

"There's got to be somewhere with an open room."

"I'm listening."

Mack shrugged his shoulders. "I don't know. I spend my time over in the fog." He tossed his head back a notch, to Fog Island.

Tanner shook his soaked head and continued to brace himself on the bridge as the boat rose up and dropped down waves. "For God's sake, why won't you just tell me what the fuck is up with you, Dreavor, and Shakespeare?"

Mack fought to keep the wheel steady. He checked his dials for depth and direction. "Fishing should be decent in most of the best spots in the morning."

"Great. Great." Tanner switched between huddling and bracing himself as they continued to battle a mogul-infested chop for what seemed an interminable time.

"Land ho." Mack pointed straight out over the bow.

Tanner squinted and saw what looked like a graham cracker on the water lit by a couple of attached white lights. "That's not the main dock, is it?"

"No, that's my friend Sam Neil's place. I don't know if he's home or not, but town is just a short spell away, off to your right when you get in front of his house."

"I don't believe this—you're not even taking me to Patterson?"

"Oh, Sam lives in Patterson."

"Mack, do you ever get the feeling that you didn't learn enough of the language growing up? Like you're speaking English and everyone around you can only understand every fifth word?"

"Nah, can't say I've had that problem." Mack repeatedly checked the rearview mirror. "You'll have some privacy going through Sam's place."

"Privacy? In this knucklehead weather, I'll have pneumonia is what I'll have."

Mack eased the throttle back, his eyes dipped back and forth between the depth gauge and the dock. As its speed slowed, the boat rocked higher and higher, subject more to the vicissitudes of the waves.

"I'm gonna pull up alongside, but she's a bit cranky tonight. Think you can jump it without me tying off?"

Tanner slugged his bike and backpack onto his shoulders. "Yeah, why not?"

As they drew within a few feet of the dock, Mack shouted down to Tanner, "You gonna give up on this Dreavor guy?"

Tanner laughed. "Just about to." He braced himself as the boat kissed the rubber ties bolted to the dock.

"Okay, *now!* I can't hold her here for long. Mind the gap."

Tanner slid his bike over onto the dock. Then he tossed his knapsack over, grabbed one of the dock's pylons, and pulled himself out of the boat.

Mack called out, "But what trade art thou?" After Tanner leaped over, he turned. The boat had shifted back to the channel and away from the dock. Mack worked the steering wheel and shouted to the storm above him, "A trade, sir, that, I hope, I may use with a safe conscience; which is, indeed, sir, a mender of bad soles."

By the time Tanner had suited up with his knapsack and lifted his bike, Mack's boat was an intermittent hum in the stormy distance.

Chapter 13

Despite his nylon outer gear, Tanner still felt cold and wet. Now, two days without sleep, exhaustion was creeping in. The roads were dark, slick, and silent, like a pack of thieves. It was somewhere near dawn when he saw the first of the road signs he was looking for: "Welcome to the University of Maine." Having spent the previous four years there, he knew where he could find a hot shower.

Tanner felt a little guilty pulling George Pile out of bed so early in the morning. Tanner had biked north nearly four hours to reach his old team in their off-campus house. He knew about a third of the team from when he rode with them. Pile had been the lucky son of a bitch whose room was nearest the front door. He was a senior at the university.

Within the first minute of being in the house, Tanner stood under a steaming hot shower. After five minutes, a bare three hundred seconds, it took every ounce of his energy to pull himself away from the streaming, soothing warmth that kneaded his muscles. He didn't want to zap all of the house's hot water for early morning. There were four other residents who would all need to tap the same hot-water tank.

Tanner rubbed a towel across his head and followed Pile into the kitchen, where he watched Pile proceed with his morning routine. Pile was a pale, shirtless stick in sweatpants, the typical cyclist physique. He stopped at the counter, grabbed a coffee can-sized plastic bottle of Advil, poured five or six into his palm, tossed them in his mouth, and followed them with a slug from an already open Red Bull can on the counter. "You hungry?" he asked.

"Yeah, starved. You have a big night?"

"Finster had a gathering last night. Tequila. I planned to sleep a bit longer than this."

"I'll be out of your hair in a minute."

Pile opened the refrigerator. Tanner saw a rather detailed collection of drinks, fruits, vegetables, yogurts, sauces, and salad dressings. The bikers were the healthiest amongst the university tribes, despite the odd binge. Pile pulled a blender to the edge of the counter. He put two long carrots into the blender and then a green pepper, stem and all. "How's your bro?"

"He's good. That reminds me—I need to call him when it's a reasonable hour."

"I'm glad you admit you're being unreasonable at this hour."

Tanner ignored the comment. He knew that on any other day of the week, someone, usually more than one, in the house was up and already on the roads of Maine, getting in a workout. Tanner waved his chin at the blender. "You gonna share that?"

Pile nodded. "Rack called last night."

Tanner instantly felt like shit. "Oh?"

"Yeah, he said you went postal after he told you he was driving for Marty."

Tanner rolled his eyes. "I don't know if I'd say 'postal.'"

Pile plucked the stem out of a tomato then dropped the tomato into the blender. "Said you burned down a house?"

"I didn't. Someone jumped me in the house I was working at." Tanner didn't sense Pile believed him.

Pile's glassy eyes bounced from vegetable to blender. "Said the cops called *him*."

"They probably did. They're conducting an investigation." As Pile continued with the vegetables, Tanner updated Pile on his previous twenty-four hours.

Pile flipped the blender on. "He says you're avoiding the bike."

Tanner started to respond, but then he settled back and squeezed his towel. "Look, Pile, I need to borrow an ID to get into the library. Can I have yours for a few hours?"

"Library?"

"Yeah. Just some books I want to take a look at."

Pile laughed. "I thought you would've read all of them by now."

Tanner had a legendary reputation as a reader—a bit of a forest fire, burning fast and broad through sections of the library. Tanner smiled and watched Pile pour a brown liquid, much like a chocolate milkshake, into a tall glass. He poured another for Tanner.

"Thanks. So, about your ID?"

"I've got to plant myself early, but I don't suppose Jeff will rise until nighttime. He'll be in no condition to read."

"That bad?"

"You sticking around tonight?"

"No, I've got to get back south. I've got a burned-out house to explain to the boss."

"I've got an Econ exam next week. Now I don't feel so bad."

"Great." Tanner had a momentary pang of melancholy. He missed interaction with housemates. Life now was a more independent existence, with free moments siding in Jimmy's favor.

Pile chugged his veggie mix. With the back of his hand, he wiped the brown residue from his upper lip. Tanner sensed an opening. "What was the name of that English Lit professor you and Rack had—the one who was obsessed, used to write with a quill, had the mustache and beard, wore the dagger?"

"Rack and I had a class together?"

"Focus, Pile."

Pile smiled, but then he squinted as if the effort hurt. "Oh, ah, Arbough."

"Right."

"I think he has an early-morning seminar."

"Okay, all I need is the ID."

"Hold on, I'll go pilfer Jeff's wallet. If I'm not back in five minutes, run for your life."

Chapter 14

His keys rattling as he locked his office door, Professor Daniel Arbough asked, "How can I help?"

"My roommate said you're an expert on Shakespeare," Tanner said.

"Your roommate? I thought you said you graduated." As they walked down the corridor, Arbough's loafers echoed around them.

"This was last semester."

"Who was your roommate?"

Tanner was afraid it might go this way. "Uh, his name was, is, uh, Rick Manning. Sometimes he was referred to as Rack."

"Rack? As in lamb?"

More like tits, six packs, and bed. "That's right."

"Wait a minute, the tall, fat one?"

"Yes, he was sort of circular—"

"Smelled like cheap whiskey?"

"I believe that was just Mondays and Wednesdays."

Arbough chuckled, or coughed, Tanner couldn't tell with the man's fourteen-foot-deep, throaty voice. Arbough dressed like a professor—a tweed jacket, olive pants, buckskin shoes, and a cordovan tie. The man was remarkably trim, and despite his age, which Tanner guessed must have been mid-sixties, his skin was tight to his cheekbones. Tanner knew his credibility was in deep jeopardy and dropping.

"I've been working for the state for the past six months." Tanner gave a three-minute summary of his role in locating Dreavor's heirs. He walked at Arbough's side as they crossed a courtyard, cut through Rawley Hall, and dipped onto a short road that led to another building. Tanner wanted the professor's undivided attention and hoped that neither of them crossed paths with anyone either of them knew.

"Interesting couple of days you've had." Arbough focused on the path ahead of them. "How can I help?"

"Shakespeare."

"Is that a question?"

"He was born in 1564. North of London. Stratford."

"Stratford-on-Avon."

"Right. Seems like his dad did all right for the times. Shakespeare went to a good school, learned Greek and Latin. Had exposure to a decent range of books, especially history."

"I know all this, Mr., ah—what did you say your name was?"

"Cook, Tanner."

"Tanner," Arbough repeated, as if trying out the name to see if he liked it enough to use it ever again.

"What I meant to ask is why people are so down on Shakespeare being Shakespeare, the true author. Most say he didn't have the education and life experience to write about kings and queens, law and politics."

"Ah, yes, now I see your question."

"Do you think Shakespeare was ... well, Shakespeare?" Tanner asked.

"I never preoccupy myself with the question."

Keep trying, Tanner told himself. "Okay, but for those who do, is there anything in particular that keeps them preoccupied?"

"In addition to the fact that the timing doesn't work for his publishing, he never had a library at home, never bequeathed a single book to his children, and his daughter grew up not knowing how to read. There are some mysterious inconsistencies about the man."

"Why would the true author be so secretive?"

Arbough gripped an iron stair railing as they rose up a flight. "Life or death."

"Death?"

"Do you know that Queen Elizabeth removed the hand of a man who wrote a play she found seditious? Find anything, oh, I don't know, antiestablishment about any of Shakespeare's plays?"

"Maybe."

"Maybe? Maybe most of them. Not that Elizabeth, Henry before her, and James after, didn't fuel the fire."

"So, if Shakespeare wasn't Shakespeare, then who was?"

"Most argue for Edward de Vere, the seventeenth earl of Oxford."

"Because he was royalty?"

"Yes, and because he was well groomed. He had the best tutor in all of England, a master in languages, math, arithmetic, law, and philosophy, with a private library of four hundred books. Folks back then usually enrolled in college in their teens. De Vere was eight. By the way, Shakespeare's parents and siblings were illiterate. We can see Ovid's *Metamorphoses* in almost every Shakespearean play, and de Vere was tutored by Godling, the man who translated Ovid into English. We have no proof that Shakespeare ever met royalty, even though most of his writings involved them. De Vere first met Queen Elizabeth when he was eleven. He was educated at Gray's Inn Law School. He traveled to Spain, France, and Italy, visiting the *Two Gentlemen*'s Verona and the *Merchant*'s Venice. There is not a shred of evidence that Shakespeare ever ventured past the Thames."

"Okay, okay, I got—wait! Did you say, 'Gray's Inn'?"

"Yes, it was one of the Inns of Court, the collection of schools where the youth of the elite were educated."

In his mind, Tanner saw the image of the Gray Inn clapboard on Fog Island. *Sonofabitch!*

"But de Vere went and died before several plays were published, maybe even written. Not overwhelmingly the best candidate. This is why I don't bother with these things. I just enjoy the words."

"The play's the thing, huh?"

Arbough stopped on the bridge between Reilly and Wentworth. He turned to Tanner and smiled. "Exactly. You sure you weren't in one of my classes?"

Tanner shook his head. "Who else could have written Shakespeare's works?"

Professor Arbough coughed into his gloved hand. "Well, there's speculation that Ben Johnson might have. And there's a big cheering section for Francis Bacon."

"Bacon? The writer?"

"Don't let him hear you describe him that way. He was a bit more rounded than that and truly believed he was a man of actionable solutions."

"Right," was all Tanner could muster.

Arbough kept one step ahead of him as they trumped up a concrete stairwell. Tanner's mind swam forward for the next question. "Regardless of who wrote the plays, do you think there was something within the pages of his plays?"

"You mean in addition to the perfect imagery, the deep psychological mastery, and the crafting of so many new words for our language?"

"Uh, yeah."

Arbough shrugged. "It's been four hundred years. People have been searching for secret messages for most of that time. Drove a few from around here nearly insane just trying to prove that. And what do we have? Nothing."

"Would life really change if we knew Shakespeare had another identity?"

Arbough shrugged again. "Not really. Oh, with proof that someone else wrote the stuff, I suppose there's a book in it, network news spots, a Discovery Channel piece, and maybe even a new walking tour. But the cannon would still be the cannon."

Tanner nodded.

Arbough's head waved to the side as he considered a new thought. "Of course, maybe Shakespeare's true identity might reveal the location of his original drafts."

"What's that?" Tanner reflexively reached for Arbough's arm, as if to say, *hold on.*

Arbough checked his watch. "The original drafts."

Tanner waited for more.

"Oh, come on, Cook, don't tell me you don't know what I'm talking about."

"I'm afraid I have to."

"No one has ever seen an original page of Shakespeare's works. Not a poem, a play, or a scrap draft. No diaries, no correspondence, no doodles—nothing from William Shakespeare's pen."

The courtyard warped, and Tanner's mind spun 360 degrees.

Arbough stopped in front of Root Hall. "Sorry, son, I have a seminar. Good luck—"

"Wait, please, just one more—"

Arbough kept his momentum shifting into the building. "If you want to talk later, come and see me."

"Sure, thanks."

"You said it was Tanner, right?"

"Tanner Cook, right."

"Good to meet you, Cook." And with that, Professor Arbough slipped into Root Hall.

Chapter 15

After Professor Arbough closed the door in his face, Tanner turned back toward the library to retrieve his bike. He started walking, but soon he broke into a jog and then a full-out sprint, splashes from puddles spraying across his pant legs. When he entered Fogler Library, he ignored the stares he got as he sprinted across its great hall. Like a seaman aboard a battleship, his feet sprayed out in front of him as he slid down the metallic stairway to the lower stacks. In the biographies section, his finger raced across volumes. He stopped short in the D's and plucked two biographies on Oxford's seventeenth earl, Edward de Vere.

His eyes soared up and down pages of the first book. His fingers flipped pages almost as fast as he could cleanly separate one from the next. In Tanner's head, words never registered individually—rather, they assembled in packs and bunches, in thought-scenes. Often, Tanner could tell where the author was going early in the chapter, and sometimes he knew how the second half of the book was going to unfold; in his brain, reading was more like completing a jigsaw puzzle than painting a picture.

The theory on de Vere/Shakespeare was that it was dangerous for the earl to have the reputation of a writer back in Elizabeth's time. Back then, the social standing of writers was akin to pedophiles and punishable by all means. As Professor Arbough had mentioned, her majesty had taken the hand of the playwright whom she thought had penned *Richard I*, seditious to her mind. So, Oxford hired out for a pen name. To Tanner, the curious thing was why Oxford didn't eventually reveal himself, even sometime after his death. Tanner kept flipping pages. Faster.

Oxford died of unknown causes. He left no will.

Tanner raced through the pages. There was no record of a funeral. No one could confirm where his corpse was. It was a good profile for someone who wanted to disappear across the ocean.

Okay, so maybe he didn't speak to later generations through a will. Maybe it was through some directive at some point after his death. To not do so would be like winning the Tour de France or the Giro d'Italia while wearing a mask. But again, given the low esteem in which writers were held, such a victory would be like crossing the finish line wearing nothing but a mask.

Where were the original drafts? Oxford died with a relatively small estate. Because of his profligate ways, he had sold all of the properties the previous sixteen Oxford earls had accumulated. He left behind two children. Nothing was willed to them—at least nothing the public knew about. No original papers existed to identify a writing sample. No overt statements from de Vere claiming authorship. No one who knew him claimed it for him. It was amazing how concealed he and his were able to keep it. And how far had we come? Today, those who achieved the slightest bit of notoriety seem to immediately saturate the media industry. A successful TV teleplay writer could make national, no, make that global headlines over revelations of the type of coffee she drank.

Was it possible? Could the most famous writer of the Western world keep his or her identity secret, a secret that would last for centuries? Until Frank Dreavor.

What was Dreavor after in the text of the plays? Would de Vere have revealed his secret in those lines? Would he have identified the location of the original drafts? If he did—a big *if*, but if he did—was that location likely to be in the United States or the

United Kingdom or somewhere else, for that matter? Hamlet's Denmark? Romeo's Verona?

De Vere captained one of her majesty's warships on a campaign against the Spanish. How far he traveled past the Canaries was not mentioned. But wouldn't that show he had the means to come across? Was that it? Tanner knew the trip back in the 1600s was perilous. Maybe they crashed. But how would that make itself known in print, post facto? Tanner kept flipping, filling in the puzzle.

De Vere owned ships. He lent his own ship, *Edward Bonaventure*, to the government for the purpose of exploration. He financed a voyage to America. He was appointed to a committee in the House of Lords that considered petitions for adventurers seeking to explore the New World. Tanner's mouth was dry, but his palms were wet. *America!*

In his mind, Tanner began to weigh whether Shakespeare's original drafts would be among the most valuable works in the world, each one a masterpiece on par with the finest Renoir, da Vinci, Michelangelo—you name it. What had he told Lieutenant Clay two nights ago? A good piece of art could go for twenty million dollars? But wasn't the recent record for a single piece one hundred million dollars? For an early Picasso? And, although he didn't know the exact number of plays and poems, there must have been at least twenty. Back of the envelope, provided most of Shakespeare's writings were in the same place, one billion, two billion dollars? Worth killing for? "Me thinks so," he whispered.

The energy with which Mack described Dreavor leaving Gray Inn and his lack of as much as a sleeping bag painted a picture for Tanner of someone in a hurry, someone motivated ... or someone being pursued. A fraction of a bounty like that could pay for someone to care for Jimmy and for all of them to live under the same roof. Maybe he could even pursue archeology ... A new brand of adrenaline began surging through Tanner.

Tanner closed *The Invisible Pen*. Students drifted across the great room, loose backpack straps swaying, their footfalls swallowed by the silver, industrial carpet that ran everywhere—underneath the computer catalog terminal table to the librarian station and down the stairway to the lower level. Through the enormous, surfboard windows, Tanner saw the sky was pushing back straggling clouds.

His phone rang. Heads turned. The law had been broken, not that it wasn't broken seventeen times per hour, anyway. Tanner saw that it was Rack calling.

Tanner cupped his hand over his mouth and dipped his chin into his chest as he answered. "Thought you'd be timing Marty."

Rack burped. "You need to let it go."

Rack was drinking. What day was it? Actually, did it matter? "I'm at UM," Tanner said.

"Where?"

"I'll give you one guess."

Rack was silent. Then, his answer came in a blast. "The library!"

"Bingo."

"Dude, I thought you read all of those."

"They got a new shipment last Tuesday."

Rack's tone became deeper. "Dude, did you burn down that house?"

"No, someone jumped me in the attic. They knocked over one of those candles and it was burning when I got there. The place went up quickly."

"Are you hurt?"

"No, I'm fine."

"Are you done with this yet?"

"Actually, I was just speaking to one of your old teachers."

Rack was silent.

"Those are the people who stood at the front of the classroom—"

"Hilarious."

"We discussed Edward de Vere, seventeenth earl of Oxford."

"You're not done with this."

"I don't know. Could be a lot of money riding on who is at the end of Dreavor's trail of bread crumbs."

"Did you say, 'riding'?"

"You call for any specific reason?"

"I just heard you burned down a house and thought I might be able to help the cops apprehend you."

"Okay, well, I gotta go."

"We didn't see any Edward de Vere books in Dreavor's attic."

"He may have taken them with him."

"The guy had no friends, no family, and no job of any interest. He had a life as dull and lonely as the tomato soup in his cupboards. Looks like he spent all of his free time in his attic scribbling notes. You think he knew where he was going?"

Tanner felt rage rising. What was Rack trying to do? Then he looked up at the cream-colored library ceiling and the rage faded.

What was he doing there? Was he simply hoping on a fairy tale? Was he making this all up? "I've gotta go. In this place they call a library they have rules about talking, especially on cell phones."

"Calm down. Look, I'm bringing my grandmom down to her house tonight. On my way back, I'll have to pass near Kargil. I'll stop in that tavern we saw, where the tree cutters get bombed every night. I'll ask if anyone knew Dreavor."

Tanner laughed. "You'd do that for me? You'd duck into an irregular bar and nestle in with the locals, just for me?"

"What are friends for?"

"Maybe you could send Marty?" Tanner didn't know what made him say it. The conversation was just turning kindly. As the words left his mouth, he knew it was a grenade.

It went off inside Rack's mouth. "You stupid son of a bitch! At least Marty would go!" The line went dead.

Tanner tucked the phone into his pocket. What the hell was he thinking? Rack was just trying to help—

Some junk in his pocket crackled like a pack of Skittles. No, not junk—letters, envelopes, rather, soaked from his time in the rain. The first was a solicitation from the Red Cross. The second was one of the pieces of mail that Tanner had found in Dreavor's horizontal mailbox buried in Dreavor's uncut lawn. Tanner read the return address.

No, it can't be.

Chapter 16

The bell dinged on the door, which stuck in its backswing on the uneven floor. Tanner was greeted by a bubbling lobster tank with green glass sides. It housed three rusty, two-pound lobsters stacked on one another.

"Help yeh?" asked a voice in a rich, homemade Maine accent.

Tanner searched for the source of the voice. Past the *20,000 Leagues Under the Sea* diving suit, past a row of used snorkels and a rotating rack of wet suits—some black, some blue—past a pile of dirty, orange life jackets and a large bucket of flippers, and behind a cash register atop a makeshift store counter of stacked lobster traps, stood a tall man with long, pony-tailed gray hair and an exploding mustache.

Tanner advanced. "I think so."

"Didn't hear yeh drive up," the man said.

"That's because, you know, I've got a ... quiet engine." Tanner stepped around the bucket of flippers and then reached down to pull a stray one from the floor and put it back in the bucket. "I picked up an overdue notice for some equipment that was rented from you guys."

"You the one who called?"

"Yeah, I'm Tanner Cook."

The man behind the register nodded. "I thought you'd be older."

"I get that a lot." He didn't really, but he thought it sounded like the right thing to say. Tanner stood on the opposite side of the NCR cash register, a 1960 model, if that. "You must be Paul Knox."

"That's right." Simple answer, but with an edge. On the ride up, Tanner had thought about the directions this might take.

"Well, I'm just trying to help you recover the proper value of your gear."

Knox leaned over his counter. "How does this work?"

Tanner was driving wildly through bullshit territory. "Well, if I can report with confidence that it actually was Mr. Dreavor who was your customer, then I might be able to help you with your claim against his estate."

"What more than the invoice do you need?"

Tanner took his small notepad from his rear pocket. "Mr. Dreavor was seventy-two. It will seem a little odd for a man of his age to be diving. Anything you can tell me about what he was trying to do?"

Knox smoothed his mustache against face and looked down on Tanner. His forearms were sledgehammer solid. "I don't know. He said he wanted to explore Lake Manfred."

Tanner scribbled to make himself seem authentic. "Did he say why?"

"Nah."

"Did he strike you as someone who had experience diving?"

"Sort of. He knew what he wanted. When he came back for a refill, it sure seemed—"

"Refill?" Tanner couldn't stop himself.

"Yeah. He came back two days later, wanting more air."

Tanner's brain was recalibrating. He had envisioned Dreavor dying in some sort of beginner's bad-luck scenario. Nothing ruled out a partner yet, but if it were Dreavor who had expended the tank the first time, then ... he knew how to scuba dive.

"Did he remark on the lake?"

Knox sprang forward and smacked his hands on the register, leaning in close to Tanner's face. Tanner recoiled. Knox's right hand had a fading scab over the nubs of where his pinky and ring finger used to be. "If you're going to hassle me about letting an unlicensed solo diver go out, do it now and knock this shit off!"

Now Tanner understood.

"Hey, I investigate estates for the state of Maine, part-time. I don't know what the laws are about renting to anybody. I just want to finish up with this open file and get back home."

Knox stayed over the register. Tanner thought he looked like a pointer sniffing out his prey. "What else?" Knox barked.

Tanner checked his notes. "Did he say anything about the lake?"

"Like what?"

"I'm trying to find someone who knew this guy. As far as we know, he has no relatives, but if I can find out who he dove with, maybe there is a friend or—or somebody. Did he say anything about where he was diving? If I can identify that, a campsite director might have seen him with someone or someone might have talked to him."

Knox eased. "You do this for everybody?"

"Just the ones who leave us without a will. So, what'd he say?"

"I've got to fill a few tanks. Let's finish this out back?"

Tanner didn't want to go out back, but he took a bit of comfort in judging that he was faster than the pony-tailed proprietor.

Knox filled his tanks at the bottom of a large box of water, like a shopping-store ice cream freezer on its side. Tanner remembered learning that this was how it was done, but he couldn't remember why. He knew it had to do with pressure.

"When he came back ..." Knox secured the line from one of the shop's Scuba tanks to a pressurized tank the size of a Ford Focus. "He complained of the water being dark and rented a couple of large flashlights."

"That strike you as strange for the lake?"

Knox's arms tightened as he hefted one tank out of the box and secured another to the air hose. "Nah. The lake is dark and dangerous. Don't know how he got along without light the first time around."

"Sounds like a rookie mistake." Tanner's mind raced to find the next best question. "When he returned, did he rent anything else that he hadn't taken the first time?"

Knox bent forward over the box, as a few bubbles rose from the tank re-filling on the bottom. "Yeah, funny you should ask. He bought four cords of red, three-quarter rope."

Tanner's eyes brightened. "Rope? What do you use rope for when diving?"

Knox grinned. "Hanging people."

Tanner grinned, optimistically hoping that Knox was joking. But he cautiously shifted his weight to his heels should Knox's explanation suddenly give the man ideas.

Then Knox laughed and pointed at Tanner. "Got you, junior, you should see your face!"

Tanner laughed, more as an escape valve for his bottled nerves.

"He said, although it was more of, ah, you know, that he needed it for the current." Knox waved his chin as the signal that he was letting Tanner in on the revelation. Given the freak scene, it took Tanner a few seconds to do the math.

"There are no currents in a lake," Tanner said.

Knox saluted Tanner with open-palm courtesy. "And that's when he more or less gathered the refilled tank and his stuff and high-tailed it."

"And you didn't read or hear about him in the news?"

Knox shrugged. "Bancher is kinda far. The news doesn't interest me. I think I might have heard about an old guy drowning, but I didn't pay much attention because there was no mention of scuba. When do I get my money back?"

"What do you estimate the total charge is?"

"The suit, tank, regulator, fins, mask, lights, all probably total about seven hundred dollars."

"Seven hundred dollars? That new or used equipment?"

Knox straightened. "Insurance is insurance. You gonna help get me my stuff reimbursed or not?"

"No, yes, of course." Tanner tugged out his wallet and gave Knox his business card. "I'm going to keep trying to find people who knew him for another week, and then we close the case." Tanner was back on the road of bullshit. "I'm sure between my efforts and your insurance company, we can find a way."

"Good." Knox punctuated the air with Tanner's card. "I'm going to hold you to that, you know."

Tanner backed away, bumped his ankle on a wagon, and nodded. "Okay, thanks for your help."

He turned to the door and then stopped. An image flashed in his mind—the raw muscle flexing on Knox's arm under the strain of lifting a scuba tank out of the water. Reversing direction, he called out to Knox, "Hold on, just how did Dreavor get around?"

Knox sucked snot through his nose into the back of his throat and then roughed the bundle up on to his tongue and spat it across the rear patio. "What do you mean?"

"I mean, the list of his possessions doesn't include a vehicle."

"Then maybe he borrowed it, but he showed up in a shitbox Pontiac, a green sucker. Suited him fine."

"Thanks. I'll keep an eye out for it."

"Yeah, do that. Even that piece of shit might be worth seven hundred dollars."

Chapter 17

Tanner biked into the small town of Washkill. He knew that in theory he should be tired, but the speed at which his mind was running through ideas kept his legs pedaling to keep similarly active. The sidewalk was buckled every hundred feet or so where the root systems of fat maples had thrust the concrete upward, looking like jack-in-the-boxes half-sprouted. He thumped down off the sidewalk onto the street, gliding with his thoughts, the gears clicking like crickets. The lobster smell of the low tide drifted inward with the westerly wind.

A seventy-two-year-old man. He spends fifty years on a lawnmower and shoveling snow, and then he takes up scuba diving. Strange. He rides an ancient Schwinn bike across his one-story town for decades and all of a sudden buys a car. Well, there was no proof *yet* that he had bought a car, but where the hell had this recluse gotten the disaster of a green Pontiac that Knox said he pulled up with? Tanner passed the CVS Pharmacy and a needlepoint store and dismounted at the screen door entrance to Frank's Eatery.

Tanner squinted inside to try to accelerate his adjustment to the low level of light. Hamburger, somebody was cooking hamburger, Tanner's nose told him. Against a side window, the silhouette of a bartender unloaded the miniature dishwasher behind a chest-high bar. Paper tablecloths and place settings covered the ten tables.

"Hi, you open for lunch?"

The bartender was a tall, blond haired man in a button-down, jeans, and an apron. Maybe mid-forties, one of the area's ex-football players who never could get far from the bars they so loved. "Yep, and I think we got room."

"Great." Tanner moved to one of the tables toward the far side of the room. He put his backpack on the chair.

"Just you?"

"Yeah."

"Something to drink?" He dried his hands on the apron at his front.

"Um, you have apple juice?"

"Cranberry okay? It's fresh off the bog."

"Sounds great." Tanner gestured toward a hallway that cut into the back wall, where a "Restroom" sign hung. "I'm just going to wash up."

"I'll leave you a menu."

A tall set of swinging doors stood still on his left, and his right shoulder clunked against a public payphone. The hallway ended with two doors, sporting eye-level signs. Tanner entered the one labeled, "Men" to find a tiny bathroom, one toilet, circa 1950, and a pure white slab of a sink with rust stains around the drain.

Just as Tanner closed the door, it exploded inward like a locomotive, crashing into Tanner, who fell back, his legs not able to keep up with his momentum, down onto the toilet seat. His hands slapped at the walls as he tried to brace himself.

A Roman column of a man jammed a piece of rubber under the closed door and then turned. His eyes bulged, ready to spill over his sockets. He seized Tanner's jacket, jerked him up, and rammed Tanner's back against the wall, rattling his teeth. Tanner sucked to get breath back in his lungs.

Tanner thought the Column was going to gnaw his nose off. "Listen, you goddamn jack-off! What was Dreavor doing?"

Tanner inhaled. "Wh-what are—"

The Column's catcher's mitt crunched Tanner's throat and slapped him against the wall, up off his feet. A tattoo of an anchor ran across the man's forearm. In the tattoo, the anchor snapped a lightning bolt in two. Tanner felt his own Adam's apple squish against the back of his throat. The edges of his vision were blurring. Across the room, the crusted hand soap dispenser faded in detail. Tanner wasn't sure if he should resist.

The Column drew to within inches of Tanner and shouted in his face, "What the fuck was he doing?"

Tanner tried to answer, but his words collided with the roadblock at his tonsils. His voice crashed in a squeak. His vision narrowed. He felt himself about to shit.

"You're riding a goddamn bike! No cop rides a bike!"

"Keehck!"

"He was after something, what was it!"

Knock. Knock.

The Column jumped at the sound of knuckles on the door. It was all Tanner needed. He drove his knee into his attacker's lower jaw, sandwiching the man's tongue between his teeth. Then, Tanner's heels rocketed out, launching the Column backward. Tanner dropped to the tile.

Choking and coughing, Tanner reached over and removed the slice of a rubber fin stopping the door, releasing the knuckles inward. An Asian twenty-something with an apron fell into the tight space.

"Whoa," the Asian said. Tanner gripped the Asian's leg with the hand that wasn't on his neck. "Heh—hey!" the Asian said and waved his leg as if Tanner were a cockroach.

On his back, Tanner watched the Column forearm the aproned man into the open door. Tanner's attacker stumbled into the dark hallway, holding his bloody mouth. Tanner rolled onto his back and coughed … as normally as he could.

Given the apron, Tanner concluded that the Asian worked in the kitchen. He rubbed his chest and looked down at Tanner. "What was that all about?"

Tanner massaged his neck and tried to suck in fresh air. He laughed inside to himself. "I'm not sure, exactly." Despite feeling a bit lightheaded, Tanner moved to stand up. "You guys have any specials today?"

Chapter 18

Tanner finished his soup. It was the only thing he could swallow. He must have downed four glasses each of cranberry juice and ice water, although he'd be damned if he was going back into Frank's men's room again. He felt safe in the dining room with the larger-than-usual barkeep. Tanner checked to see that his bike was still locked to the town bench out front. No one in the restaurant asked any questions.

The entire episode made him think about Jimmy, his only kin. His mother and his father had come from small families, each an only child. Tanner had been nine years old when his father never came back from a Sunday-morning newspaper run. The challenge of raising Jimmy had been too much for him. More than once, Tanner had heard him through the floorboards crying at night after trying to calm Jimmy down, often resorting to the shot. He knew his dad hated to give Jimmy the shot.

Not long after his dad left, Tanner's mother soon grew a weird shade of yellow, shuffling around inside their house all day, every day. She would send Tanner out on his bike into town to do every sustaining task for the family, like shopping for food and Jimmy's diapers—and to pick up liquor. She had standing orders with Martin's Spirits to allow Tanner to mule her supplies back home. She claimed that arthritis in her shin kept her from being able to drive.

Nine years later, Tanner found his mother on her back in the basement, in the dark. The tool and paint supply shelf had tumbled with her. The Cold Creek vodka bottle was nearly drained at her side. She had vomited into the laundry basket, and a trail of drool connected the puke to her lip. She somehow sensed Tanner had quietly approached and looked up at him through her cobweb hair.

"You were born with it all. Now, you have it all—he's alllll yours."

At the funeral, it seemed to Tanner as if every sixth adult male first asked if he had heard from his father, and second, if his mother had any life insurance. He answered no to both, but as he learned later in the unair-conditioned courtroom during custody hearings, his mother did have a life insurance policy, but she had let the premiums expire.

Jimmy had been in state-run institutions ever since. What little earnings Tanner had made from racing, he plowed back into his equipment and Jimmy's care. He also managed to take out a one-million-dollar, twenty-year-term life insurance policy. It cost him six hundred dollars per year, and the first six hundred dollars Tanner made each year he put toward that premium. If anything were to happen to him, Jimmy would inherit the policy proceeds, to be administered by Rack's dad, the only functioning adult Tanner knew well enough to trust.

Not long after his stop for lunch, Tanner found himself cruising into Reveler Notch, a steep, zigzag road that cut through the union of Mount Pine and Mount Reveler. Tanner loved the Notch. The pines dripped down the towering mountainside above a road, which was more like a path that broke hard left for maybe twenty yards, barely a decent car length, before it would jag ten yards right. Whoever put that blacktop down did so without any well-though-out plan. For better or worse, it was a remarkable example of man's mark on nature. If both vehicles held their breath, two cars could pass side by side. Needless to say, in a month's time, when temperatures would consistently drop below freezing, any patch of ice could prove fatally unreliable.

On marathon training runs, Tanner used to love the challenge of the Notch. This was where he would shame his teammates, where they would shake their heads at the rocks under his skin, the pistons that ran from his ass to his toes, at the masochistic zone he slipped into when he hit the rise. Run after run, he would eventually view the rest of the team as little men in his rearview.

His phone rang. A Bluetooth receiver sat securely in his helmet earpiece and a transmitter in his chinstrap. During races, this was how he communicated with Rack in the minivan. "Hello?"

"Tanner? Where are you?" It was a raspy man's voice, his manager Jack Purcell. "Mr. Purcell, hi."

"Tanner, this is a first—"

"It wasn't my fault, Mr. Purcell." Tanner was losing breath due to the incline, and he tried like hell to keep his voice from sounding strained.

"The police told me what happened. How do you feel?"

"Physically, I feel fine. A lump or two. I'll heal." Tanner turned his head and breathed deeply. An SUV, an Explorer, sat in the half-dollar-sized rearview mirror attached to his handlebar. *Great—traffic, an incline, a boss, and a cover story for hooky all at once.*

"I tried to call you yesterday, but I just kept getting voicemail."

"I was up late Tuesday night with the police. I didn't get home until late. Yesterday I slept most of the day." As fat a lie as any told on the planet.

"Well, don't feel like you need to rush in today."

Tanner tried to play up his devotion. "Oh, I don't mind. I'm out now, biking trying to stretch my leg, the one that got banged up."

The SUV grew larger in his mirror.

"Well, take your time."

Tanner wished he could. As he neared the Notch's rise, he had nowhere to pull to the side. He heard the Explorer's engine grumbling behind him.

"I'll call you … in a little … while." He was vertical on his pedals now as he hit the crest. He checked his mirror, and the SUV's grill grew larger and larger as it neared. It was maybe forty yards behind and not giving him a lot of room to step aside. Then, his front tire cleared the apex, and in one more rotation Tanner was staring downhill. He checked over his shoulder and saw the SUV was coming faster than before.

It isn't going to stop!

Tanner's pulse skyrocketed. His slope was a frightening downward angle—a wagon set off alone would become recklessly fast in seconds. He cranked his pedals and leaned into the first turn. He heard the SUV, now just a car length behind him. Its tires squealed like a terrified baby.

Tanner wanted to stretch the distance between them, but he was going too fast for the hill. He squeezed his brakes. His rear tire melted in a skid. The big car had a moment to add speed—the engine revved. The pitch of the road became even steeper.

"Shit!" Tanner hissed. He spun the back end of his bike sideways to keep control around the next turn. A burning scream came from under the car as it sailed through Tanner's wake.

The ground began leveling. The SUV jumped forward like an alligator waiting in the grass. Its bumper seemed to chomp just inches from Tanner's rear tire. In a flash look at this rearview, he saw a female neckline and wave of dark hair through a break in the glare of the SUV's windshield. Tanner's cheeks fluttered. He squeezed his handlebars, the road bent. There was too much ground before the turn—the bumper would plow through him.

Tanner looked left, at the edge of the road, toward a drop with dark teeth of pines just below the shoulder. The SUV centered on Tanner's rear wheel. Tanner sliced hard left, off the road … and dropped.

His bike sailed off the side of the road.

Tanner opened his arms, and released the bike from his grip. He covered his face as he and the bike sailed off the road's edge and into a collection of trees on the mountainside. His feet kicked and fought for traction on pine branches as he dropped. His arms locked around branches in a grip that would have choked the life out of most living things. He dropped through dozens of snaps and crackles. Then, his body jerked to a stop.

Above him, the SUV cut back toward the mountain. It had already been lured too close to the edge, however, at too fast a speed, and the left wheels slipped over. And that was it.

The Ford Explorer rolled. It tipped over, and the engine whined loudly as the undercarriage was exposed to the sky and trees. It rolled in a metallic crunch—glass crackling and popping—in what seemed like slow motion. The tumble accelerated as the car completed two rolls before the roof folded around the base of two thick pines. Glass chips tinkled to the ground and water leaked from the radiator, hissing as it fell on hot parts of the engine.

Tanner froze. His body was a tight band of muscle vice-gripped on the branches. As echoes of the rolling car faded, his heavy breathing slowed. Tanner peeked over his arms as smoke or steam drifted out of the wreckage. Otherwise, there was no movement.

Tilting his head back over his shoulder, he could see that he was about forty feet from the ground. His pine was thickly filled with branches. Tanner edged his foot toward the tree's trunk and found the thicker, sturdier portion of a branch and stabilized his weight there. In seconds, he was stepping down the natural ladder the tree offered him until he pushed away and jumped to a pine needle-laden ground that slanted up the mountain.

There was still no movement from the SUV. His bike had stopped tumbling halfway between him and the SUV. Tanner hesitated but then went to salvage it. He didn't feel the ground he was walking on, and his vision shook.

He reached his bike. The front rim was dented. He looked twenty yards to his left at the broken, steaming wreck. Cautiously, he moved toward it.

Chapter 19

Tanner's face and his body leaked perspiration. His hand shook as if he were wobbling on a tightrope as he tried to reposition the Bluetooth receiver on his ear. He barked into the mouthpiece, "This is fucked."

The hissing, intermittent voice of Pile was in his ear. "Easy, dude. Calm down."

Tanner pulled at his hair. His retinas spasmed. Tanner had taken refuge up the hill from the wreck, closer to the road. The police sirens flashed, and the Explorer's engine steamed like a dying horse's last breaths. The exposed white of the broken tree limbs above outlined the SUV's path.

The back of his hand wiped the sweat from his upper lip and then his forehead. He wrapped his arms around himself and squeezed. *It was a drunk. Must have been someone bolting from a tavern after too much cider. That was it, maybe it was a mistake!*

Twenty yards in front of him stood two coke-machine state troopers. They angled backward at the hip to read the mountainside and the Explorer's path. One pantomimed the trajectory he imagined the car would have needed to take.

"I can outrun *them!*" Tanner shouted into his phone. "Good fucking luck trying to catch me!"

"Tanner! Mellow! Your heart rate is top-lining."

Tanner covered his face with both hands. He sucked deep breaths, as deep as his lungs would allow. His hands smelled like bike grips and tree sap. Exceeding his target heart rate was a no-no. Ease back. Don't let in the evil lactic acid. All of this was training speak, language he and Pile had lived on for years. During training runs, Rack followed him in the minivan and monitored riders' heart rates and provided feedback via their headsets.

"Find somewhere to sit down. Okay? T?" Pile asked him.

"Yeah, yeah. Okay, okay."

"You and I both know the Notch can swallow the best driver."

Tanner heard the echo of a dog's bark. He opened his eyes to see a trooper photographing the Explorer's wrinkled front end. Tanner poked his finger through the hole in his jacket arm. His bicep ached. "Yeah, yeah. Maybe."

"Stay put. Harry is MIA, so I'm gonna see whose car I can grab to pick you up. If you move, call me."

"Okay, okay. I'm here. Thanks, I'll talk to you later."

Tanner stared at ants chaotically skittering across the ground. Then the paranoid horses broke the corral in his mind. What if she were really trying to run him down? Why? Was it connected to Dreavor? Had he been murdered? Had people gone lunatic for Shakespeare's shit?

A fire engine's motor grumbled. He looked downhill toward the wreckage. Firemen were slugging a hose up the drop. They had doused the Explorer to make sure there were no seedling fires. Tanner had a cut across the left side of his neck, but bandage and gauze seemed too car crash-like, so he had waved the EMT off.

A state trooper approached and stood tall above him, his leather bomber jacket showing signs of faded weathering at the outer elbow. "You need a lift?"

"I've got a friend coming to pick me up."

"We've got one trooper headed south and one west. You could catch a ride with either if you'd like. Save your friend the trip."

"Yeah? Who's going south?"

"You get my reimbursement yet?" called a voice from across the slanting road.

Paul Knox sat in the front seat of his Chevy pickup, an early 1970s rust bucket. Three Scuba tanks were harnessed to the sidewall.

Tanner's mind zigged toward an angry reply, then zagged toward a neutral response, and then stopped, stuck between the two. Knox pulled to the side to allow the congregating traffic room to pass and continue down the mountain notch.

"You know this gentleman?" the trooper asked.

Tanner nodded. "This is my, um, Mr. Knox. He owns a dive shop in Washkill."

The trooper nodded under the brim of his cowboy hat. Another large state trooper jogged toward them from his cruiser. Tanner read his nametag: McEvoy.

"You leaving now, Mr. Cook?" McEvoy asked.

Tanner wasn't sure how to answer. He nodded.

"Okay. The teams have reported in." McEvoy removed his hat and slapped it to clean off the pine needles and other debris from the woods. "We cannot locate the driver."

Tanner blinked, hoping a fresh focus would clear reality. "What?"

McEvoy pointed out into the distance. "Even the dog team on the outer rim has run cold."

"Could—could she have out-run you? In her condition? I mean, that was a serious crash."

McEvoy shook his head and tucked his hands into his massive belt. "Not likely. It's a little ... curious."

Tanner twisted toward the dense woods to his right. Given the mountains and the thick of the trees, light was scarce.

"You need a lift?" Knox asked.

More like a rewind button.

"Where are you headed?" Tanner heard himself ask.

Chapter 20

Tanner watched the side mirror and then shifted around backward, looking over to Knox.

"You always drive this slow?"

"I don't need to go fast." Knox stroked his mustache.

Tanner felt like an itch, unable to sit. "Listen, someone tried to run me off the road. It wasn't by accident."

Knox shot a look over at Tanner. "You told the cops—"

"I wasn't thinking. I'm still not."

Tanner checked over at Knox and saw that he was studying the road. Tanner tried to fasten the seatbelt across his chest, but the belt wasn't capable of that. The Chevy was so old it offered only lap seat belts.

"Is this what happened to the old man?" Knox asked.

Tanner put a hand through his hair. "If you had asked me six hours ago, I would've said no. Now, yeah. Maybe they did kill him."

"They? Who are they?"

"I don't know. *They* is a guess."

"What do you mean, a *guess*?"

"A feeling. Intuition." Tanner dialed Rack on his cell. "It's me." Tanner spoke into Rack's answering machine; he left a message asking if Rack would return the call. Tanner gave him Knox's address and asked if Rack could pick him up. At best, Tanner knew if Rack left at that moment, it was a three hour drive.

"You gonna come clean with me?" Knox asked.

Tanner checked the side mirror. "There's not much to tell."

Tanner sensed Knox check over at him. "How about the highlights?" Knox pushed in the cigarette lighter—the lap belt's accompanying vestige.

For the next twenty minutes, Tanner explained events that led up to the crash in the Notch. Knox interrupted a few times with questions.

At the end, Knox asked, "You think Dreavor was close to something?"

"I don't have enough to even venture a guess."

"Well, they didn't try to run you through because you take up a lot of the road."

"That's what scares me." Tanner reached over and turned on the radio. AM only. Squawks and bleeps—nothing solid. "I don't know who they are, and I haven't got a clue what they think I know."

Knox himself flicked a glance at the rearview. "You think they're watching you now?"

"Shit, I hope not." Tanner looked back over the truck's rear bed and saw exhaust rise up blue behind them. "Tell me, what the hell is there to dive for in Maine?"

Knox laughed. "You mean, what *isn't* there?"

Tanner looked at him with the forced beginnings of a smile, wanting, hoping Knox was being sarcastic. But Knox glanced over as if to say, *seriously.*

"You mean rocks?" Tanner asked.

"I mean, Biker boy, sunken ships, fallen lighthouses, underwater caves, whale skeletons, and, yes, world-class rock formations. Am I leaving anything out?"

"Drafts of the original works of Shakespeare?"

Knox flipped the radio knob, silencing the horrible static. "Haven't heard that one yet."

The Chevy slowed and then crawled as the wheels rumbled over the planks of a short bridge. It stopped at a low-rise seaside shack extending out over the water. "I suppose you need a place to crash."

Tanner froze with his hand on the door handle. His face broke into a dozen smiles. "I think I've crashed enough in the past two days. *Sleep*, now that would be novel." The scents of the shore greeted him as he followed Knox from the crushed seashell driveway to the house. The front door squeaked like a poorly played violin.

"Want a drink?"

"Water would be good." Tanner saw the sun reflecting off the ocean through the window in the far wall. The floor had a hollow sound. A staircase led to a loft area above. Thick, insulated wires snaked along the ceiling. Four corner nails plastered a detailed ocean depth chart to the wall between two oversized windows that looked east over the ocean. An odd collection of items were scattered across the house—a couple of scuba tanks, one with a regulator and one without, the front half of a flipper, and an umbrella in a holder made from cork. He stepped over a beach ball of fishing line.

"Are we on stilts?" Tanner asked. He walked past a crusted metallic boar's head on an end table.

On the right, Knox stepped into a narrow kitchen—a refrigerator's width—and removed a plastic Domino's Pizza cup from the cupboard. He filled it from the sink. "Yep. It was originally a boathouse for the harbor master." The refrigerator door *smucked* open, and Knox selected a tall-neck Budweiser for himself. "The original dock came down fifteen years ago. I bought it with the money I got from a find of cannon balls on the harbor floor."

"Cannon balls?"

Knox entered the main room, handed Tanner his water glass, and then took a long suck of his Bud. "Yeah, just your typical coast of Maine diving trophy."

Tanner laughed.

Knox nodded and turned to the window. He rested his bottle on the sill next to an upright telescope, an old one with engraving of birds along its sides. The sun's reflection off the water highlighted the crests on Knox's face and also shadowed the ridges. Tanner counted at least five open clam shells scattered around the house, open and filled with cigarette ashes. "You dive a lot yourself?"

"I haven't been down for a couple of months. A string of bad luck. I got caught in a blast underwater and damaged my ear canal." He lifted his three-fingered right hand. "Didn't help my claw, either."

"What was it?"

"We're not sure exactly, but my partner and I think he accidentally punctured a submerged propane tank. The explosion rolled the old tug we were exploring. In addition to my ear busting out, the ship rolled over on my hand." He dropped into a captain's chair. "Partner's fine."

"You lose consciousness?"

"I think for a moment or two. My regulator was shot. In order to get out of there, I needed to cut myself loose."

Tanner eased into the chair across from him. Knox flopped one foot over the other on the top of a lobster trap. Tanner did the same. His right thigh burned as he lifted it. Tanner noticed that Knox's flip-flops were worn cracker-thin. His toenails had bleached white centers and corn yellow rims.

Knox swallowed a slug of Bud. "It was either lose the digits or lose my life."

The glass of water tasted salty. Could have been the glass, and could have been the plumbing. "So what kind of old ships have you seen out there?"

"Lots of fragments. Hard to survive as a wreck on the bottom here because of the rocks and our storms. But there were a lot of early voyages that learned the hard way how rough our coast is."

"It must have been hell at night trying to navigate without even a lighthouse."

Knox nodded.

Tanner walked over to the depth chart. "How much do you know about the old traffic that crossed over?"

"I don't dwell on the stuff that made it safely back home."

Tanner felt a cold chill. One might make the argument that he was an archeologist, but to Tanner, Knox appeared to be more like a grave robber.

"I don't know where our friend would've wound up," Tanner said. "If we restrict our thinking to the time just around Shakespeare's life, we're probably focused on a period of twenty-five years beginning about 1590. If we presume Dreavor was diving near here because he used your shop, then our area of interest narrows."

Knox pushed up from his seat, and it crackled like an old lady's osteoporosis. He opened his desk drawer and removed a long, flat book of wrinkled pages. He flipped through them.

"You ever hear of a Captain Richard Hanham? Here." He slapped the book on the lobster trap table and flipped open the pages. The book smelled like cigarettes and beer. "There weren't *that* many. Cobran was early in 1602. Then, Raines. MacCauley, Berensford, Pring, and Waymouth. What in particular are you looking for?"

"Anything manned by Shakespeare?"

Knox turned back to the kitchen and walked with his head cranked back, sucking on the bottle. Tanner ran his finger down a page of written notes. Knox's script was neater than Tanner would have expected. The page had a column of dates, a ship column and its captain, a column of locations, and a section of comments, mainly descriptions of sites. He hoped he might recognize a name.

"You want a beer?" Knox asked from around the corner.

Tanner had determined that the saltwater was not healthy. "Yeah, I suppose. Anyone ever told you that your water tastes salty?"

"I think the pipes have been infiltrated. I stick to beer and orange juice."

"Oh, I'll take an orange juice."

"We're out." Knox returned and put a Budweiser in Tanner's hand. He set his bottle on the sill again and opened the window. He spit out the window and watched the lump fall, and then he snapped a pack of Camels out of his chest pocket and slapped them up against his wrist.

Tanner put the book aside. He looked out the large window. *It must get dark at night here.* Why hadn't Pile called? He hoped Rack picked up his message.

A cigarette jumped up from Knox's pack. "Maybe that lady was just trying to scare you."

Tanner laughed. "I tend to think she had loftier goals in mind."

"Oh well." Knox selected a single cigarette. "I guess you better find out why they want you dead." He took a seat in the captain's chair again.

"It would probably help to know where Dreavor was diving."

Knox flipped the top of a Zippo lighter and lit his Camel.

"Where is the closest collection of wrecks?" Tanner asked.

"Most of the sites worth exploring are concentrated near the bend before Miller's Cove. Before the Hurricane of 1834, there was an enormous collection of rock lurking just below the surface. From a thousand yards out, it looked like a peaceful, welcoming harbor. In the end, it castrated many a ship. They tended to fall one on top of the other."

"Is that far from here?"

A slow grin broke across Knox's face. "Two miles down the coast."

"What'd you see when you dove it?"

"Lots of fragments. It's been worked over pretty good."

"Who was the first to discover it?"

Knox scratched his head and his finger snagged on something. "Oh, I think the Deffle Museum has a good chunk of relics." Knox pinched his scalp and brought his fingers around to inspect something too small for Tanner to see from across the lobster trap.

Tanner looked away. Knox's home grew nastier by the second. "Deffle?"

"Named after the old man who dove the waters. He's dead. It's a town museum now."

"And how far is the museum?"

"Next town up. It sits on a quiet piece of land on a hill. I don't recall Shakespeare being among his collection. Been a while since I've been there."

"Any other sites in this vicinity where we might find wrecks from around that time?"

Knox tilted his head back and inhaled the Bud. When he finished his sip, he belched. "Not really. Not in this area. There are other dive shops he could've rented from down south to explore spots outside Portland."

"Wanna go to that museum?"

"I'm telling you, there's not much worth anything. Town sold off anything of real value over the years to help pay for stuff. I think they sold the ship's wheel to help pay for a new flag pole."

Tanner spread his arms to the room. "Well, if cannonballs can get you this, a wheel should clearly carry a flagpole."

Knox laughed and flicked his spent ash outside the window with a casualness that showed he'd done it a million times before. "Right."

"So, you wanna go?"

Knox checked his watch. "My partner is gonna be wondering where I am."

"That's all right. I can find it." Tanner took a long plug of beer.

Knox inhaled two complete lungs of cigarette smoke and then pitched the stub out the window. "Nah, I'll take you. You've got me intrigued."

"I can't say we'll find anything."

Knox rested his empty bottle on the lobster trap. "Now you're sounding like a treasure hunter."

Chapter 21

The museum was in a nearby seaside town called Chestnut. It sat up on a hill on the far side of town, up off the coast. Knox wound the pickup through the tall trees and the thin road that led to the museum, which was housed in an old colonial. On the ride, Tanner sent an email over the phone to his boss. Knox yelled at a couple of cars on the road while Tanner typed.

"Tell me some more about this de Vere character?" Knox said with both hands on the pickup's wheel. The cigarette in his mouth waved up and down as he spoke, and ashes sprinkled across his lap.

"There's not much more I know about his time at sea."

"Well, give me the basics at least."

"He led a division to fight the Spanish in 1588."

"Really?"

"He never saw combat, either in the sea or on land, yet became heavily involved with expeditions to explore the new world."

"Here?"

Tanner nodded. "He financed them. A venture capitalist. It was the growth industry of the day."

Knox's eyebrows peaked. "So he was rich?"

"He never made a dime at it. And as far as documents show, he never traveled with any of them."

"Where did these explorations go?"

They slammed into a parking space amidst six or seven empty parking slots carved into the backyard of the old house. Tanner had come to observe that Knox liked to park the same way he drove: every turn or application of the brakes appeared to be a last-second thought, grudgingly applied. The pickup tended to jerk into turns or lurch forward at red lights.

"The fleets sailed west trying to find a shortcut passage to China. I don't know anything about those efforts."

Knox stood from the truck and pitched his cigarette stub. "Doesn't sound too promising."

As they walked around to the front of the house, Tanner saw a short man in a navy blue wool coat sitting in a fold-down chair at the front of the house. He wore a policeman's cap with a badge that said, "Security."

"Afternoon," the man offered. His nametag said, "Roy." Tanner thought he must be in his late fifties. He had a few days' growth. A newspaper and *Sports Illustrated* sat under his chair. He had a small radio next to him, and *Tea in the Sahara* was winding down.

"Museum open today?" Tanner asked.

"Sure is. Till five."

To Tanner's immediate right was a Lucite box on a three-foot stand with a couple of dollar bills inside. "Is there an admission fee?"

"Entirely voluntary," Roy said. Knox plowed into the house past Tanner, who stopped to fish a dollar out of his wallet.

"Are you a Deffle?" Tanner asked as he fit two dollars into the slit in the box.

"Nope. Mr. Deffle died a few years back. I'm just security."

Roy had neither gun, nightstick, nor radio. "Anything to keep in mind as we pass through?" Tanner asked.

Roy turned in his seat. "Yeah, we close at five."

The house smelled like must. The windows were open and a breeze blew through. There were no carpets, and Knox's boots echoed as he walked.

"Come on, most of the stuff is in here," he said. Tanner followed him into the first room on their left.

A sad room. Bands of sun came in through the front windows. Natural light provided the only source of light in the house. A long, flat chocolate timber ran the length of the far wall, a piling from a ship's flank. Thin glass cases stood against the walls. A few small items lay on the shelves. They appeared to be broken cookie pieces.

Tanner listened beyond Knox's footsteps for other movements in the house. He heard the metallic clip of scissors. Knox had flipped his lighter under a cigarette in his mouth. He slipped the Zippo into his jeans pocket and drew the cigarette a quarter of the way down. He coughed.

"Ah, they probably don't want you to smoke in here," Tanner said.

"I told you, this is crap. Couldn't buy a paper with proceeds from this."

Tanner looked through the cabinets. The first object was a single farthing, which looked like the pennies that he and Jimmy used to leave on the train tracks to be smooshed by a passing diesel. Tanner actually thought that the similarities were kind of cool. Next, he panned by a half of a teacup with a slight design that ran the circumference. Then he breezed by the head of a pipe, barrel braces, a shrunken, black boot heel, and a pistol barrel.

"See any of Shakie's stuff?" Knox's cigarette flapped when he spoke.

Tanner continued to walk the room. The round edge of a port hole. An oar tip. A framed sketch of a schooner's cross section hung on the side wall.

Tanner stepped into the wave of dust motes highlighted by the afternoon sun beaming through the window. He slowly walked by another case holding a blackened tin cup. "This thing looks burnt."

"Yeah, there appears to have been a fire on one of the ships. Given the overlap of wrecks on the point, it's hard to tell which one went down in flames."

Tanner stopped under a single shelf on the wall. He stood under a partial cannon barrel, rusted and with a cracked tip. "Is this a cannon?"

Knox *klunked* up behind Tanner. "Deck gun. Also called a verlas."

"Cool."

"Dime a dozen." Knox moved on.

Tanner kept walking. There was a table whose stand was formed from ballast stones. On top was the bottom half of what may have been a sugar container. A painting on the wall displayed a well-dressed sea captain pointing out to sea as one of his crew steered.

"Well, what do you think? He remind you of anything?"

Tanner scanned other recognizable items across a few of the other shelves. A pulley wheel. A lantern top. A key lock. The arc of a backstaff. "Nope. You were right. I didn't know what I was thinking we'd find. Sorry to bring you out here."

"I told you. Amazes me the town keeps this thing open. Measly dollars in the bin up front can't pay the rent." Together they walked toward the exit.

"Maybe they get tax breaks. You know, historical landmark status or something."

"My house ought to get a tax break."

Tanner refrained from saying that Knox's house ought to get dynamited.

"Where do you wanna go from here?" Knox asked.

Tanner stopped and slowly turned back to the room. He walked to the far side.

Knox called after him, "Hey, what are you doing? I've got a business to run ..."

Back in the main room, Tanner looked up at the shelf with the cannon. "Can you give me a boost up?"

"What?"

"A boost. Just get me up there. There's something about that cannon."

Knox stood still. "Are you kidding? What the fuck do you want with that piece of shit?

"It's shiny inside."

Knox came into the room. "What are you, a two-year-old?"

"Humor me for a second."

"Humor you? Sure."

Knox walked over to the trash can and kicked it over on its side. It was empty, and it made an awful lot of noise. Tanner looked around the room and into the hallway, expecting Roy to pop around the corner. Knox kicked the can across the floor toward Tanner.

"Roy's not gonna like that," Tanner said.

"There's your boost."

Tanner bent over, turned the can on its mouth, and stepped up on its bottom. He was eye-level with the cannon. He steadied himself on the wall with his right hand and poked into the cannon with his left index.

"It's smooth. It's—it's glass."

Knox shrugged. "I heard of 'em tarring front and back to seal in maps. Protective. Makes a good hiding place too."

Tanner squinted to see if he could detect anything inside. "They usually line it in glass?"

"Here." Knox handed his lighter to Tanner. "But careful, I don't think they want you to smoke in here."

Tanner smiled and held it close to inspect inside. "Glass or ceramic for certain." He shifted the flame to the front of the cannon. The light made it possible to see a spread of black fudge at the seal. "You're right about the tar." Tanner stepped down. He felt a buzz rising. "It would work for documents, right?"

Knox looked at the cannon again. "You think you could fit a whole book in there?"

"I don't know. Maybe. How many of these did they find?"

Knox walked to the front of the room, cigarette smoke trailing him. "Weren't Shakespeare's books, like, long?"

Tanner straightened the trashcan and carried it back to its original location. "Yeah, regular plays, but I bet you could've rolled up an individual play and fit it inside of that."

Knox read a laminated poster listing all of the recovered items. "Says here they uncovered three of those. Could be more on the floor. I've been down there. Lots of folks have. It's true there could be more down there, but I'd say they're well hidden. I don't remember anyone mentioning glass inside the deck guns or papers being recovered. Unfortunately, if water were to break the tar seal, bye-bye Shakespeare."

"You think there's a basement to this place," Tanner whispered.

"I've been there, it's empty. They really cleaned this place out when the old man died. I came to the estate sale. Nothing. I would've remembered deck guns."

Tanner peered down the hallway that led into the house. Gray walls, old wooden floors. There was nothing more here for him. He and Knox walked past Roy. Knox pitched his cigarette nub onto the grass from the front porch.

"Can't see that they had room on any ship to house thirty heavy guns with plays in them. That's a lot of weight. And a bad use of weaponry."

Tanner nodded. The deck gun had looked heavy. And the only thing it could have done to conceal Shakespeare's true identity if they had been discovered would have involved tossing it overboard in deep water. If this was the way that Shakespeare brought his works across the Atlantic, then did this mean that those works had found their way to the bottom of the ocean? Was it likely that if other deck guns or cannons were cracked like this one that Shakespeare's original writings were gone?

129

Knox lit another cigarette. "You look like someone kicked you in your gut."

Tanner shrugged. "If this is what became of any cannon they had on board with documents inside, then the prospects don't look good."

"Our prospects never looked good. That's the nature of treasure hunting. I'll do some digging on where the other relics from this ship went. Maybe someone has an old, sealed-up cannon sitting on their mantel somewhere and doesn't realize what they've got."

Tanner stared at his Nikes. "Not encouraging."

"Did you actually think that we'd just waltz in there, a graveyard of a graveyard, and uncover Shakespeare's stuff?"

If Tanner had started off feeling shitty, Knox had just made him feel juvenile for his initial optimism.

Knox fell in behind the thin, wide steering wheel. Tanner plopped down, once again Knox's passenger. Cigarette smoke swarmed. Tanner felt tired, and his joints ached.

"I'll take you to my place, and you can wait for your ride there. Then, I've got to drop these tanks at the shop."

They drove for ten minutes. Knox worked a new Camel to life. Tanner felt vibes of irritation pouring out of the man with every puff. Maybe he should try interrupting.

"So, which ships went down at the point?"

Knox coughed. It sounded deep, from the bottom of a lung and rough like granite. "Does it matter?"

"You're starting to sound like a treasure hunter."

Knox coughed again, or was that a laugh? "You're starting to humor me."

Tanner bit down. *Humor you!*

"Ever hear of the broadship, *The Charge*?"

"No, I—"

"I didn't *think* so, genius. Done for the day?"

But there was something, something he read once. Tanner spun his memory reels. *The Charge ... The Charge ... The Charge ...*

"This is obviously past you—"

"Captain Mealey, April 1781, no survivors," Tanner said. He felt the truck slow. Knox squinted and eyed him up and down. Tanner felt the need to check where the pickup was headed. "I've got a good memory," Tanner said.

Knox puffed out a wig of smoke. "I'll say." He slowly turned his attention back to the wheel and straightened out the Chevy. Tanner's head nearly knocked the window when the truck burped back on line. He could tell, even behind the heavy smoke, that Knox was stewing.

"So … do you know any other wrecks that went down near *The Charge?*"

"Others?" Knox coughed, and a puff of ashes sprinkled on the steering wheel. He shook his head in a way that showed bewilderment. "How about *The Reliant?*"

Tanner thought. The bumps in the road jiggled him, but his mind stayed focused.

"George Rainey, I think."

"You'd be right. Again. That was the end of him."

"See, I didn't know that. I don't know that much detail. Just the big items. I read a book on sea disasters once."

Knox nodded. "The big items. Of course." His cheeks worked the Camel like an incinerator. "How about *The Halbeard?*"

Tanner thought. Cigarette smoke mummified him. After a minute, he opened his eyes. "I don't know that one."

"You sound sad. You're not gonna cry on me, are you?"

Tanner shook his head. He moved to turn on the radio but then remembered the static and withdrew his hand.

"Just a cod ship, no one of notoriety."

"Oh."

"And *The Broadside?*"

Tanner closed his eyes and nodded. "I recognize that one."

"Great." Knox stabbed his cigarette butt in the overflowing dash ashtray. "Let me save you the trouble. It was part of Gosnold's fleet."

"Gosnold …" Tanner pivoted to the side. Sometimes the hunters in his memory ran wild with nets through the hollows of his mind. A name like that stood out.

Knox's shoulder rose and sank as he lowered the window. The diver's scraggy, hay hair and crusted face mop rippled in the oncoming wind. He turned. "You must think I'm a total hick jackass."

Tanner thought Knox's eyes had turned the color of bourbon. "Wh-what?"

"You come to my store with some story about working on the old man's estate."

"That's no stor—"

"*That* front disappeared quickly!" Knox's acid breath slammed into Tanner. Tanner inched toward the passenger door. "And all of a sudden you're able to recall ships' captains from four hundred years ago?" Knox shook himself on the steering wheel. "Are you fucking kidding me?"

The Chevy turned down Knox's road. Tanner saw another pickup parked in Knox's driveway. It was an older Toyota, and most of its original red paint had been worn down to rust. Something about that Toyota Tanner didn't like.

"Now, we're going to go inside and have a talk. And your memory better work a little bit faster." As Knox parked behind the rust bucket, another vehicle pierced his peripheral view: a Jeep Wrangler sliding to a stop in front of Knox's dead front lawn, perpendicular to Knox's truck. Tanner watched as the driver stepped out. He couldn't believe it.

Kyle Murray.

Chapter 22

"Sorry, chief," Tanner said, bounding out of the pickup. "My ride's here." He heard Knox exit fast.

Kyle popped out of the Wrangler and closed the few feet between the vehicles, holding her cell phone to her ear. "No, thanks, Sheriff. I found him."

Perfect. Tanner knew Knox heard her loud and clear.

"He's right where he said he would be," she said, "out on Raven Way. Yep."

Knox stopped moving. He married lighter to cigarette and leaned back against the bed of his truck. His eyes stuck to Kyle's chest; he made no move to lift them. Tanner stepped forward to meet Kyle. She drove a Jeep Wrangler. Of course she did. Anything else would be out of alignment. The Portland Sea Dogs cap allowed wisps of her dirty blonde hair to curl from under. She was cute on cute.

"Thanks for your help … Okay … Bye." Kyle ended her call. "Howdy," she said to Tanner and Knox.

"Friend of yours?" Knox asked.

"Sort of," Tanner said. "Rack with you?"

"No, just me. Leaves me room for your bike."

"Nice, yeah. Leaves room for a lot of things." Tanner couldn't resist. He walked to the spot next to Knox, bent over, and drew his knapsack and then his bike from the rear of the pickup. Tanner nudged his head toward Knox. "This is Paul."

"How do." Knox nodded, and his eyes worked Kyle's body.

"Hi."

"I suppose Rack ..." Tanner started.

"Agreed that it wasn't necessary for me to drive all the way down south with his grandmother." She shifted on her feet and took in the entire scene. "Cool place."

"Thanks." Knox flapped a hand toward the house. "Like a beer?"

Tanner backpedaled toward Kyle's Jeep with his bike over one shoulder and his knapsack over the other. "I think it's time I left you with a bit of your day to yourself." Tanner waved to Knox. "We'll have to finish our discussion some other time. But thanks for the ride and the tour."

"Sure. I'll see you soon."

"Great."

Kyle gave Knox a finger wiggle wave. "Nice meeting you."

"Pleasure." Knox held a cigarette between his lips and returned his lighter to his pocket. "Let me know if you think of anything else."

Tanner loaded his bike into the rear of Kyle's Jeep. "Likewise, you've got my number."

Knox tapped his finger to his explosion of hair. "Oh, I got it right here."

When Kyle opened her driver's door, she nodded her chin at Tanner's bandaged bicep poking out from his shirt. "Man, did that happen from the accident?"

Not quite Valley Girl wonderment, Tanner thought, but Kyle had that California-fascination-overload nonetheless. "Actually, I hit an old lady who was walking her dog. She took up too much of the sidewalk and, well, you know, it was her or me."

"Not funny. Get in."

Kyle honked and flashed a smile at Knox as she drove away from his house. Then, she backtracked to 95. It took fifteen minutes for Tanner to fill her in.

"So, this guy sounds like a nut job. Not that he looked like an appeals court judge."

"This entire case has that sense—nut job, not judge."

"But it sounds like you've got another connection in this Gosnold name."

"Yeah, maybe. I haven't really thought it through."

"Who was he again?"

"He was one of the first to explore the coast of America. He captained the crew that named Cape Cod, Martha's Vineyard, and Cuttyhunk."

"Never heard of him."

"The crew went on to the Jamestown settlement. Ring any bells?"

"You mean like John Smith and Pocahontas?"

"Right alongside them. Gosnold is somehow connected to *The Tempest*. I'm sure of it."

"The Shakespeare play?"

"His last."

"Hmm." Kyle kept her eyes on the unfolding road. "You remember anything else about him?"

"He was a friend of the earl of Southampton, who, now that I think about it, was a lifelong friend of de Vere's."

Kyle turned toward Tanner. "No shit."

Tanner's sat back. There was still more, and he waited for it to connect up. "*The Tempest* … is thought by some to have been based on one of Gosnold's sea journals."

"So you have Gosnold, an early visitor to the coast and a friend of a good friend of Shakespeare. This is where Shakespeare got his ideas for *The Tempest* and where he learned where a good hiding place for his original drafts would be. There's your link. Not bad for an afternoon with a nut job."

"Unfortunately, though, I've told you about all I know, all anybody really knows, and the guy's ship—not really his ship—is sunk and buried in the ocean."

The dark night slipped past them as she drove, fast but in control. The highway wasn't crowded this Sunday night. As she passed a Corolla, she spoke, giving Tanner another excuse to stare at her.

"I've been meaning to ask you about that camera in your head," she said.

"Yeah?"

"Like, before a test in school, could you just zip through the pages and then walk into the test?"

Tanner shook his head. "I'm afraid it doesn't work like that. It takes time to digest. It works best, like most things in life, when you're alert and focused."

"And Rack was your roommate."

Tanner laughed. "Enough to dull the senses of any right-minded individual." *How do beautiful girls keep their skin so clean?* Tanner fiddled with the radio. He settled on WNBF 89.7, a hole-in-the-wall station from up north that broadcast whatever the Eskimos wanted. Now, it was Bob Dylan's "Desolation Row."

"So, where would you like to go?" she asked.

"Me? Back to my apartment is probably best." Tanner hoped against hope that she would pull two plane tickets to a warmer climate from her back pocket.

"I wasn't sure if you had another stop on your investigative route."

"Oh, ah, no. I'm fresh out of leads."

"Maybe something will click with Gosnold."

Tanner's eyes felt better closed. He eased his seat back and a weight lifted off his chest. "I don't know. Maybe, yeah." His words were taking longer to come out. "But I wouldn't … know where to begin to make … connections. I just kind of have to go with what …"

Tanner shook awake. He was still in the passenger seat of Kyle's Wrangler.

He pinched his eyes. "Sorry, did I fade on you?"

"In mid-sentence." Kyle smiled. "It's okay."

"Where are we?"

"I pulled off at an exit for Danton. Ever hear of it?"

"Vaguely. Think we'll find anywhere to—" And just then, around a bend in a road, bracketed by tall, dense forest, stood a small sign cut in the woods.

The Carlysle House.

Kyle turned down a long driveway penetrating deep into the woods. A two, maybe three-story colonial spread out before them. "Thought you might be hungry."

"Thought right." Tanner's stomach gnawed on itself, and Carlysle House looked nice. Credit card was his only possible means of payment. He had found a bank that came to campus last year and was foolish enough to hand out credit lines of fifteen hundred dollars. He signed on.

The restaurant was in an old bed-and-breakfast. The lights were low, emitting a golden glow. Tanner tried to see through the curtained windows as they stepped up to the porch.

"Something smells good." He held the door for Kyle—anything to catch an added view of her caboose.

Just as he expected, the inside was a home. Paneled walls, doily table tops, baskets hung here and there. Rich molding enhanced the seam of the wall and ceiling, and the oil lamps on the half dozen tables in the dining room glowed gold.

Tanner leaned close to Kyle's ear. "I feel better already." She had a warm rose scent, and between that and the heat from the scattered fireplaces, the cricks in Tanner's back melted away.

"Can I pick 'em, or what?"

Again, with that ceaseless enthusiasm. What was in the water out west?

They were greeted by a matronly woman in a dress that bunched in a double wrinkle at her hip. "Good evening."

Her excited greeting jolted the tired Tanner and called for a reciprocal level of enthusiasm. "Hi."

"Two for dinner?"

"Very much."

Tanner ushered Kyle ahead first. This was too easy. He watched her move across the dining room of a half dozen tables, two of which had middle-aged couples already seated. Tanner watched the man in the couple nearest him lock on Kyle. Tanner's pride grew, and he sat across from her in a corner table. The hostess handed out menus.

Make polite humor. "I'm tempted to say just yes to the menu."

"Actually, everything is delicious and fresh. I'll be right back with some water."

After the hostess walked away, Kyle asked, "Hungry, huh?"

"I had a bit of an unconventional lunch." Tanner explained being jumped in the tavern men's room.

"Christ, did you manage to avoid any crisis today?"

They ordered wine, a sauvignon blanc—a forty-two-dollar bottle, Tanner noted. The lamp's hue made Kyle seem tanned, as if she needed it. The first part of their conversation was dominated by Kyle sharing her view on the advantages of pinot grigio over sauvignon. Tanner was happy to let her talk because he had the chance to see the full sky of her eyes when she became excited about the dryness of pinot.

As soon as he noticed she was winding down, Tanner asked, "So, where did you learn so much about wine?"

"It seemed like when my dad came home, he came home with a different bottle every night."

Tanner thought about his package-store vodka runs for his mother. Every night? Maybe, just about. At the time, he had no awareness of his role in her demise. Since then, he had kept trying to put it all out of his mind.

"He used to talk to mom about them at length ... and then he asked about my day."

"Your dad an accountant too?"

"No, an investment banker. We grew up north of LA."

"So Stanford was a great getaway, huh?"

"Hey, they had a very decent volleyball team. I was good player. It fit at the time."

Her dad had a way, Kyle said, of knowing how to move men and women to action. He could persuade them to focus on certain things. "But more than that, he knew what motivated people."

"Did he understand you?"

"Not if I could help it."

Tanner sensed one part spite, one part pride. "You didn't want him to know you?"

Kyle took a full swallow of wine. "That's something you have to work at."

He was poking around too far too fast. He eased back. "What are you gonna do for Thanksgiving?"

Kyle's eyes seemed to volley the idea in her head. "I'm not sure yet. That's a ways away."

"Okay, let's start with Halloween."

Kyle's face brightened. "Right. Who are you going to be?"

Tanner's mind flashed to a series of snapshot memories of Jimmy: as Frankenstein, Bigfoot, Batman. Tanner's chariot bike transformed into a spaceship, a rickshaw, a stagecoach.

"I hadn't thought about it. It's been a while since I've dressed up."

"I used to love costume parties."

"Yeah?"

"All the initial mystery and the laughs."

She was looser, she broke into a smile easily, and her hands became more animated. *What's not to adore?* Tanner could not hold off asking any longer. "So, are you seeing anyone now?"

Kyle smiled. "Not now. Last guy I dated was back in DC, about two months ago. He found someone else whose vision of the future was more in line with his. No big deal."

"If there's a bar somewhere called 'Regret,' I'm sure he'll be a frequent visitor."

Kyle laughed and almost fell out of her chair. Tanner fell in with her wave of laughter.

"*Ohmygod*, that's awful," she said.

How could he argue? It was. "You're right, you're right."

Later, as they ate their salads, Kyle said, "So, Rack says you have a pretty little sophomore that you sneak away to see on weekends. Does she know what you're up to?"

Tanner coughed, and as his hand rushed to cover his mouth, he knocked the table, clinking the silverware. "What?"

"He told me all about her. How you met her as you were graduating. She's a biology physicist. Frankly, I've never heard of—"

Tanner laughed deeply, unabashedly.

"What?" Kyle asked, seeming genuinely surprised.

"I don't have a girlfriend," he managed through his laugh.

"You better not let her hear you say that."

"No, no. There is no sophomore, no nobody." He dropped his head into his forearm to recover. "Nobody outside Rack's feeble imagination. A biology physicist? God." And he started laughing again.

Although smiling, Kyle asked, "And he did that because ..."

"He must really like you. Anything he can do to cut back on the competition."

She laughed and stuck her salad with her fork. "And I believed him. I even asked how you two met."

"Don't feel so bad. I'm the one who really loses when you think about it. How good-looking did he say she was?"

Kyle lowered her fork. "Mocking doesn't help."

"Right." Tanner lifted her beloved bottle. "More wine?"

Chapter 23

Rack's minivan rolled to a stop in front of the pharmacy. His headlights shone on a sun-aged sign for hemorrhoid relief. He had been driving for two hours without a stop, and more importantly, without a beer. All that would change. Next door to the pharmacy was the Bull Hollow, a fifty-by-fifty pub with a brick facade and a neon "Rheingold" sign in the window. The street spots were occupied by twin Toyota pickup trucks. Each could've used a bath. Rack stuffed himself into his field jacket and went in.

Rack Manning grew up in Maine. Unlike Tanner, he rarely exercised. He was a Playstation baby, a couch potato's envy. His father, George Manning, was a commercial real estate lawyer. Under the blessing of good timing, his father came into his prime during an upswing in the economy, when lending rates were low and capital was available. His father worked on deals raising hotels, smaller fifty-to-eighty-room plots, north of their home on I-95. He also helped usher in three strip-mall properties in the upcoming towns of New Digger, Helsing, and Betran. His father was a busy man, often on the road, and more often on the phone. When he arrived at the dinner table, he usually had the impression of the phone on the skin of his cheek and ear. Given his schedule, George Manning was never Rack's baseball, basketball, or soccer coach. Rack never even benefited from late-afternoon games of catch. While the Mannings managed to ski together at least two weekends of the season, that damned cell phone found reception almost all the way to the top of the mountain. Rack Manning grew up with a shadow of a role model.

His mother? Laura started out bubbly. As George's business prospered, she grew in enthusiasm for town tennis leagues, her bridge club, Rack's school, the design of her home, and vacation planning. When the bottom dropped out of the real estate market, the same leverage that buoyed George Manning on the way up swamped him on the way down. Laura was slow to adjust, but smaller bank accounts and rising bills-to-income ratios have an inherent self-correcting mechanism. In the prolonged recession that spanned Rack's high school years, the Mannings became a quieter family.

Soon after Rack started at the University of Maine, he and Tanner collided at a keg during a fraternity party. Despite their differences, or maybe because of them, they clicked. Tanner was one who wore the weight of the world on his shoulders. He constantly fought to become more competitive on the bike. At the same time, he battled to make time to see Jimmy whenever he could. He had to navigate his sponsorship as well as his grades, all the while worrying about what he would do for a career, conceding that eventually his legs would grow weaker.

But Rack, he knew how to relax. He was good for Tanner in this way. In a similar vein, Tanner had a positive influence on Rack. Tanner was a discipline machine, an early riser who pinballed through the day and finally came to rest late at night after connecting with Jimmy either on the phone or in person. Tanner's nonstop way swept Rack up in its wake. After a while of observing Tanner in hot pursuit of many things for fourteen hours of the day, two hours of study didn't seem so demanding to Rack. And that was the pattern that eventually drew Rack to become Tanner's road manager. Besides, Rack had the minivan, and he was happy to have a companion to talk to. There wasn't too much more to it. The long road trips they took to races left them lots of time to talk. It wasn't long before they knew most every memorable moment of each other's childhood, cementing their friendship. And that's why Rack embarked on the kind of effort he did the night in Kargil.

The inside of the Bull Hollow was bar-dark, with perhaps a shot of Southern Comfort. Rack moved aside a broken bear trap hanging from a chewed leather belt attached to the ceiling. He thought the place smelled as if a bear had been caught yesterday and left to struggle overnight and had only recently been removed. The walls were punctuated with other hunting implements, an old tin coffee pot, and an ancient, dismantled shotgun—stock, trigger, hammers, and bore. The floor had been nearly worn to the dirt. The bar itself was felled oak and the size of a taxi cab.

Four trolls hung over the bar top, firmly planted in their stools. Rack slid onto a stool and spun toward a skinny, oily man thumb-pumping a clicker pointed at a TV mounted over the Scotch shelf in the far right corner.

Rack waved at the bartender. "Bud, please." Rack nodded at the man to his right, who scratched his head with the loose finger of the hand that held his smoking cigarette. A smile of gumdrops—no, make that teeth.

The stool sitter spoke. "Evening."

"Hiya," Rack said, and with that, he began his reconnaissance.

Chapter 24

After dinner, Kyle and Tanner were encouraged to take their drinks out on the back porch, where an outdoor fireplace issued a blanket of warmth against the cool September wind. The house backed up to a pond that stretched for a quarter mile in either direction. Across the pond, they saw the distant twinkling porch lights of two or three houses. The crickets were clicking steadily.

Kyle and Tanner were leaning against a chest-high railing, watching evening birds skim the pond's surface. Tanner spoke first. "What a brilliant find."

"Thank you."

"I've got to remember to bring the sophomore here."

She punched him in the arm.

He grabbed his bicep. "Ow, the bandage, woman, remember the bandage."

She stayed close and kept her eyes on his. Tanner thought he heard the crickets hush. *She is perfect.*

"So …" Tanner sipped his wine for something to do to relieve the awkwardness.

"So …" She turned back to the pond.

"You have your mind set on becoming an accountant, huh?"

"Just the current path I'm on. Like you."

"Me?"

"You're not going to be an estate custodian your entire life."

Tanner watched a swallow skim the surface at a breakneck speed. "I'm not?"

"Nah. You're too smart."

"Thanks. Out of curiosity, what am I going to do with myself?"

"Probably a detective, at this rate."

"I can appreciate that."

"What do you think I'm going to be?" she asked.

"You? I don't know you enough—"

"Venture a prediction."

He turned to her and took the liberty of looking her up and down. In the firelight, she was a goddess. How to keep control?

"You, from what I know, can be anything you want."

"I was looking for something more specific."

"That's just it. You're smart, funny, beautiful. I don't know, to me, you could be anything."

She was watching him now. Her blue eyes, greened by the fire.

"Of course, that's just a venture."

Her teeth lost no brightness in the night. "Thanks."

This time she did not turn back to the pond. The better part of his conscience was tugging his face away. His heart braced with full-body resistance. He smelled the port on her breath. Her face inched closer, her eyes steady.

"I think ..." he started, and he brought his glass up for a sip. Then, mustering all of his energy, he turned to the side. "I'm going to have a busy day tomorrow."

"You think too much."

He finished his port. "Can't help it. It never turns off. *Julius Caesar*, by the way." He was grasping for words to put between them. *She's Rack's, she's Rack's.* Rack thought she was his, so she was.

"What?" She stayed close enough for him to see the curvature of her lip.

"You think too much. The phrase. From Shakespeare's *Julius Caesar.*"

She leaned in and kissed him … and he let her. The crickets hummed, the night watched, and the fire applauded. Kyle turned away with her port. Tanner felt as if he were viewing himself from above the patio. He watched her smile over the pond. Then her eyes met his.

"Okay, well," he said, "this is trouble."

"Trouble?"

"Let's just keep this between us and the crickets. If the swallows let it out, we'll come back for them off-season."

"You're worried about Rack."

He nodded.

She smiled and sipped her glass as she looked out over the pond. "I've got news for you. Rack and I never went as far as this."

"You were jumping all over his back at Dreavor's."

"So?"

"You two drove home together that night."

"So?"

"You're helping him by giving me a lift."

"Your point?"

"Never mind." He was sure Rack would see it differently. The moon's glow shone across the liquid glass before him. "This is not black-and-white accounting."

She punched him in the shoulder. "Well, thank God I'm not going to be an accountant."

Shit, she has a strong punch.

"You folks want something else?" The voice behind him broke them apart. It was the hostess. They turned.

Tanner looked at Kyle. "Want some coffee or something?"

Her look quickly passed Tanner and met up with the hostess's. "Yes, actually, do you have any vacancy?"

Chapter 25

The National Security Agency (NSA) was born in 1952. Officially. From America's earliest days, before the country organized itself, some of its first freedom fighters were doing intelligence work, such as cracking military codes of the British enemy. Ever since then, the United States of America has maintained code makers and code breakers, always more critical to the protection of the nation than commonly understood. The headquarters building at Fort Meade is an intimidating structure of black glass and gives off a "don't fuck with us" aura. The Agency's stated mission was to achieve "global dominance" in cryptology. No other U.S. government agency expressed its mission in terms of global dominance. Around the clock, whether it was in the wee early morning in the Philippines or late at night in Frankfurt, its teams were always chewing on data and signals traveling through wire and space. And its members had a broad mandate to achieve its mission through many means, including those clandestine.

Under its shadow, Randall Levine and Mark Miller sat in a Mitsubishi Eclipse down the street from the Carlysle House. Miller pried a pistachio apart, and the shells fell into the collection on his lap, where some stayed and others rolled to the floor mat. It was a rental. "Think she'll fuck him?"

"Nah."

Miller cracked another pistachio like a split pencil. "I don't know, this guy's a stud. She might just make a workout of it."

"You know, the old colonel was a nut for this stuff." Levine adjusted the focus of his binoculars as he trained them on the upper floors of the inn.

"I heard that." Miller chewed the daylights out of a single pistachio. "Can't believe the entire thing runs deeper than he would've ever imagined."

Levine turned to Miller and wiggled his eyebrows. "That's what he might've wanted you to think."

Miller laughed. "In any event, it's ironic that we're involved." His hand rustled in his pistachio bag.

"Ironic to you—goddamn spooky to me. I'd just as soon be back at Meade when this thing blows."

"You and me both. Speaking of blow, how's our boy doing?"

Chapter 26

The door opened with an orchestra of squeaking metal. The municipal garage was large enough to support a 24/7 echo. Crandall braced his walrus frame on the door handle. "Wait 'til I get the lights." He slurred as he spoke.

With his hands in the pockets of his field jacket, Rack followed Crandall inside. The garage was the antithesis of the Bull Hollow Pub, big and lifeless. Not that what congregated in the Bull Hollow was lively, but the garage's oil smell was far from the bar's odor of organic decay.

As the fluorescent lights blinked to life, Crandall staggered over to the far side of the garage. He hip-checked stacks of rock salt and pushed aside the handles of snowblowers and a green plastic barrel of snow shovels.

"Your uncle's rig is over here." Crandall barely assembled the words in the right order.

Rack followed with a touch more balance … just a touch.

"He loved his Deere." Crandall collapsed on the blade hood of a tractor mower that lurched under the weight like a horse, initially shaken but then calmed at its master's touch.

Back in the bar, Rack had inquired about "Uncle Frank," embellishing as the night developed about their Thanksgivings together when he was young. The bar crew showed their surprise that "Dreav" had any family. "He used to live like a zombie," they told him, "coming and going, mowing, raking, shoveling, planting. No friends, no drinking. Didn't even follow the Pats or the Sox."

Rack stepped up to the seat of the John Deere and slid behind the wheel. "So, this was his throne?"

Crandall sat staring at the ceiling. "Yeah, 'cept for winter. He was pretty handy at tuning it."

Rack pretended to steer. A well-worn steering wheel. "Who did he talk to the most?"

"Himself. We'd always see him driving around with his lips moving. Most of us would bring ear wear, but not Frankie."

"He gay?"

Crandall sat up, and his face flattened. Rack felt perspiration break out across his entire body. In a flash, Crandall sat back and his expression seemed to say that it was a fair question.

"Not that I know. Most of us thought he was just retarded."

Rack smiled, but his mind immediately flipped to Tanner's brother Jimmy. Good thing Tanner wasn't there. "Where'd he go on vacation?"

Crandall shook his head and paused. "Inside. Literally. He would just spend more time in his house. He didn't travel except for last month. Said he was going upstate."

Rack ran his hands over the face of the fuel gauge, the engine temperature gauge, the gear shift, key, and steering wheel. He looked around the garage. Old nameplates from other garden equipment were tacked to the wall next to him. Honda, John Deere, Black & Decker, Toro, Craftsman, Lawn Boy. "This Uncle Frank's steady parking spot?"

Crandall nodded. "All his."

Rack looked over at the signs again. The "a" in Honda was blackened. "So, did he get excited about anything?"

"Not so far as I can tell. He liked to go home at the end of the day. *That* I know."

Rack was drawn back to the tin plates on the wall. The "l" in Black & Decker was blacked out. The "a" in Lawn Boy. The next sign had the "r" in Deere blackened. The final sign: a darkened "C" in Craftsman.

The squirrels in Rack's brain fought on their exercise wheels through the sludge of jerky, pretzels, Jack Daniels, and Bud. What did the letters A L A R C have in common?

"Time for bed," Crandall said. "You ready to blow me?"

Rack slipped on the driver seat and caught himself on the steering wheel.

Crandall held his gut and laughed deep, like a moose yawing. "You shoulda seen your face!" His shoulders pumped up and down between laughs.

Rack forced a smile and righted himself. "Yeah, you got me. Damn."

"Come on, I gotta be back here in four hours. I need *some* sleep. I'm doing the high school football field. Gets a lot of wind. Going to be cold tomorrow, and maybe wet."

Rack stepped down from the rig. His body was charged with feelings of accomplishment and subversion. "Tanner better appreciate this," he mumbled to himself.

After they said their good-byes, Crandall threw himself into the driver's seat of his old and angry-looking Ford pickup. Crandall shouted from his front seat, "You're gonna let me put outta here before your sorry ass, right?"

"Sure."

Crandall's tires coughed like sandpaper as he dropped the Ford into gear and it spit out of the parking lot. Rack counted to ten and then slowly pulled onto Route 332, hoping that he could weave accurately toward home.

Chapter 27

She walked down the inn's hallway, her feet noiseless. They had taught her more than a decade ago how to walk without sound. It was an ancient technique that involved shifting the tendons in her feet so that her soles never met an object to which they could not yield.

The old house was equally silent. She knew the owners were downstairs—the old man washing the last of the evening's dishes and his wife laying out breakfast settings in the dining room. A sixty-something female hired hand was rotating linens from the washer to the dryer in the laundry shed near the kitchen door. Before entering, she only needed to circle the house twice to make certain she knew where its occupants were. They hadn't locked the front door yet, and opening it and slipping through without jolting the bell was easy.

The upper hallway smelled of pumpkin and cinnamon, a wonderfully nutty scent she loved but had rarely encountered. The house warmed her, not just against the 52 degrees outside but in the years the place communicated. As she walked, she let her eyes settle on the photographs on the walls, scanning them a moment longer than was prudent. Color photos of a family on vacations, a group of five parked atop a mountain under the sun, wide smiles underneath ski goggles, and a collision of tanned bodies on the beach. This had been a home for more than one generation, a home of hardworking families much like her own. But there was a comfort and warmth in this family that the state had robbed from her by taking her away from her parents and sister at such an early age. Perhaps her sister Daes might see such a life with her new husband. As she inched down the hall, she told herself that all she needed was to be there at the conclusion of this puzzle.

She passed two rooms until she stopped at the one she knew to be Cook's. She shrunk to the floor and attached a small disc to the bottom of the door. Her earpiece crackled to life. She knew she was in for a night of passion—she could tell from watching them on the patio. What had she read recently? "How silver-sweet sound lovers' tongues by night, like softest music to attending ears!" Too bad she had her two colleagues with her. Otherwise, she might synchronize an orgasm with the pair of them.

No matter, tomorrow she would end this, retrieve the package, and return home. This tranquil land was making her too melancholy.

Chapter 28

Tanner rolled over in bed. What a massive dream! His heart rate was still elevated. Wait! This wasn't his wallpaper, and he didn't have an old English fox hunting painting. Then it became clear: he was naked under the bedspread, and on the edge of the bed lay the tangle of a white bra.

Holy shit.

He inhaled deeply, as if that would ignite the senses of the memory, her perfect skin, tight limbs, and petal lips. It had been a night for the ages. Then came thoughts of damage control. How far did they?—rubbers?—she enjoy it?—effective rubbers?—where was she?

At the moment, he was the only one in the bed. He remembered flushing the rubber now. The race of his pulse eased. He listened. Birds outside. Sunlight peeking from behind the window shade's border. Kyle's jeans were lumped on the floor near her side of bed.

She was lying on her stomach on the rug, her knees bent, ankles crisscrossed, head on her hands, reading a hardcover.

"Um … good morning," he said. She was wearing one of his old racing T-shirts and a pair of his boxers from his knapsack. Her rump greeted him.

She turned and smiled. "You sleep this late during training season?"

Tanner pushed himself up and walked over to the couch. "No. And thank God it's not training season." He sat down on the couch, and Kyle rolled over to face him.

"I made coffee," she said.

"This is awkward."

"Deal with it."

"Right. Will you marry me?"

"Not now. I smell pancakes."

"Right. Well, then, maybe we should go get breakfast."

Kyle closed the book and pushed herself up. Tanner watched her loose breasts move under the T-shirt and extended her a hand.

"Thanks," she said softly.

"I-I had fun. Last night."

"Rack will get by."

"He'll rage, he'll hate me. I think this plays into his greatest fears about me."

"An inferiority complex?"

"Of sorts."

She popped up, sat on his lap, and began kissing him.

"He'll get by," she said between kisses.

As they broke, Tanner asked, "Who?"

Chapter 29

Before going to breakfast, they decided to take turns showering. Tanner leaned against the metal railing that encircled their room's balcony and stared out at the Maine countryside. Off in the distance were the vanilla ice cream peaks of mountains. The wind tousled his hair and howled across his ears. Behind him, he could hear the whisper of the shower. Kyle had insisted that he go first. Rather than push his luck and suggest they economize and shower together, Tanner went first. In the space of a few hours he had gone from cursing Dreavor's existence to blessing the old man.

The hell with the old man's treasure hunt—now there was Kyle. Adrenaline surged through his limbs. The lean flesh on Kyle's ribs under her breast flashed in his mind, the tight skin of her perfect thigh. Good grinding, as Shakespeare might call it. Life seemed to have a fresh buzz to it.

Then he remembered he needed to call Jimmy. In that moment, Tanner wondered if Jimmy ever got horny. Were there girls in the home that excited him? Did he get action at night? Would he know what to do if given the chance? Would instincts take over and—

"What light through yonder window breaks?" Kyle slid up behind him and squeezed him around the center. She kissed him on the cheek.

That rose scent again!

"What're you doing?" she asked.

"Just thinking." The flushed face of Rack in rage snapped before him.

"What about?"

"About seeing Mr. Manning."

"You think too much." She slapped his butt. "Come, on let's go."

He smiled. But then his face twinged. His hands gripped the sides of his head. It was "the feeling," as he called it.

She stepped toward him and put her face in his line of sight. "What's the matter?"

"You think too much," he mumbled.

Kyle glanced behind her. "Are you okay?"

"Brutus said it to Cassius. 'He thinks too much: such men are dangerous.'"

"Christ, can you quote any line now?" The wind bent her short hair. She wrapped her arms around herself and checked left and right, as if someone were responsible for turning on the breeze.

"In *Julius Caesar*. Shakespeare's."

"Yeah? So you said last night."

"Mack."

Kyle cocked her head. "Mack?"

"The innkeeper from Fog Island." Tanner turned and searched the trees and mountains. "When he dropped me off in the storm, he said, 'But what trade art thou? A trade, sir, that, I hope, I may use with a safe conscience; which is, indeed, sir, a mender of bad soles.'"

"Okay, that's a long, non-sequitur good-bye. Sounds like Shakespeare."

Tanner nodded. "*Julius Caesar.*"

"Did you just place it? Is that what this is all about?"

157

"No—I mean, yes. I mean, I think I knew it was Shakespeare and, for that matter, *Caesar* all along, but now I wonder if I'm missing something."

"And?"

Tanner hurried into the room. He unzipped the front pouch of his knapsack, dug his hand in, and then withdrew a small pad of paper and a BIC pen. He scribbled Mack's quote, broken apart by line. He placed it on the rug and sat across from it.

So what? The wind built outside. The walls rumbled a little as if they were on a bus.

Kyle stepped inside and looked down over Tanner's shoulder. "It's not strange that Mack quoted Shakespeare. You told him why you were after Dreavor. You said he was a closet Shakespeare fan. You think he was hiding stuff from you?"

"But why *Julius Caesar*?" Tanner tapped the pen to the paper. "Why this?"

Kyle shrugged her shoulders. "What does this have to do with de Vere?"

The room spun. The deer antlers swooshed from above the bed to over the door, pushing the fly fishing illustration through the mirror above the bureau, shifting the wooden duck decoy into the forest outside. The feeling came in spades; he felt as if snow ran through his arteries.

The lines in the lighthouse basement! The words etched in the foundation of the lighthouse! Holy shit! Holy, holy shit!

Kyle had walked into the bathroom. He heard her stuffing her toothbrush into her duffel bag.

The inscription, the lines ... Holding his breath underwater in the lighthouse basement, Tanner had traced the lines of the inscription with his finger: *I come to bury Caesar, not praise him.* The line that followed was the famous: *Friends, Romans, Countrymen, lend me your ears;* again, *Julius Caesar*! Tanner's mind rushed to cram the puzzle pieces together. He shifted them up, down, and sideways, hoping they would click together to form a clear picture. But the ends did not fit ... another piece was missing.

Kyle popped out of the bathroom, zipping her duffel. "I'll tell you what. Let's get some breakfast. That ought to grease the gears."

Tanner stared down at the page with his handwriting.

> *But what trade art thou? Answer me directly.*
> *A trade, sir, that, I hope, I may use, with a safe*
> *Conscience; which is, indeed, sir, a mender of bad*
> *soles.*

His brain stirred a mix like a cake batter. His cerebral cortex turned the idea around and around itself until it thinned to its roots, its simplest form. Suddenly the quatrain became clear, and the message within the lines spoke.

"Whoa."

"What?" Kyle asked as she pinched her T-shirt to adjust a bra strap on her shoulder.

Tanner glanced over at her and then picked up his pen and circled the first letter of each line. Kyle sank to her knees and looked closely at what Tanner had done. Tanner could tell from where he sat, by her silence and slowed movement, that she had fallen under the spell of the message.

> *But what trade art thou?*
> *A trade, sir, that, I hope, I may use, with a safe*
> *CONscience; which is, indeed, sir, a mender of bad*
> *soles.*

Bacon.
Francis Bacon.

Chapter 30

Tanner stood in line, tapping his foot. The man in front of him licked his fingertips as he peeled dollar bills from his wallet. Back at the inn, they had decided to take breakfast on the road so Kyle could get to work on time. On their way into Portland, they stopped at a coffee shop called Caffeine Joey's.

"Relax, we'll be there soon," Kyle said as she read her email on her blackberry.

"Something is weird." He looked over at her—she wore his Red Sox cap and no makeup, no matter. He wasn't sure what she did with her bra, but he didn't care.

"You need a cup of coffee to settle your nerves." She clicked through her messages. "Here's one from Rack. Said he had a wonderful night at the Bull Hollow last night. When he was shown around the garage where Dreavor stored his stuff, he found the letters A, L, A, R, and C, each blackened on a different logo plate on the back wall of the garage."

"Logo plates?"

"He said they were for brands like John Deere and Honda."

Tanner dug a hand through his hair. "Glassed cannons, Francis Bacon, Julius Caesar. Can you make sense of it?"

She didn't respond. Her eyes locked on her phone screen, but it was not the reading kind of stare where the eyes jitter, taking in words.

"Bad news?" Tanner asked. "Did he propose too?"

That seemed to shake her out of it. "Not Rack. A surprise, that's all."

"Surprises can be happy." Tanner stepped up to order. "A medium black and ..." He turned to Kyle.

She looked at him, but her gaze was empty.

"*And?*"

Kyle breathed in. "Um, cappuccino."

"That'll work." He ordered.

"My parents are next door," she said.

Tanner shifted his eyes toward the entrance.

"No, I mean in New Hampshire. They just emailed that they're vacationing in New Hampshire."

"So ... that's a pleasant surprise."

Kyle tilted her head and tossed an eyebrow.

"Or a damn shock?" he added.

"No, no, it's all right. Just a surprise."

"Would you consider meeting up with them? How often do you get to connect?"

Kyle took her cappuccino and followed Tanner to the milk and napkin bar. "I see them fairly often. Just saw them in August before I came out here. They're typical parents. I just didn't expect them to visit. They say they're here to see the foliage."

"Well, their timing is a little off. Peak foliage is a month away."

"Right. Right."

"Well." Tanner turned to the cafe while Kyle sprinkled cinnamon on her cappuccino. Through the crowd, through the front window, he caught a glimpse of a woman just before she moved down the sidewalk and out of view. *Was that*—He spun to the rear of the shop. "Come on." He bolted down the shop's back hallway.

Kyle rushed to cap her cup and scrambled after him. "Wh-what!"

He called over his shoulder. "Come on, we've got to go." Kyle shuffled toward him with her cup outstretched, not trusting the lid. He shoved open the back door.

"Tanner, what?"

They were at her Wrangler in seconds. He jumped into her passenger seat, keeping an eye on the rear door of the coffee shop. "That lady."

She climbed in after him and sat behind the wheel. "What lady?"

"There was a lady across the street from the front of the shop."

"Who? What about her?"

"She's following me." He stared at the steering wheel as if he were trying to start it by command.

"I know we just met, but you don't strike me as the paranoid type." Kyle put the key in the ignition. "In fact, just the opposite."

"You're right."

"Okay, right. Why do you think she's following you?"

Tanner turned to Kyle and paused for a moment. He smiled and let his shoulders relax. "What they don't know and what you're forgetting is that I don't forget."

"Forget what?"

He pointed to the building. "That woman, she was on the ferry with me heading out to Fog Island. She was behind us last night at the red light in Danton." He tapped the side of his forehead. "It doesn't all surface all the time, but when it does, it's unmistakable."

Kyle started her Jeep. "Okay. I believe you, I really do. Just one thing. She's Asian. You know what they say, you know, about them all looking familiar. Could—"

Tanner shook his head. "Position of the pupils, length of nose, hair length, depth of chin, weight in the cheeks, fullness of the lips, scale of the ears. It's her."

"Who?"

"I don't know her name. I never spoke to her. Call her the Grocer, for short. Now, can we get out of here?"

Kyle gave him one last questioning look and put the Jeep in gear. Tanner kept his eyes on the rearview mirror more than the road unfolding in front of them.

"You think she's following you because of Dreavor?" Kyle asked.

"It's the only mysterious addition to my life. I didn't see anyone following me last week."

"Maybe she's a sex-starved biking fan from when you were on the circuit."

Tanner smiled. "That would put her in a unique class. Bikers don't typically see any extraordinary share of sex."

"Worked for Lance Armstrong."

"What didn't work for Lance?"

"Good point. So, if she's following you because of Dreavor, then all the more reason to drop the whole thing. Who needs Vera Wang creeping behind you 24/7, right?"

Tanner weighed what she said while checking his side mirror. "If she's following me because of Dreavor, does that mean I'm closer to some dark root of this thing?"

"Tell you what, let's go to the police. Have them pull her over and give her a thorough questioning. They can ask her where she's been for the past few days. It would certainly help me sleep better."

Tanner wasn't sure what the police would or could do. Nonetheless, the sound of reinforcements sounded comforting. "Good call."

"I got to admit, I can't believe you were jumped again," Lieutenant Jerome Clay said as he poured coffee from an old Mr. Coffee pot in his small police station's pantry. "A men's room? Locked in a flooding lighthouse basement and driven off a road?"

Tanner nodded.

"You sure you don't want some?" Clay arched his eyebrows, shifting his gaze from Kyle to Tanner and back again. Clay had spent much of Tanner's storytelling watching Kyle.

"No, thanks, we filled up at—"

"Caffeine Joey's," Clay said. "Right, right."

Tanner had been apprehensive about visiting Clay, but he knew Clay wouldn't have to struggle to come up to speed. Clay with his fifty-ish face, cheeks beginning their age melt into jowls.

"Now, did this Asian woman approach you?"

Tanner shook his head.

"She holler at you, threaten you in any way?"

"No."

He led them down the short hallway to his modest office. "Did you happen to catch her license plate?"

Tanner closed his eyes and ran through his memories of the Asian woman's car. He opened them. "There was no front plate. She must have removed it."

They entered Clay's office. There was a small collection of book cases and lots of three-ring binders shelved neatly. Clay eased into a tall seat behind his desk, careful not to spill his coffee on the way down. Two steel chairs offered seating to guests.

Clay sipped his coffee. "Now, bring me back to the motivation."

"Always comes back to money, doesn't it?"

Clay put his coffee down. "Or revenge, or love, lust, something. In this case, sounds like there could be a lot riding on whether your man Dreavor was onto something with Shakespeare."

"Well—"

"Hikers found Dreavor downstream in the Kennebec River. Do you know any more about where he was specifically searching?"

Tanner shook his head.

"Anything about what kind of success he had with the supposed riddle within Shakespeare's stuff?"

Tanner shrugged. "I'm really not sure. All I've got is this theory that maybe someone other than William Shakespeare wrote his plays and poems, and that that person might have come to America. And maybe that person brought with him the original drafts of his works. It's pretty thin."

"He landed somewhere around here?"

Tanner bounced his head back and forth. "Maybe. I don't have anything that says yes or no one way or the other."

Clay looked over at Kyle and smiled at her.

Does anyone not smile at her?

Clay came back to Tanner. "You think all of your ... your mishaps are related?"

"I mean, don't you?" Tanner knew he let himself get a little too excited.

Clay shrugged.

Tanner looked down at his own hands. His mind drifted back to his last race in Madrid. The day before he plunged off the embankment. *Should I tell them? It would feel good ...*

"Look, if she threatens you, call me." Clay handed over his business card. "If she comes onto your property, call me. Naturally, if she gets violent, call me. Until then, I can't do anything to or with her. And, practically speaking, I don't have the manpower to cover you or investigate more."

"Doesn't this all strike you as strange?" Tanner asked. "I mean, we're dealing with a dead body—"

"You want me to call in our sketch artist? She can do the lady and the guy that jumped you in the men's room. Nice artist—she lives over in Gibly. A bit slow, a bit chatty, but she'll get the job—"

Kyle leaned over to Tanner. "I've got to get to work. Don't you?"

Tanner knew she must have thought this was bordering on a bit much. "No, that's all right," he said to Clay. He looked at Clay's card. "I'll call you if anything pops again."

"What I can tell you is that most people who come in to see us with the fear that they are being followed do not return because the perceived stalker never materializes in a harmful way."

Tanner eased in his chair. "Really?"

"Seriously. And this isn't just a Maine thing. It's the same no matter what police station you visit in the country. Coincidence is a much more powerful phenomenon than we give it credit for. Someone actually told me recently that it's less coincidence than the odds playing themselves out. Take this lady, for example. Now, I'm not saying this is the case, right? But it could be possible that she visited Fog Island when you did. She traveled home on the same route—there are only a few logical paths. And if she lives in the vicinity, she goes to Joey's for java. In the morning, of all times!" Clay smiled. "Then again, she may be lining you up to slit your throat at night."

Kyle laughed, and Clay did as well. The officer kept his eyes on her, her chest, and her crossed legs just a moment longer than a neutral law officer should have.

"Okay, Lieutenant. I hear you. Maybe I'm still spooked from the arson, the lighthouse, the tavern men's room, and the bike ride."

"I don't blame you after what your past few days have been like."

Tanner pushed himself up. "Sorry to take your time up, Lieutenant." He shook hands with Clay across his desk, knocking into a stack of papers in the process.

Clay caught them. "Whoa, I don't want to go through these again. Insurance company reports for traffic accidents. You talk about haunting nightmares."

"God willing, maybe this woman will take a swing at Tanner and we can rescue you from that," Kyle said.

Clay laughed and took her in.

Tanner broke their communion. "Thanks."

"Yeah, see what you can arrange," Clay said to Tanner. "Anything but murder. The paperwork for that is hell."

Kyle was laughing, a scratchy, sexy giggle.

"Nonfatal knife wound, garrote across the throat are okay, then?" Tanner asked as he backed out of the office. Kyle trailed, still laughing.

"Perfect! Guaranteed to keep me out of the office for a solid afternoon," Clay called after them.

"I'm glad you two had such a good time with my paranoia."

Kyle scooped his arm in hers. "Come on, I've got to get to work. I'll drop you. And make sure you get in safely."

"What a terrific boost to my manhood this entire episode has been."

When they emerged from the police station, Tanner scanned the street. No sign of the woman or the blue Taurus he remembered her driving. They stepped down to the front curb and Kyle's Jeep.

Kyle paused at the driver's door and looked over at Tanner. "We still have ten minutes left on the meter if you want to go back in and page through rap sheets or something." She cracked up so hard that it took her a moment to put her key in the door.

"Funny, very funny. Let's go. Think you can pull yourself together enough to drive?"

Kyle buried her head on her arm on the side of the car. "It ... might take ... a minute. Watch my back!"

Tanner's feigned pride broke, and he started laughing. When it ebbed, he spoke first. "I can get out at your office. Mine is a quick few blocks from there."

"Don't be silly. I'll take you to yours first."

"But that's needlessly out of the way. It makes no sense."

"You've got a busted rim."

"But—"

"That's the last of it," she said with a smile.

As they drove to town, Tanner stole what he hoped were casual glances in the side-view mirror. "Tough job Clay's got."

"What do you mean?" Kyle said. "He's a cop. He helps people."

"No, I mean, every day people bring him problems."

"Some of them are even real."

"Are you ever gonna let this go?"

"You brought it up."

Deep down, Tanner recognized that she was enjoying the moment. "No, I mean, it just seems that it's problem after problem, and then stacks of paperwork to explain the problem to others and more paperwork to explain the solution."

"Most things are like that, no?"

Tanner started to object, but then he fell back in his seat. He gripped the door handle. His eyes fell to the glove compartment.

"What is it? You look like you've seen a ghost ... or worse, a Korean grocer."

Tanner looked over at her with a blank face. Then he looked to the road ahead. His mind whirled like a camera rewinding a spent roll of film.

"Clay's stack of insurance papers," Tanner said to himself as much as to Kyle.

"Frightful, I know."

"A stack just for that." Tanner thought about the last time he had seen stacks of paper and work.

"We just agreed paperwork sucks—"

"No. Not his ..." Tanner reached into the backseat for his backpack.

"What're you doing? Did you lose something?" Kyle tried to watch the road and Tanner at the same time.

He scrounged through it. "It couldn't have been there the entire time ..." Tanner pulled out *The Complete Works of William Shakespeare* and his camera and thumbed the camera's dials in his lap.

"What are you doing?"

"Dreavor."

"I thought we were going to let that die."

"You work your whole life, day, night, no family, no other interests, no TV, movies, or love interests, and you're focused on just one puzzle ... When you find the answer, do you just get up and leave?" He watched her eyes, hoping she'd join him in his thought, but she was still trying to catch up. He'd have to show her.

"I don't know. I haven't had a lifelong quest."

"But if you did?" He continued scanning through the pictures on his camera.

"If I did ... what is with your camera?"

"His invitation to the next generation."

"What?"

"When we were first in his house, he left a string of breadcrumbs."

"The only strings in that place were the curtains."

"Not quite." He stopped flipping through images. His eyes paged across a single image: Dreavor's hidden attic room, the first photo Tanner took as he entered the cryptic study.

"What is that?" Kyle shifted her eyes from the road to the camera in Tanner's lap.

Tanner stared at the photo. "I can't believe it ..."

Chapter 31

"The letters 'F' and 'B'? You think those stacks of books represent a 'B,' as in Bacon?" Kyle asked as she steered over the Shandon Bridge.

"Can't you see it? Even from the driver's seat?" Tanner raised the camera to her eye level, in front of the windshield.

"Maybe when we crash I can focus better."

"Okay, okay." Tanner brought the camera down. "But would you agree that if those stacks of books formed an 'F' and a 'B' this would be another arrow pointing toward Francis Bacon?"

"Seems awfully coincidental, if you ask me." Kyle shrugged her shoulders. "What was it Rack was saying about the letters in the town garage where Dreavor worked? Did those letters spell anything? A—L—A—R—C. Alarc? Is that someone?"

Tanner had forgotten. Alarc. Reels of tape and film streamed forward between his ears. He knew the name. Or … almost.

"Alaric, with an 'I,' was the first Gaul to have penetrated Rome during its empire."

"Say that again?"

"Rome. The Empire. Lasted some four hundred years. But, like the smallest of hamlets, even an empire has its boundaries. There was always a battle being fought to push back or protect those boundaries. The Gauls were early Germans. Their first successful leader during the time of the Roman Empire was Alaric. He wound up sacking Rome. He eventually retreated, but he later went back for seconds."

"Some people don't take no for an answer."

"In any event, he died a pretty rich king."

"I suppose. Was he Shakespeare?"

"Ah, no. This is a good thousand years before Shakespeare was born."

"Okay. Soooo why did Dreavor care about him?"

Tanner shrugged.

"Did he come to America?"

Tanner laughed. "Alaric? Not quite. He died at something like thirty-four. Not sure even the Native Indians knew where America was then."

Kyle seemed to weigh a thought. "He died pretty young, huh?"

"Young and rich. They said his sack of Rome brought him two thousand pounds of gold."

"Maybe that's why Dreavor was interested in him."

Tanner smiled. "Maybe. When Alaric died, a caravan went out into the wilderness. His lieutenants ordered the damming of a river so that his body and a hunk of his fortune could be buried in its basin. When that was complete, the dam was removed and the river flowed freely again. Then the workers who dug the grave were all slaughtered so the grave's location would be protected."

"Whoa."

"Today, somewhere in Central Europe, a river runs above his undisturbed grave."

"How's this relate to Shakespeare? Did he write about being buried underwater?"

Tanner shrugged. "Not that I know of." He closed his eyes and fanned the pages of *The Complete Works*.

"This is spooky cool," Kyle said.

Tanner opened his eyes and looked over at her. "Maybe." That neck, that sexy collarbone. *Did we really fuck last night?*

Kyle pulled the Jeep to the curb of a cobblestone street and put it in park. "Well, here you are." She nodded at the windshield.

Tanner looked through the glass. Kyle had parked outside the office building where he worked. In Portland, much of the office space was converted fish warehousing, and the Office of Trusts and Estates was no exception.

"Jeez, you're good. How'd you know?"

She smiled. "Yesterday I looked it up in the phone book. To be honest, I didn't believe that such a place existed."

"You thought Rack and I made it up?"

"I've had weirder lines thrown at me for a date."

He couldn't fault any man. He sucked in a chest full of air. Time to make the donuts. "I guess it's never too late to say you're sorry about burning a house down."

"Relax, you didn't do it." She leaned over, cupped his cheek with her hand, and kissed him softly and deeply. "See you tonight? Drinks at six-thirty at the Sea Chianti?"

He may have tumbled through the woods, been caught in icy water, pedaled all night, and leapt into pines, but her touch soothed him all over.

"Make it six. I'm in the public employ." He popped out of the Jeep.

The tires squeaked as she popped out of her parking spot. Tanner stopped himself on his way into his building, set his bike down, and punched in a number on his cell. Ten seconds later, he was connected.

"Good morning."

It was the voice Tanner was looking for. "Professor Arbough, this is Tanner Cook."

There was a chortle. "Cook, ehh? Find me a first-edition *Richard I* yet?"

"Not exactly."

"Too bad. What can I help you with, Tanner?"

No mention of his first class or impending seminar. This is a good sign.

"Bacon, you knew him—er, know him, know of him, no?"

"Did you just ask me a question? Francis Bacon, is that what this is about?"

"I was hoping you could tell me about him."

"He lived a long life …"

Tanner entered through the main doors of his building. "Just the basics." He set his bike down.

"Mr. Cook, I've got a class to conduct in a few minutes."

Across the lobby, Tanner saw the Asian woman reading the building's white push-pin directory. He froze. She had her back to him. He hefted the bike back on his shoulder and swung around back to the door.

"This'll just take a second, Professor."

Arbough sighed. "Bacon was born the second son of Sir William Francis Bacon, Lord of the Seal to Her Majesty Queen Elizabeth. More or less the equivalent of attorney general and chief justice of the Supreme Court."

Tanner checked over his shoulder as he jogged down the sidewalk, juggling his knapsack and his bike. "Was he as powerful as he sounds?"

"Yes. You see, in some ways the world back then was more defined than ours, and in other ways there was less definition. These chaps used to take gratuitous stipends from citizens of all classes for case strategy and consulting on matters of law. These were folks whose cases were currently in the courts. Needless to say, if done properly, one could grow quite wealthy as lord of the seal."

Tanner turned down an alley, again checking over his shoulder. "Uh huh."

"I mention this because this was the kind of wealth Bacon was born into, that he was raised under. In fact, this practice eventually caused his impeachment when we fast-forward thirty years and he holds the same position his father did."

"Seriously?"

"I'm going to consider that rhetorical and move on."

173

Through the phone, Tanner heard clicking—keyboard keys. He crossed in the middle of the block, pacing himself against the cars turning the corner.

"Gorhambury, the country home where Bacon grew up, was filled with enormous gardens. It housed real and stuffed samples of species of animals from all over the world—well, as far as Mother Britannia had traveled through the late 1500s."

From across the street, now up against the brick wall of a medical office building, Tanner saw his office building's door open. "Sounds like Neverland." The pause over the line revealed the limits of Arbough's contemporary knowledge. "Michael Jackson's old place," Tanner added. He opened the medical office building's front door. As he wiggled his bike through the door behind him, he saw the Grocer trying to cross the street in his direction. His heart fell down the stairs in his chest.

Arbough clicked his tongue. "Same scope, different class."

"Got it." Tanner went quickly down the hallway, passing the elevator bank and office doors. At the end of the hall was another door.

"Bacon had some of the best tutors in the known world. He attended Cambridge and then law school."

Tanner checked over his shoulder. "Cambridge had a law school?"

"No, his was called Gray's Inn. It was more a country club-cum-college-cum-residency."

"Isn't that the same law school as de Vere?"

"Yes. Good memory."

"I get that a lot."

"Bacon did fine there, but his father died when he was something like nineteen, just about to emerge from law school and begin life in the good old real world."

Tanner exited through the far doorway and crossed through an alley. Two filthy, concrete buildings rose more than five stories on either side of him. "How big was his inheritance?"

"Nothing much to speak of. In those days, men born into a comfortable state of being found it difficult to pare back. You know, his dad had seventy servants, land in multiple counties, and the country home, Gorhambury House, had the requisite chapel, stables, mill, acres and acres of impeccable gardens, banquet hall, and personal brew house. Something like forty fireplaces. You get the picture."

Tanner ran down the alley. "Royalty."

"More or less. Where are you, Cook? It sounds like you're on a treadmill."

"Just making my way through Portland, Professor. So, now, Bacon, why was he so special?"

"Special?" Tanner heard a file cabinet draw open. "Why does the Hope Diamond have a name? Bacon was the Renaissance, as multi-dimensional as da Vinci, and in some ways more so. Philosopher, artist, writer, scientist, lawyer, physician, historian. When he took the job of chief justice, he cut through a five-year backlog of undecided cases. He adjudicated more cases than all of his predecessors combined. He weighed in on innumerable royal decisions, and he wrote dozens of essays, philosophical works, plays—you name it. He ran models on Britain's tax revenues, on which lands to annex. Here's a guy who advised King James on his plantations in Virginia and Ireland—what crops to plant and which types of workers to send to populate the land. It was said there was no busier mortal man."

"Jeez, a true multitasker." Tanner sprinted out of the alley and took a hard right. His biking sneakers slapped on the sidewalk.

"Yeah," Arbough laughed, "he used to have secretaries trailing after him, men, mostly, jotting down his thoughts and whatnot. The immortal Thomas Hobbes not the least of which."

"Genius, then, huh?" A street full of shops. A few pedestrians. Tanner was up on his toes, careful with his momentum and the front and rear tires of the bike, trying to steer clear of a wide woman in a parka and around a thin college student in a UMaine sweatshirt, and he nearly clipped a wobbling gray hair who took up most of the sidewalk.

"Well, you know, he had all the ingredients. He was born into wealth, not just a wealth of money and comfort, but of exposure—exposure to music, animals, religions, sciences from all over the world. His mother was fluent in Latin, Greek, Italian, and French. He landed at Cambridge's Trinity College just after Henry VIII's reign, when the battle for the correct way to worship God was still hot. So, you've got this baby of the family, with a highly trained liberal-arts mind, set loose on the world. He had spent enough time coloring inside the lines, if you will. It was time to bust out."

Tanner heard the other line on Arbough's phone beep. The bells on the door of a familiar shop tingled as Tanner ducked inside. His bike clanked on the ground. Tanner looked up to see dozens of other bikes suspended above him to his left and right. A black man with cornrows looked up, and the man's smile ignited. He saw Tanner on the phone and dipped back down to his paperwork.

Arbough continued. "Before law school, he had been an emissary to Spain for a few years."

Tanner put his cheek flush with the store window so he could see down the sidewalk. "All teenagers should be," he said.

Arbough chuckled. It sounded more like a *hurumph* than a back-breaking laugh.

Tanner peered out the store window. "Remind me—what were his writings about?"

The chair squeaked again, and Arbough groaned. Tanner guessed the old man was pushing himself up.

"Bacon wanted to change the world. He wanted a new approach to education and thought. This was the backdrop of his *Great Instauration,* a tome about a new intellectual empire. He wanted to recast all the universities in the world and create places where people ignored what Aristotle or church leaders had to say and explore the mysteries of the earth, the human body, plants and animals, the truth in math, the stars. And while Bacon lived in a town that hanged eight hundred people a year for pilfering the likes of a loaf of bread, it was more risky to bypass the church, which was the ultimate core of beliefs and the tuning fork of royalty."

"So he never got caught?" Tanner asked. From the store's front window, no one on the street looked out of the ordinary. Tanner dropped to his knee and began unlocking his damaged front wheel.

"Depends on your definition. Some say he was a tremendous loser." An automatic pencil sharpener whined behind Arbough's commentary. "Of the seven siblings, Bacon got the least from his father's will, in fact very little at all. Even his stepbrothers and sisters made out fine. Bacon's uncle was a powerful minister to Elizabeth, but Bacon got nothing from him either. He lost a series of open positions to Edward Coke, and he was arrested in the streets twice for debts he couldn't and didn't pay."

"Broke?"

"Deadbeat. As one avenue to escape debt, when he was forty-five, he bloody well nearly arranged his own marriage to a fourteen-year-old. Not as odd then as we view it today, but not a highly respectable move either. The only progress he made was on his own merits, a slow road in those times. He finally became a well-respected lawyer and congressman of sorts."

Tanner lifted the wheel free and put it on the clerk's table. The clerk was entering data on the computer in front of him. When the wheel hit the table, he looked up and exchanged smiles with Tanner. Tanner continued his conversation with Arbough. "So what was the catalyst for his success?"

"The catalyst," Arbough said, "was Elizabeth's death. James I ascends, and so rises Bacon."

"And he became attorney general?"

The clerk picked up the wheel, and with his pen pried the tire from the rim. He didn't look up at Tanner nor interrupt his phone conversation.

"Not that quickly. He maneuvered for it. He had a strong track record as a lawyer and representative."

"And he was impeached because ..."

"Took bribes, tribute. He was careless, thoughtless with his health, his finances, and the monitoring of tribute. In the end, he was banished from the courts and from London. Couldn't get within twelve miles of the place."

"Back to being a loser."

"Depends on your definition. He entered one of his most prolific writing stages. He dug deeper into scientific experimentation."

Tanner pulled his wallet from his knapsack and removed his Citibank credit card. "Was he Shakespeare?"

"Maybe. If he was, this was the time when the *First Folio* was printed."

Tanner shook his brain. "You mean the first book of collected Shakespeare works?"

Arbough sounded taken back. "Mmm. Are you sure you were never in my class?"

"No, sir. Now, you mentioned that every state in the union had its Shakespeare conspiracy theory wackos."

"And then some."

"Anyone here?"

"Here, as in Maine?"

"Yes."

"Well. Hmm. Yes. A while ago. There was this gym teacher, no, wait, librarian, from down south, near Portland. He went crazy from it, I think. Total nervous breakdown—found him one dark night sniffling in a corner of the local library. He was pissing on a collection of Elizabethan-era works and eating the cover of *The Tempest*, or something of that sort. This was in the children's section."

"Um, maybe he's not the best reference."

Arbough laughed, a hard crackle, like the crunching of a brown paper bag. "Let's see. There was an old man many years ago in New Hampshire, up near the Old Man in the Mountain, but I heard he died of cancer a couple of years ago."

"Shit. Oh, sorry, Professor."

"The nut in Gloucester, I think it was. His name was Saint John or James or something apostolic. I have a class that's coming up, Tanner. Anything else?"

"No, no, thanks, Professor—"

Tanner froze with the phone to his ear. A city block away, just edging out from the corner behind Beals Ice Cream store, was the face of the Asian woman.

Chapter 32

Tanner strode into Sterling Falls Convalescent Home. *Be steady, steady.*

Sweat dripped down his spine and caught in the waistband of his Hanes. Tanner's eyes locked straight forward. He had never done anything like this before. Inside his jacket pockets, his fingers were slick against his palms. Rye-rye, the bike store owner, was a long-time friend of Tanner's, and while fixing Tanner's wheel he had let Tanner Google the news story of the Gloucester police arresting a man in a library. The mailing address came just as easily. Tanner spent some time researching St. James' past as well.

A receptionist with thick, black-rimmed glasses sat behind a tall lobby desk. Tanner walked past her, never slowing his pace.

"May I help you?" The woman spoke loud enough to catch his attention, yet not loud enough to come across as threatening.

Tanner turned to her but kept up his pace. "Just visiting my uncle, Henry St. James. Room 212. Hope he's awake."

Her head dipped in half a nod. Her eyes dropped to a screen or paper or list on her desk—Tanner couldn't see. In seconds he was past her and down a linoleum hallway. He had gotten the room numbers on the fly from the mailbox listings just through the front doors.

Tanner slipped out of his jacket as he walked. The building felt about 102 degrees. It seemed that insensitive temperature control was standard operating procedure for institutions. He shot a breath through his nose. He expected the ammonia scent but hated it. Jimmy flashed in his mind.

He passed rooms on his right and left. Most of the wood doors were closed, but an occasional one was open. Narrow rooms, yet deep—maybe a couple of couches wide by forty feet deep. In one, a man, no more than a trash bag of wrinkles, slumped in a recliner and stared out at the hallway. A woman, nearly two hundred, gawked at her ceiling. Unfortunately, she was naked. Room 206. Tanner remembered her name—Carmichael. The numbers took too long to accumulate.

Then 212 arrived, a closed door. Tanner checked left and right. The hall was empty. He knocked and twisted the handle.

The room smelled like shoes worn all summer without socks. Sweet Jesus, he had to get out of there. Tanner slowly crossed the toasted crumb-colored shag rug. He flashed his eyes over at the bed, which was a mess of sheets and spread. Nearby was a small bookshelf with discombobulated, scattered volumes. To the right was a recliner, 1978 model, the same plastic green as down the hall, with a thin be-sweatered stick figure engulfed in it.

The gnat voice of a baseball announcer came through the small Sony radio on the table next to the stick figure of a man. "Why they sent Riley, I have no idea. He's one for fourteen this year in stolen bases." Henry St. James sat hunched over in his chair, his back curved forward and his shoulders folded in like a weary sparrow.

A different voice responded over the radio, "Novatno will need help from the bullpen if they plan at all on saving the season."

Tanner debated whether to wake the man up or not.

St. James' head slowly sprouted up. His eyes had an empty focus. "Junior drugged somebody."

Tanner stepped back. He froze. The words came from the body, the mouth of St. James, where Tanner had expected only a catatonic silence.

"Sorry?" Tanner said after a good six-second buffer.

The old man turned, from the hips, like he had an enormous stiff neck.

"Who—who are you?" His voice sounded like rocks knocking together in a garbage disposal.

Tanner held up his hands, the international communication that he was unarmed. "I'm Tanner Cook. Just a visitor."

"I don't get visitors. Wrong room." St. James turned and mumbled, "Jackass." Anger—not what Tanner expected. He didn't advance.

"Mr. St. James, I was wondering if you could—"

"What'd you call me?"

"Mr. St. James."

"Mister? I haven't heard that one in some time."

"Professor Arbough, from the university, suggested I … catch up with you. I was nearby, so I thought I would drop in." Tanner hoped that he sounded honest, harmless, and earnest. At least it was harmless and earnest.

"Arbough? I don't remember an Arbough. Did we ever work together?"

"No. He was aware of your work, your work on Bacon."

"Bacon?"

"Yeah, Francis Bacon. Your excavation—"

"My excavation?"

"In Wales. The River Wrye?"

"It's an excavation now?" St. James' eyes took on angry wrinkles.

Tanner didn't know where to go. He thought he'd try once more. "I thought you led the expedition."

"Excavation implies we found and uncovered something."

"That's not how the *Tribune* described it. It said that there were characters carved on the ceiling, that there was evidence that Bacon had used the cavern—"

"I'm tired. I need a nap. Good-bye." With his hands on the chair arms, St. James pushed himself up. His arms were like rotted birch branches, white and thin. They fluttered when St. James increasingly settled weight onto them. Tanner stepped forward to help, but the old man barked, "Get away! I don't need a fireman!"

Tanner stepped back. "Sorry, I-I just wanted to see if I could help. I didn't mean—"

"Shut up, will you, Gloria." St. James stood free from the chair. He was bent forward a few degrees. "You never let me alone. Always fucking chim-chammering."

Tanner stood still. He had never been one on one with senility before. When St. James turned to face him, it took about seven different shift-steps. The fly to his trousers was down, and skin and light-colored underwear flashed in the opening.

"Did we have lunch yet?" he asked Tanner.

Tanner had no idea. His mind rewound everything he knew about the facility. He replayed his path to the room. The heat, the hallways, the open doors, the attendants' section. No food trays anywhere. His watch said 11:30 AM.

"Not yet. I think they are coming, though. I saw them beginning down at the other end of the hallway." As soon as he said it, Tanner realized that they may not even serve door to door here. They might eat cafeteria style. Shit.

St. James stopped his inch-by-inch shuffling and looked up at Tanner. "I hope they hurry the hell up, I'm fucking starved."

Tanner stifled a sigh of relief.

"Okay, I'll go tell them." It was all Tanner could think to say. He badly wanted St. James to think of him as an ally.

St. James pitched forward, continuing his toe-by-toe step toward his bed.

"You want me to fix the bed any special way?"

St. James shook his head … and continued shaking it for a solid fifteen seconds, a mix of emphasis and forgetting to stop.

The heat, the smell, and the grouchiness were smothering Tanner. He didn't know how to stand. He tried his hands in his pockets, but then he thought he should have them out to catch St. James should he fall. He tried them on his hips, but he didn't want to seem the interrogator. He clasped them behind, against his butt, but then he felt like an orderly, so he moved them to the fig leaf role. Too queer. He settled with them tucked into his armpits.

What the hell am I doing here?

"When you went to the River Wrye, what was the number-one thing you were hoping to find?" It was a go-for-broke question.

"A hole."

Tanner laughed … quietly. The simple honesty of the answer struck him.

Tanner stepped to the door, wondering if someone might truly be bringing lunch. "When did you know you had the hole?"

Tanner eased just a bit. St. James didn't seem to mind Tanner's pushing for more detail. He rested his cane against the night table and drew up to his cheese slice of a pillow, stained with a dozen different drool spots.

"I was never sure until we found a way in."

"What was the key?" *Keep the questions broad.*

"The key …" St. James took a deep breath. His eyes took on an energetic focus at his knees. "The key was a dial."

"Like a combination lock?"

"You know, all this stuff … it's been a while since anyone has discussed Bacon with me."

Tanner sensed a warming. "I've come across a guy, a guy who seems to have thought the way you did."

St. James rubbed his chin. "There are fewer of us now. In fact, I didn't know there was anyone left." St. James wiggled his head and seemed to change channels. "It's gone now. What does it matter?"

"How many holes do you think Bacon constructed?"

St. James rolled his head from side to side. "I don't know. At least one."

Tanner nodded, stepped back, and bent to take a look in the hallway. It was empty. And hot. "Did anyone ever come as close as you did? Did anyone ever find another?"

St. James shook his head.

"Did anyone ever find a crypt under a river for any reason since your venture?"

St. James shrugged his bony shoulders.

"What were Bacon's traveling capacities?"

St. James' face pruned. "Cat cities?"

"No, capacit—I mean, did he have the resources to cross the Atlantic?"

St. James blinked at Tanner. His eyes lost their focus. He withdrew into himself on the bed. Then, without warning, he shook his head.

"Cross the Atlantic? Here?" His eyes darted from left to right to left. "How?"

Tanner didn't know what to say. It was just conjecture on his part.

"No, nothing. It was just a hunch. But I've only been at this for a few days. You've studied the question for years."

"He was missing for a chunk of years ... there are no strong records during his retirement, just his books."

"Was he a seaman of any experience?"

St. James shook his head. "He did travel to Europe as a teenager. Attaché to Spain. Never came to the new world."

"Could he have hitched a ride?"

"Hitched—no."

Tanner looked out the door and down the hall again. After he was certain the hallway would allow him a clear, quick exit, he asked, "Why?"

St. James scratched his head and looked at his toes. He tugged at his cheek as if trying to jump-start his mouth. His hand stopped there. His eyes stayed with his toes and drifted back inside his head.

Tanner stepped closer to St. James's bed. "He was as curious as they come, no?"

St. James grabbed his toes and dropped his head. "I'm really hungry. If you don't get me my fucking food, I'm going to scream!"

A voice responded behind Tanner. "What's going on?"

Tanner spun and stepped back, like a burglar. At the door stood a wide man holding a green plastic tray and wearing sky blue scrubs. The man was a tall chimney and balding.

"Who are you?" The chimney asked Tanner. Then the man looked over at the despondent St. James.

The old man's head poked up. "Finally! I don't know this guy. What is it? Oatmeal? Is that cinnamon raisin?"

The chimney stayed on Tanner. "Are you a relative?"

Tanner put his hands up and nodded. "No, no, not real—I mean, I work with the state."

"Charlie, give me my food for Christsake!"

"I'm going to have to ask you to step outside for a moment," Charlie said to Tanner as he walked to put the tray on St. James' side table.

"I-I was just asking Mr. St. James if—"

"Outside." Charlie said over his shoulder as he turned from the tray.

Tanner nodded and looked over at St. James, who was already gripping the plastic fork and eyeing the yellowish mound in a pink plastic bowl. Tanner backed out of the room. "I'll come back."

Charlie moved toward him, but then St. James shouted with a mouthful of yellow, "Turn up the radio!" which reeled Charlie back into the room.

Tanner flashed his eyes over his shoulder as he jogged down the hallway.

Chapter 33

Tanner biked alongside traffic with an eye over his right shoulder at the sidewalk pedestrians and another on the cars in his rearview. He squinted at the passenger-side windows on his left. At the red lights, he left himself lots of room to maneuver his front wheel in multiple directions.

He didn't know shit. Fog Island? Shakespeare? Was that worth running him over for? In his mind, he saw St. James's yellow toes, his shaky pretzel body atop his cane.

A dial ... a hole. St. James's words replayed in Tanner's head amidst the engines, the horns, the tire shushes, and his own clicking chain. If anyone could piece together Dreavor and Mack, it was St. James. Maybe if he just simply explained the entire sequence of events and his thinking to him and that orderly, Charlie, they'd try to help him.

Tanner's hands squeezed his brakes.

Minutes later, he locked his bike to a three-prong rack in front a "No Parking" sign five blocks from Sterling Falls. When he drew to within two blocks, he saw the red siren flash and the ambulance's open rear doors awaiting a patient like an oven begging for a loaf of dough. A team of policemen directed pedestrian and automobile traffic.

Tanner stopped and drifted backward into the shadow of the nook between two old, brick buildings. He inched his way closer to Sterling Falls, taking stock of each passing car. Only a handful of pedestrians came and went. Not many seemed to care that an ambulance would be removing someone from the rest home. Tanner kept his head down, his Red Sox cap greeting those who passed him.

"Sir, you'll have to take a step back." The first policeman extended an arm in front of Tanner's torso. Tanner was breathing heavily. He didn't realize that he had run the last block and was at the door of the rest home.

"What happened?"

"Sir, you'll have to keep back."

Tanner spoke even louder. "What happened?"

"Do you know someone inside, sir?"

Tanner's eyes stretched down the corridor. Far down. Just about where he knew Room 212 was, a crowd was growing, including a couple of police officers and two men in suits, one of which was taking flash photography.

"My—my uncle lives down there," Tanner heard himself say without directly engaging the policeman.

The officer lowered his arm. "What's your uncle's name?"

Tanner's brain thumbed through a recent memory file. "Conzelman, Room 210."

The policeman nodded.

Tanner feigned alarm. "That's where everyone is down there! Is he okay?"

"Relax, sir. He's fine. His neighbor is missing, though."

"Henry St. James?"

"Yeah. You know him?"

St. James? Missing? Tanner's breath was jagged. He interlocked his fingers behind his head. He looked up and down the hall. "The—the—ah, the three of us play cards every now and then." Tanner wanted out.

"Ever see anyone suspicious around?"

"In this place? There are a couple of old ladies on the second floor that scare the shit out of me." Tanner forced a smile. "If St. James is missing, what's with the ambulance?"

"There was an incident with one of the staff."

"Charlie," Tanner felt it slip out of his mouth.

The policeman nodded. "He was stabbed by an intruder. Not before he delivered a beating, though."

Tanner wiped his sweaty face with his jacket sleeve. His eyes quickened their pace up and down the hallway. "Can I see my uncle?"

"There's quite a mess down there, sir. The crime scene folks are going to need more time. Think you can hold off for a bit?"

Tanner was already backing away. "Sure, no problem. I can't really stand the sight of blood anyway. Uncle will understand. I think I need fresh air." Tanner turned and trotted away.

Tanner sat on the toilet in Sterling Farm's first-floor men's room. Had to be a coincidence. Had to be! They got St. James? An old man who said he didn't know anything, but since Tanner came back for him ... they did too. He heard the hum of the bathroom's fluorescents above him. How valuable could those pages be?

The officer said "missing" and that there was a give and take. Maybe he was just missing—maybe St. James escaped during it all. Great, now St. James was—was whatever he was. But St. James was imbalanced on a good day. *Good luck*, Tanner thought. *Now, where the hell should I go? The police station?* Portland was bigger than Gloucester. The police here would be more willing to listen—Hold on, Portland was bigger, a regular city with lots of ... attractions.

Tanner jerked his body and leaped from one foot to the other. He led with his face, always trying to see beyond the person in front of him. His eyes were desperate. The baseball stadium's interior stairs opened to the broad view of the field. He added his hand to his visor to help him make a compete scan.

There he was, several gates away in the first-base upper bleachers. A minute later, Tanner folded down the short stub of a bleacher seat and dropped himself next to St. James. "Reilly score?" Tanner asked, keeping his eyes on the field. He thought that would be more natural, less threatening.

With his elbows perched on his knees, St. James held his chin on his interlocked hands. "On a walk. Matson batted him 'round with a double. Got here too late to see it, though."

Tanner watched the stadium empty, as did St. James. "How did you get out?"

"Charlie told me."

"Told you? Told you what?"

"Told me to run."

Tanner nodded. He didn't know what to say about Charlie.

"There was a lot of blood. Is Charlie okay?" St. James asked.

"I honestly don't know. I got back and there was an ambulance pulling away."

St. James shifted forward. "Well, I suppose I should be getting back. Dinner's soon."

Tanner rose and put a hand on St. James's shoulder. "I'll help you. But you can't go back."

St. James looked at Tanner, his face asking it all.

"Because you might know something that people are willing to kill for," Tanner said.

St. James' pale face shifted to gray, and he turned to Tanner. "You'd kill me?"

"No, they're after me too. And don't ask me who, because I don't know."

Tanner had him by the arm and slowly, painstakingly slowly, guided him down the steps to the nearest exit. Each step down, Tanner's eyes searched: by the scoreboard, into the dugouts, the custodians. Who looked normal, who didn't?

"Do you have any relatives in the area?" Tanner asked as they turned into the inner stadium.

St. James shook his head.

"Nobody?"

"Do I need to spell 'no' for you?"

"Okay. How about any relatives anywhere?"

St. James shook his head.

"In the entire country?"

"My wife divorced me after, well, you know … and I've lost track or contact with anyone remotely related to me over the past forty-seven years."

Tanner tried to disassemble and then reconstruct what St. James was trying to tell him. The expedition was a failure, and he came home ashamed. The stress took its toll and accumulated in some form or another. It bubbled over back in the children's section of the library. So, what to do with St. James?

"Well, let's get you to the police, they—"

"No," St. James said, tugging his arm in Tanner's grip. The old man wasn't strong enough to rip free.

Tanner stopped and turned. "Why?"

"Don't like them."

"Hey, I'm not a great fan, but—"

St. James grew tense and red. "I'm not going to spell it out."

Tanner looked at him for an added moment. If he had wanted to, the old man could have refused to accompany Tanner anywhere. He could've staged a protest simply by sitting down where he stood. His agreeing to accompany Tanner this far was a strong sign of some level of trust, even if it was just to get back to the home.

"Okay, let me ask you—do you think Sterling Falls is a safe place?"

St. James looked at the ground. He turned his shaking hands inside one another. He shook his head and bit his lip. A wave of sympathy flushed through Tanner. No family whatsoever, his only friend in the whole world might have been Charlie, and in one afternoon, his complete foundation had been cut out from under him. Tanner wondered how much of this was his fault.

"Well, let's keep moving." He put a light hand on St. James' upper arm. "We'll figure this out."

They kept their slow pace through the stadium. Tanner searched for a darkened exit. "Let me ask you—did you have any theories about where Bacon might have dug another hole?"

"I had a lot of guesses. In the end they were just guesses."

They came to a turnstile exit/entrance. Tanner wondered whether St. James would have the mass or energy to propel himself through. But the old man approached, and with what might have been fifteen steps, was able to crank the spike enough to pass to freedom.

The crowd had thinned considerably from when Tanner first hopped the gate. They stood a few feet from a family—father, mother, and two sons—debating where to grab a bite. Tanner noticed St. James eyeing the boys. Tanner felt dizzy trying to keep watch in a 360-degree radius. His hand shot up for a taxi. A white Portland Express cab steered toward them. Tanner braced St. James under both arms as the shaky man practically dropped into the backseat. Unfortunately, he hadn't lost his stinky shoe smell. Tanner jogged around to the other side. He had no idea where to go and about forty-five dollars in his wallet.

"Can you take us to the Hilton?" Tanner asked.

"Been a while," St. James eked out. He was breathing hard from the turnstile and the taxi.

"You think Bacon would've dug a hole somewhere closer to London?"

St. James shook his head back and forth in a near fit. He had both hands on the crank of his window. "After his banishment, Bacon couldn't stand the fucking *sight* of London. He hated that wretched place."

Hated? The committee members of Tanner's frontal lobe all turned toward the head of the table. A new idea had entered the room. "Francis Bacon hated London?"

"Who's partially deaf here?"

"But he was once the lord chancellor—"

"They treated him like a cancer the minute he was born. He was her bastard son. She pawned him off on her chief justice, Nicholas Bacon, a man whom she trusted, who—given his position—owed her everything. He had comforts and the means to support another son. And since Papa Bacon was within shouting distance, she knew she could keep tabs on Francis."

"She?"

"Elizabeth, Elizabeth, for Christsake! But then the old man dies. She can't help the young boy or everyone knows something's going on. Suspicion was already roaming through the upper circles. If she had a son, a would-be king, the devious ones in her inner circle would have had all the more reason to kill her."

"And after Elizabeth died, Bacon still couldn't say anything?"

"Not if he didn't want the new king on his tail. Bacon's jackass father left him nothing." St. James wiped his nose with the back of his hand. "Made him scavenge. Arrested, humiliated. No one stood up for him during his impeachment. I'd run from that."

"How far would you go? If you were in Bacon's shoes, would you come all the way across the Atlantic?"

Tanner could tell that the old man was thinking about it. While St. James stared out the window at Portland passing by, he didn't seem to focus on any item in particular. St. James broke the silence. "There's no mention of him doing that anywhere. No books, no journals."

"Did he even know much about America?"

St. James looked into his lap. His fly was open, but he made no movement to adjust it. "It all got a bit crazy in the end." St. James' attention drifted to a teenage girl walking on the sidewalk wearing a flannel shirt open low down her front. "The king's royal circle was hunting him in the end. I nearly escaped with his life. But they got him in the end."

Tanner kept his knees close together and on his side of the hump. Had the old man just said, "I nearly escaped with his life?"

"I'm sorry, did you say they got him in the end?"

St. James rubbed his eyes with the heel of his hand. Was he crying?

"The books will tell you he had leaped from his coach in a snowstorm with the idea of preserving flesh with ice. He caught a cold and died two days later of congestion complications."

Tanner read the taxi driver's ID inside its plastic mount. Fred Lexow. "Francis Bacon didn't die of natural causes?"

St. James looked over at Tanner. "How many royalty did back then? There were a bunch who wanted him dead. As chief justice, he learned way too much about those who had been brought before the court. His randy parties brought out the deviance in the higher circles. Many knew he was the bastard son of Queen Elizabeth and entitled to the throne. The question isn't who wanted him gone, but who didn't?"

"I see. America is looking more attractive by the moment."

The cab slowed to a stop in front of the Hilton. Tanner fished out the proper payment.

"He advised the king on the Virginia colonies," St. James said to the window, as much muttering to himself as answering Tanner's question.

"So, maybe Bacon dug a crypt in Virginia?" Tanner asked as he stepped out of the cab and walked to the other side to help St. James do the same.

"Francis Bacon traveled to Virginia and you're looking for his crypt?"

Tanner gripped him by the elbow and led him toward the hotel's main doors. "Sometimes you can find royalty in the strangest of places."

The hotel reception agent greeted them with a smile. Tanner used the hotel's cash machine and paid for one night's stay. The receptionist looked at him strangely when he said he would bring their bags up later. As she took note of him helping St. James up toward the elevator, Tanner hoped her concerns would be dismissed.

The room was no improvement on St. James's old quarters.

The old man took a seat in the room's only comfortable chair. "How long are we going to be here?"

Tanner checked the charge on his phone. "I don't know. Until I figure out how to stay safe."

"If you're waiting for someone to find Bacon's crypt, I think I'll head back to Sterling Falls."

"There'll be another way." Tanner stood. "I just don't know what it is yet." He left one of the room keycards on the desk. "I'll be back in an hour or so. If you're hungry, just order room service."

St. James sighed. "I'm not hungry."

"Mind if I ask how you calculated where the Wrye crypt was?"

St. James' eyebrows arched in surprise. "You don't know?"

Tanner shrugged. "I'm learning as I go here."

St. James stared out at the lightly busy traffic moving on the street below. "Bacon included code in all of his writings."

"What kind of code?"

St. James kept his eyes on the street below. "Not kind. Kinds."

"How's that?"

"You'd have thought you would have at least done some minimal amount of research before bothering me."

"You know, normally I do. It's—"

"In the most interesting of Bacon's works, there are three kinds of code, sometimes all going on at once. Sometimes he used simple anagrams throughout a single play. In his case, these were compilations of passages that didn't quite fit. When you put them together, they tell stories. One told the sad story of his illegitimacy."

"This goes on in the middle of Shakespeare's plays?"

James nodded. "Plays, poems—all his writings. Sometimes he uses a biliteral code, colluding with printers on out-of-place typeset words or individual letters."

"Just scattered throughout the text?"

"Not scattered. Usually in a sequence that made sense if you followed along, plucking out each letter in order."

"Seems obvious."

"Maybe today, but not then. He also used simple substitution codes. So, just sequencing together oversized letters didn't amount to anything until you figured out the code."

"In the same writing?"

St. James turned. What looked to be six-week-old oil clumped his hair in chaotic patches. His eyes opened with a heated glare. "Brilliant, wasn't he? Fucking brilliant. We won't see his kind again."

Tanner nodded. He started to back out of the room. "Use room service if you need it. I'll be back in a little while." As Tanner slowly closed the room door, he saw St. James staring at the carpet with his shoulders slumped, like dripping maple syrup; he carried the look of defeat.

Tanner jogged back to the stadium. He had locked his bike to a fence nearby. As he squatted to insert his key, he pictured St. James as a librarian reading to a half circle of three-year-olds sitting on the miniature wooden chairs in the young kids' section of the library. St. James' bug eyes spent more time on the audience than they did reading pages. He was a smart man, but his mind and his judgment were dented, definitely dented.

Suddenly, a point that felt like a scissors' tip poked Tanner in the scruff of the neck, forcing his head forward.

"Mr. Tanner," a female voice spoke behind him. "Please don't turn around." An Asian voice. *Please* vocalized as *PRease*. Tanner's fingers froze on the key in its lock. "I would like you to explain to me what it is you and Mr. St. James spoke about. Your side of the story, please."

How the hell ...

"We talked about his work on Francis Bacon." The point in his neck was sharp. He felt as if he were bleeding. He wanted to put his hand there to check.

"More specifically!" *SpecificaREE.*

Tanner tensed. As sharp as the knife point was, as close as it was to his spinal column, as blind as he was to how many people might be behind him, anger seethed just atop the fear running through him. How fast was she? How fast was he? His fingers pinched the key in the bike lock.

"He traveled to England twenty years ago looking for a crypt—"

In mid-word, Tanner tumbled forward on the sidewalk, spun on his heels to face the pointed blade, and—still crouched—instantly shuffled back, separating himself from her.

He was faster.

He faced the Grocer like a monkey backed into a corner by a tiger. She had a surprised look on her face and held a short knife.

"I hope you have help." His eyes darted beyond the Grocer, searching for others. He inched back from her, still ready to spring in any direction. He dipped his eyes to verify his bike was unlocked.

"Do not be a fool. Several of my colleagues are watching you. You will be stopped within one block."

"They'd better be fast." He edged up on his toes. From as early as he could remember, Tanner had shifted into this position as a defense mechanism. The Grocer's eyes went wide as she tried to follow Tanner's center. His bounce widened in diameter. A defensive ritual for him, and a taunt for her. She moved the knife and braced herself. Tanner's bounce quickened, like a blender building speed.

The Grocer thrust, leading with a short stab of the blade. Tanner's mind synchronized with his bounce; he rolled right, matador style, seized her behind the collar, and tossed her forward with her momentum. She skidded to a stop face down, splayed flat on the sidewalk. He kicked the open bike lock away, leaped aboard his Trek, and was gone in a blur.

He checked left—a parking lot. No engine ignitions. Right—Banner Street, light traffic. No one advancing on him yet.

Just get the fuck out of here!

Buzzed on adrenaline, Tanner weaved through traffic, intent on making it hell for anyone with a vehicle to follow. He cut hard right down Mellon Lane and then left up Sprook Street.

He replayed the encounter. "I would like you to explain to me what it is you and Mr. St. James spoke about." *Where the hell is she from, and why does she give a damn about Shakespeare?*

University of Maine biking teammates described Tanner's ability to leap his bike at will as supernatural. At nearly twenty miles per hour, he leaped at a crazy angle over and between two trash cans, banking up Rosewall's Court.

The Grocer lady had a meaty, muscled neck, like a Romanian gymnast. "Your side of the story, please." As if there were two sides to the—

Brakes! The tire burned *slishhh* in the alley. Tanner stopped breathing. The only other side of the conversation was ... St. James'.

Oh shit. He leaped and spun the bike 180 degrees.

A wake of car horns trailed behind him as Tanner danced his four feet of bike between people crossing the street and other innocent bikes ridden by sub-teenagers. Between blinks of the eye, he clenched his hand brakes, fanning his rear wheel to avoid collision with a poodle on a leash. *Damn downtown pedestrians!* He vertically hopped his front tire to sail over the fire hydrant.

Despite the stop signs, the red lights, and the crosscurrent of Portland citizenry, Tanner never contemplated stopping. To the passing—and leaping—foot traffic, Tanner was a sweaty madman, a dangerous lunatic. His rear tire crunched a pigeon like a bag of Fritos as he slid around Watercrest Street and faced the Hilton a block away.

And then he stopped.

Normal traffic passed down the street, but in front of the entrance to the hotel, four men in sports coats rounded a Town Car. One of the men placed his hand on an old man's head to ease him into the rear seat. Tanner wondered what St. James was thinking as he plopped down in that Lincoln.

Had the old man called for help? Could St. James have been playing him? Had he caused a ruckus in his hotel room? Could the men helping St. James into the car be good guys? Somehow, Tanner didn't think so. He needed space. Nothing seemed good about St. James getting in that car. Something bad was spreading to everything that came into contact with Dreavor's efforts. Tanner steered back the way he had came and tore away.

Chapter 34

Tanner rode with his eyes perpetually checking his rearview. *This isn't happening!* If it had been hooked up, he was sure his cardio monitor would have been off the charts. He leaned at 45 degrees around a bend not far from the apartment, a small cottage off of a back road in Gill.

It was real—the house burning, the lighthouse flood, the Asian woman's pursuit, the road rage in the Notch, Charlie, and now St. James. But why?

What in God's name do they think I know?

Tanner's knees pumped near his chest. He formed a bullet casing, in line with his handlebars. Where the woods met the road, tree branches fluttered in his wake.

Did they see me with Kyle? He should warn her. Shit, he didn't know her cell phone! It was still three hours before they were supposed to meet. He slowed to dial information.

"Say the city and state," the automated voice began.

"Portland, Maine."

"Portland, Maine," the machine mimicked. "Say the name of the business."

"Hanely and Henderson."

After a two-second pause, the voice said, "I'm sorry, we have no listing with that name. Please try again. Say the city and state."

Tanner pumped with all he had. Maybe his huffing made his speech unrecognizable. No, idiot, she had told him they moved offices. Something screwed up with the phone lines. How the hell was he going to warn her?

He drove his weight down on his pedals as his bike soared over Strongback Hill. What was it they wanted? He'd learned that a supposed code within Shakespeare's writings pointed to an underwater crypt where his original drafts may be. But he hadn't a goddamn idea where that was! Maybe somewhere in Maine. He squeezed both brake handles to stop in time to catch the driveway. The one-story house squatted like Buddha amid a row of houses on Cherry Street. Rack shared this two bedroom shack with Jason, a friend who was currently traveling down south. Rack's share of the rent was financed by his father, the commercial real estate lawyer.

Tanner tossed his Trek to the side of the stoop and bolted through the front door, his chest heaving. When he entered the kitchen-living room, Rack jerked awake in his La-Z-Boy chair and looked over at Tanner.

"Dude, you're dripping on the carpet."

Tanner's soaked white Nike top formed a film over his taut upper body. "The Asian is back! She threatened me with a knife. They took this guy, St. James! Do you have Kyle's cell number?"

Rack struggled and then pushed his big frame up and out of the soft, angled chair. "Slow down, what are you talking about?"

"I tried calling from the road." He slipped under the side window's curtains.

"My phone's dead. I had it on all night. I was trying to get you and Kyle."

"Huh?" Tanner stripped off his soaked shirt. "Her cell was on when she picked me up."

"Well, I couldn't get you either."

"Really? My phone must have cut out during dinn—on the ride."

Rack's eyes narrowed. The expression on his face displayed one part realization, and one part disgust. "Where did you sleep last night?"

"Up in Danton."

"And ...?" Rack pushed himself up from the recliner. "Where did Kyle sleep?"

"Um, same town, I, think."

"You didn't—"

"It was late. I'd been run off the road that morning."

"*Did you fuck her?*" The batteries nearly spit out of the remote control in Rack's grip.

Tanner took a step back and put his hands up to settle Rack down. "Hold on, it's not like that."

"If you had your dick out anywhere near her body, it's like that!"

Tanner glanced at the kitchen counter. *Think.*

Rack thumped forward, his nose at Tanner's eyebrows. "I made it clear you were not to even get hard in her presence!"

"She said you two weren't ... that close, yet."

"She did, huh? Well, thanks for checking!" Rack threw the remote control ... and it took out a window in the kitchen.

Tanner waved Rack down with both hands. "Calm down!"

The countertop lifted off its supports as Rack slammed his fist on it. "You stole Kyle! She came up to me at The Overlook, not you, *me!*"

"Look, that's not the way she tells it—"

"You stole her! You gave up on yourself and me! You're still feeling sorry for your fucking self! Fuck! What the fuck am I doing, huh? Thank god I didn't wait for you!" Rack pulled at his hair as if it were burning his skull. His eyes were wildly searching the room, and they skidded to a stop on the Jameson bottle on the counter.

"Rack, settle." Tanner had rarely seen Rack so insane. A lot was bubbling to the surface, but Tanner thought there might be more to it.

Rack snatched the bottle and recklessly tossed the cork behind him. "You can go fuck yourself *and* that slut!"

Tanner backed up to give Rack a path out of the room. Rack slugged the scotch and then shook his head to hurry it down.

"Rack, settle. People are circling me, man! This Shakespeare thing—"

"Fuck up! Fucking shut the fuck up!" Rack bounced off the lintel on his way out the kitchen door.

"Rack! No! *Listen* to me!"

Rack reached his minivan, threw his head back, slugged three massive gulps of the scotch, and then flung the bottle across the driveway and fell behind the wheel.

"Rack, you want to kill yourself, is that it? If these motherfuckers find you firs—"

Rack hoisted his middle finger and floored the car in reverse. The wheels sprayed gravel.

Tanner flinched as the minivan slid into alignment with the road. The wheels hiccupped as Rack dropped it into gear and sped away.

Shit.

Chapter 35

Teck, teck, teck. Tanner was back in his own apartment, the first floor of a tiny fifties colonial. Tanner looked up and saw Kyle pecking at the sliding glass door. She was wearing her white smile and overalls and had a sailor's sack slung over her shoulder. The bagginess of the overalls highlighted how trim she was and how easily she could slip in and out of them, like a gun in a holster.

Tanner slid the door open. "You're early, and a few miles off."

She smiled her wonderful smile. "I can leave ..."

Tanner laughed quickly and shook his head. "Please don't. But you missed Rack and all the fireworks."

"You told him?" She stepped in when he opened the door. He smelled a rose baby powder that weakened him.

"He may be fat, but he's smart. He figured it out. But that's the least of my problems."

"What?"

"She was back again."

"Who?"

"The Grocer. Chased me across downtown."

Kyle tensed. "In Portland?"

Tanner pulled a fresh flannel shirt over his head and marched down the short hallway that connected the kitchen to his bedroom. Kyle followed behind him, and he told her about St. James.

Tanner stopped at the one bookshelf on the wall in his room. He twisted the head off of a gargoyle bookend and shook the monster upside down. A thin roll of bills fell into his hand. Then he sprinted back to the TV room.

He heard Kyle follow him. When the reached the living room she lowered the sailor's bag from her shoulder. "If you're kidding, this isn't funny. Is that why the curtains are drawn?"

"I've got to get help. If they tracked me from the island to Portland, if they're the ones behind Dreavor's death, Charlie's attack, and what appears to be St. James' abduction, then they'll be here any minute." He turned to her and held his hand out. "Mind if I drive?"

Kyle smiled and cocked her head slightly. After a brief moment, she shrugged her shoulders. "I suppose not." She dropped the car keys into his hand, and he broke for the door.

"Wait, where—hey!" Tanner ran to the driver's side and jumped behind the wheel. She slid into the passenger seat. "Are you going to wait for me?" The Jeep jerked backward before her door was closed. She put her hand on the dash to catch herself. The Firestones screeched across the street.

"Where are we going?"

"Freeland Institute. Just want to make sure Jimmy's safe."

"How could they know about him?"

"How do they know anything? What's in the sack?"

"It was a down day at work. I slid out to the library and did some thinking for you."

"Oh?" Tanner's head snapped forward as the Jeep dropped down a sharp incline. A sharp metal *chink* shrieked and ended immediately.

Kyle spun to look behind. "Did we just drop my muffler?"

"About what?"

"What about?"

With his eyes, Tanner traced her body under the bulky overalls. "Your library reading. Thinking for me. What about?"

"Oh. Well, did you know it was rumored Bacon was the son of Queen Elizabeth?"

Tanner glanced over at her. Sure, he knew, but he could pretend … and try to see down the front of the overalls—he had a good angle. "Really?"

"The rumor is that she gave birth to Francis and a brother Robert, who was the Earl of Essex. She threatened them with death if they revealed the secret. She was paranoid about maintaining her power and didn't want anyone thinking about installing a boy king. To admit to the world that she had a son might stir that."

"It's a stretch."

"Yep."

"But if it's true … I guess Bacon had two identities he couldn't reveal."

"It's more than that, though. Imagine you lived back then. Massive class system, and a wide gap between the haves and have-nots. Your level in society is everything. And Bacon should have been king. What's your state of mind if you're him?"

Tanner adjusted the rearview mirror. "Pissed."

"You approach the good queen and try to reason with her. She not only rebukes you but threatens that if you tell anyone, she'll have the executioner in the Tower cut you to pieces."

"More pissed."

"Might you be resentful?"

"Sure."

"Might you be enraged?"

"Okay."

"Enough to subversively work against queen mother's efforts?"

"Maybe. They took anarchy pretty seriously back then. That would get you in the Tower quickly."

"Would you write about your sentiments?"

"If I'm Bacon, probably."

Kyle pulled a thick book out of her sack. Tanner flipped his eyes over at it. *The Novum Orgum.*

"Would you advocate the abrogation of the existing school system?" She tugged out another book. *A New Atlantis.* "The total establishment of a new society with a more egalitarian class structure?"

The Jeep leaned left as they rounded a right-hand curve. "I vaguely remember hearing about these books in grade school."

"I didn't think you vaguely remembered anything."

"Not everything sticks."

"So, with such a revolutionary mindset, you think you'd be willing to leave your country, Mr. Bacon?"

Tanner's mind ran the thought forward. "So I came here to do what?"

"Bacon left England, came to America, brought his manuscripts, and then left, hid, or died with them here. That's what Dreavor was after."

"You came up with this, this afternoon?"

She edged forward and brimmed with enthusiasm. "Well, yeah. So, what do you think?"

"St. James thought Bacon was angry too."

"But obviously that's what Dreavor was onto, some American lead." The Jeep rumbled over a rough coastal road. Kyle braced herself with the safety bar above her shoulder, and Bacon's books jiggled onto the floor. "Tanner, there's no one behind us—you don't have to drive so hard." She shifted her right foot up on the glove box as an added stabilizer. "What if I told you Bacon was very good friends with Walter Raleigh?"

"Walter—"

Kyle smiled. "The naval explorer, eventually sent to the Tower and beheaded under Elizabeth's direction. Before his execution, though, Bacon spent a lot of visitor time with him—helped Raleigh write his memoirs up there."

Tanner's brow wrinkled. "The naval explorer?"

"One of the first to sail up and down the coast of ..."

Tanner took his eyes from the rearview mirrors and glanced at her. "Maine."

"And Bacon was related to Bartholemew Gosnold," she said with a smile. "Cousin on his wife's side."

Tanner didn't know what to say. "Gosnold, whose ship is in the museum, with a crew who we think were carrying deck cannons designed for hidden storage? Mind if I borrow your cell? I had to leave mine with my sack when the Grocer jumped me."

Kyle eyed him cautiously and dug her phone out of her pocket. Tanner held the wheel with one hand and thumbed the cell phone keys with the other. He inserted the phone between his cheek and shoulder.

"Freeland," said a female voice Tanner recognized. "Melinda, it's Tanner. How are things?"

"Tanner." Melinda's voice grew serious and soft. "How's Jimmy?"

Tanner didn't like her tone. "Melinda, how, wh—why are you asking me ..."

Tanner lost sensation across his body as Melinda told him about the men. The Jeep slowed.

"What is it?" Tanner heard Kyle ask from the seat next to him.

The cell phone dropped as his mind processed what he had just heard. He was aware that Kyle was speaking to him, trying to inquire, but her voice was a low, low priority.

"Tanner, what?" she persisted.

Tanner turned to her and started to tell her, but suddenly his head snapped. The Jeep rocketed forward as if a tornado had struck it from behind. In the rearview, Tanner saw a Ford Taurus shake its nose in recovery.

Kyle screamed. "Tanner!"

His hand at four o'clock on the wheel ran around to six o'clock. The Jeep rounded across the front lawn of a house on the street and then found the road again. The growling Taurus closed from the right. Tanner gunned ahead of it.

Kyle braced herself and squeezed her door handle. "Tanner!"

A short slope led from the road to the shoreline. Kyle's Jeep spanned nearly the entire width of the road. An occasional house flashed in clearings between the trees.

"Shit!" The Jeep groaned under Tanner's foot.

"Pull over! Pull over!" Kyle yelled at him.

"Are you crazy?" Tanner's knuckles bleached around the wheel. "It's them! They've killed everyone else. They want us!" He desperately searched ahead for … witnesses. The Taurus crunched the Jeep's rear.

"Do something!" Kyle screamed.

The steering wheel spasmed. "Hold on."

The Taurus bounced from the sea edge of the road to the wooded side. The car sped in and out of the afternoon shadows. Its engine's whine rose and lowered like a tiger growling over a fresh find. As the Jeep's grill turned the next corner, Tanner saw a half-mile stretch of road ahead, followed by a turnoff onto a narrow, one-vehicle lane. In the corner of his eye, Tanner watched the Taurus pull alongside, nearly driver seat to driver seat, neck and neck. A thick, sunglassed man focused on the road.

Koom!

Tanner and Kyle snapped forward. A Durango had rammed them from behind. The blow also forced the Jeep ahead of the Taurus. Tanner snapped the wheel right, and the Taurus slued.

Tanner heard a squeal and crash behind him. Up ahead on the left, the shoulder dropped down a rocky slope, and a mean hillside rose up on their right. Tanner sheared the Jeep's undercarriage as he shot down the rocky slope. He and Kyle bobbed in the front seat like popcorn. The rearview showed the Durango madly speeding in pursuit. Tanner kicked onto the single lane road. Single-story, ocean-view shacks flew by.

"Come on, come on, where are the cops!" Tanner's arms tensed as he fought to stay away from the shoulder.

Kyle kept her feet on the dash and her fist locked on the grip above her right shoulder. "Where's the next town?"

"In about four miles."

Their necks snapped forward and then back. The angry Durango rammed them again.

"Christ!" Kyle screamed.

Tanner accelerated into the darkness of a tree-smothered strip. Branches of leaves slapped at the antennae and Wrangler's sides.

Kyle shrieked, "Isn't there anything you can give them?"

"I would've tried that when the crazy Asian was poking her razor in my neck!"

"Shit!"

Tanner's eyes widened at the sight dead ahead. "Oh no." A white van sat across the road a quarter of a mile up. Something about the intentional angle of it, diagonal, with running lights on—this was no random parking spot.

Kyle shook her head. "Oh, God."

To the right of the van was the rising hillside. On the left stood a dense collection of trees and a split-rail fence marking a home's driveway.

Kyle eased in her seat. "Let me do the talking. The owner of the practice I work for is pretty well connect—Hey! Slow down!"

The Jeep accelerated sharply.

The surroundings quieted. The immovable entities that lay ahead took on the appearance of a deadened void. The air stopped having meaning, and Tanner felt surrounded by a comforting gel, just like when he approached a monolithic pack of competing bikers as he readied for a pass. Never mind the churning pedal teeth, the high probabilities of another biker slipping a centimeter and short-circuiting the pack. In a waiting room in his mind's recess, he was aware of Kyle screaming at his side, her arms flailing for him to stop, and the speedometer steady at seventy mph. To lock those in the van in place, he needed to convince them of his unpredictability.

Seventy yards, fifty, forty yards—and with a slip of breath from his lips, he tipped the steering wheel to the left.

The Wrangler cut left. It ducked within an inch of the van's ass and blasted through the split-rail fence, obliterating a mailbox and mangling a yearling dogwood. A tip of the wheel to the right and another puff of breath, and the Wrangler's right side-view mirror disintegrated against a front lawn sugar maple, the last obstacle before Tanner and Kyle leaped atop the road again. They were past the white van.

Tanner glanced over at Kyle and saw her slowly unfurl her head from the protection of her arms. Her face remained wrinkled as the country flew past at a very ill-suited eighty mph.

Droplets tinkled down Tanner's nose. The tendons and cords of muscle in his arms formed the only barrier between Kyle and him.

"Sorry about your mirror." A cheap comfort, but it was all he could produce. "We'll be at town soon."

"I … I think you should stop. We are not fit for—for each other." Kyle's hands clenched the car seat, and she pressed her back into her seat back.

"If you ask nicely, Rack would probably take you back."

"I'm calling the cops."

"Don't mention anything about stalking Asians. In my experience, it hasn't—"

"Stow it."

Tanner's eyes flipped to the rearview. "They're back."

Kyle spun to look behind her. "How far is town?"

"Soon."

"I think they're going to be here sooner." She spoke into her cell, "That's right, a white van and a gray Taurus." To Tanner, she said, "What road are we on?"

"Miller's Wheel Ridge." A sandstorm of dust broke from under the van. "God, he's fast."

"Can't you go faster?"

"Well, I could, but I'd have to ignore where the road goes. Where are the cops?"

"About ten minutes out. They're going to ram us!" She curled up her legs against her chest.

Whoom! A rear-end collision sent the Wrangler forward, and its nose skidded from side to side. With his arms jiggling to compensate, over and then under, Tanner felt as if he were holding down a crazed pit bull at a family barbecue.

"She's coming harder and faster." As the van chomped forward, Tanner veered hard to the right and avoided the heft of the van. He could see no more than a tenth of a mile ahead, and it was a wavy road. "We can't take another full-on slap."

Kyle nearly tore her seat out. "The police said they're coming!"

"Trust me."

"What? What are you doing?"

The world went cotton again, a breath slipped from his lips, and the Wrangler punctured a picket fence and tore across a front lawn. The Jeep mangled three tin garbage cans, decimated a Weber grill, and then sailed off the edge of the backyard toward the Atlantic.

For a quiet second of hang time, the rumble of the pitted road vanished. The Wrangler arced slowly down, like a dolphin, ending in a two-ton fountain splash.

The Wrangler sank quickly. Five, four, three, two ...

"Take a breath!" Tanner shouted. He sucked as big a breath as he could and unclipped his seatbelt. Kyle jerked right and then left, obviously too panicked to realize what was keeping her down. He focused on her seatbelt latch and popped it. Tanner fastened her under his arm and used his powerful legs to scissor kick upward, yanking her out of her seat. They rose steadily.

He swam away from the bubbling Jeep and into the black ahead. Could he get both of them to the surface before he sucked in ocean? His mind flashed with the image of his bicycle frame tearing his thigh to the yellow bone. Black cold enveloped them. He was dizzy but crunched another kick, then another, and then another ... Kyle started spasming at his side.

The water brightened. He kicked toward the light.

And then they burst through the surface. Kyle threw up water she had swallowed. She clawed at Tanner for buoyancy. She gagged and puked, desperately trying to cough out stinging saltwater. Snot coughed out of her nose.

"Easy." Tanner tried to tread, suck in fresh breath, and avoid her sharp nails. "Easy." He ducked her desperate flailing and checked over his shoulder.

They had swum a whole property's width away from the Jeep to the neighbors' house, to the far side of the dock that belonged to those neighbors. The dock hid their presence from anyone who might have been drawn to where the Jeep plunged into the ocean. From their spot at the far end of the dock, Tanner couldn't see the Jeep's entry point or the backyard he had driven through. He listened through his splashing for their pursuers, but he didn't hear anything. This gave him no comfort.

"Come on, we don't have time." Tanner locked his arm over Kyle lifeguard-style and swam her toward a pillar of the dock. There was a rusty ladder built into the dock that extended into the water.

He pushed her hands onto the first rung. "Come on, Kyle! Climb."

Chapter 36

Once atop the dock, Tanner latched Kyle's arm over his shoulder and practically carried her up to the backyard. This house was separated from the one whose backyard they had destroyed by a dense collection of trees, which gave them all of about thirty seconds of cover.

Tanner sounded like a hippo with a gunshot wound and asthma. Seawater and sweat dripped from his chin. Kyle's feet dragged more than kept pace. His eyes pleaded up and down the barn he approached for signs of life. *Just one telephone ...*

His leg burned so deeply at the thigh. Now they would need to listen! There was a Jeep bubbling at the bottom of the bay.

Jesus! Somebody must have witnessed that! Where are the goddamn cops?

Kyle shouted in a whisper. "Tanner! Stop for a minute!"

She staggered over next to him, bent over at the middle, her hair still dripping. "Just ... just, what did you do?"

Tanner acknowledged to himself that his chest was heaving and he could use the rest. Tanner shook his head. "What are you talking about?" Eyes ahead, eyes behind.

"What do these people think you did?"

"What did *I* do? I haven't got a clue."

She straightened somewhat and put her hands on the barn wall as if being frisked. She spit in an effort to clear the remaining taste of the bay. "Think harder." Her breaths came in heaves. "These are not book collectors!"

"I never said they were, but they've obviously got the wrong guy." Tanner looked hard at the house attached to the barn and up ahead, past the wide and deep football field lawn to the main road they had been traveling. "We should keep moving."

Kyle took her cell phone out of her pocket and tried to turn it on.

Tanner moved around the corner of the garage. "Come on, you can do that as we walk."

"Shit!" Kyle swore at the drowned phone. She fell in behind Tanner and wiped the soaked hair from her face. "Where are you going?"

"Just want to find a phone. The police will listen now."

"Maybe a tow truck first."

Tanner didn't laugh. They came to the corner of the house, and Kyle raised a hand. "Hold up."

Tanner turned around to face her but kept walking, backwards. "What's the matt—"

Headlights clicked on two houses away. The van.

"Shit." Tanner grabbed her arm. "Run!" The van's engine growled, and its tires fought for traction on the gravel road.

"Move, move!" Tanner ran strong, even though Kyle weighed him down. Her free arm flapped, and her legs slapped behind him. They circled back behind the barn.

Kyle slowed and moaned, "I-I-c-can't,"

The ass wheels of the van howled as it slid around the corner of the barn. Tanner skidded to a stop, faced Kyle, dropped his shoulder into her gut and bucked her up on his shoulder, twirling toward the far side of the property. Without a check over his shoulder, he raced ahead, carrying Kyle like a golf bag of cement.

The van threw itself across the yard, nearly shaving off Tanner's kneecaps. His momentum brought him crashing into the forward side panel. Kyle's body slammed into the side door and fell free. Tanner rebounded backward onto his ass.

His thigh—the patch over his puncture scar—was numb. He rolled onto his hands to push up. In seconds, from the corner of his eye he saw figures leap from the van. He felt flame on his back, and heated electricity sizzled from his eyebrows and nuts. He lost contact with the ground—the searing heat was all he knew. And then, blackness.

Chapter 37

The stink of urine filled Tanner's nostrils when he opened his eyes. From the chill of the room and the musty smell, he guessed he was in a cellar. Two old, lampshaded lights lit the fifteen-by-twenty room. He was duct-taped to a La-Z-Boy. There were perhaps a half dozen layers across his thighs, another patch across his shins, and another gray belt across his chest. He couldn't move, and he couldn't topple the chair. The rest of the room was poorly decorated. Bad, 1940s-ish amateur oil art, a twenty-year-old TV on a thin chrome stand. A soggy stack of newspapers and magazines. Christ, this looked like any one of several of the old, unclaimed estate homes he'd cleaned and auctioned. The lower left side of his back stung. Did they use a fucking Taser? Is that what a Taser felt like?

The room's only door opened. Kyle walked in, her hands in the pockets of a suede sport coat. Underneath, she wore a fresh pair of jeans and a collared blouse. "You're awake." She walked with a confident square to her shoulders. She didn't seem to be in a desperate hurry to rip through his restraints.

"You think you could get rid of these?"

"Sure." In a swift flash she drew a blade—a Buck Knife—from her jacket pocket. She bent to sever the chest line but stopped when the blade touched the tape. "Oh, just one thing. First tell me where the crypt is."

"What? Crypt? What did you just say?"

Kyle took a step back and locked eyes with Tanner. "Look, I'm not who you think I am. But you should know that the people who put you here are tough. They'll carve out your eyeballs inside of an hour unless you tell them where the manuscripts are."

"You're not ... wait, I don't know where—"

"Don't waste time, economize it. Tell me where in the mountains the crypt is. They told me that they've worked out a way for you to live."

"What in God's name?" Tanner pushed at the duct tape; it was unyielding.

"Knox mentioned that Dreavor had a car. Yet, you never mentioned it to me. Why?"

Tanner's world was tilting. "His car? I don't know. What was I going to do with that information? What are you? Are you serious—"

"Where was he diving?"

"Diving? I don't know!"

Kyle crossed her arms, looked at the floor, and shook her head. "You *know*, Tanner. Save yourself some pain."

"This isn't funny anymore." Tanner looked past her and yelled at the door. "Rack, you stupid motherfucker, enough already! Get your fat ass out here and let me out!"

Kyle clenched her jaw and slashed the knife across Tanner's arm.

"Ahhhh—*what the fuck*!" Tanner looked down past his chin and saw the blood. Kyle stood with a blank, serious face and a dark red blade. "What the *fuck was that for*?"

Kyle slowly, meticulously wiped the blade on Tanner's jeans. "Where is the crypt?"

He saw and felt that his jeans were wet; he had pissed himself earlier. "What the hell's the matter with you?"

Kyle clenched her fists. "Tell me where he was diving!"

He strained at the tape, veins popping in his neck. "What the hell is going on here? Who the hell are you?"

"Shut up, Tanner! They'll use acid if I let them! Where was he diving?"

"Acid?"

"It will eat through you, the chair, and the house's foundation. One last chance. They don't have to come in here. For the love of God, where was he diving?"

Perspiration poured across Tanner's body. His eyes shot around the room: the old TV, the soggy magazines, the gnarled ring rug, a warped, heavy oak door. The TV had a "V" antenna. The wall was made of thick stones with lines of cement holding them together. Kyle had no discernible bulges under her clothes.

Tanner tried to buy himself time. "Look, I've been with you for the past two days, right?"

"Except when you were on Fog Island, when you went to the university, and when you spent some time with Knox."

"But we've been desperately searching together since then! If I had something, do you think I'd be wasting time—"

The lights went out. A deep black doused the room.

"Time's up," Kyle said.

The lights came back on. She spun on her heels and stepped out the door.

"Kyle, don't, don't—"

The door *whoomed* shut. Tanner recoiled as if the sound had slapped him. He wrenched his body under the tape, throwing his shoulder out, his hips up, and his chest down. Each move ignited the laceration across his shoulder. The tape bonds were wrinkled, but otherwise they held.

What the fuck was that all about? She's fucking nuts! This has to be a joke.

He rammed against every corner of tape. His right shin felt like it earned a bit of light. Then the door opened.

The room on the other side was black, pitch black. A squeaking hinge sound came from the dark. Tanner squinted into the black.

The squeaking drew closer, closer. Then, from the dark, a gray table on wheels edged into the room. On the top of the table lay a syringe, scalpel, duct tape, pliers, drill—

Fear began rippling through Tanner. "Wait! Kyle! Let's talk!"

The table stopped. A man walked around to the front of it. He stood in fine, gray wool slacks and a black dress shirt. His body was solid not fat, but tree trunk solid. A ski mask covered his head.

"Crypt?" he asked. The word was slightly muffled and in a low, low voice. Tanner inched back into his chair. The Mask pulled the squeaky table into the room. His movements were assured. He unraveled the drill's power cord. As loop after loop fell from the drill, the Mask stood straight and sure and kept his stare on Tanner.

As the cord slapped the ground, Tanner spoke. "Wait—wait a second."

The Mask crouched and plugged in the cord. He squeezed the grip. Gears whined like a metallic cat.

"Knock it off, will you!" Tanner's scream competed with the volume of the drill. He watched as the Mask stood and advanced with it.

Tanner's face dripped. "Listen, you don't have to do this." He tried to sober his mind and buy himself more time.

The muffled voice was barely audible over the drill. "You want to tell me where he was diving?"

"How did you know?" Tanner shouted. His fevered eyes jumped across the room: the magazines, the La-Z-Boy, the ringed rug, the duct tape ...

"You've been holding out, Tanner. We've known all along."

"I'm still not sure—"

The hungry drill thrashed. "You're a fan of Lance Armstrong, right? Ready for prosthesis?"

"I—I wasn't sure at first ..."

The Mask focused on Tanner's thigh, and the drill bit gnawed on Tanner's jeans. "Faster."

"I reasoned that a seventy-two-year old man wouldn't be able to hike that far."

"Spare me the details, goddamnit!" The ski mask moistened at the mouth.

"You need to hear this. Calm down, please."

The Mask backed off.

Tanner shook his head to keep the sweat from dripping into his eyes. "I figured his range in the woods was about ten to twelve miles. I'm a pretty good judge of a man's endurance from just looking at him." Tanner hoped the Mask wouldn't realize that Tanner had never seen Dreavor in action and had no true idea what the man was capable of. Tanner made it up as he went along. "You're right about the car. He parked near where he intended to dive. The scuba tanks were too heavy for him to lug."

"At this pace, you'll bleed to death," the Mask murmured, nodding his hood at Tanner's slashed arm.

"You already thought of this, I know, but I focused on those areas of the river that would have been deep enough either now or four hundred years ago, deep enough to hide an entrance to a crypt. Those points would be ..." A thought coalesced in his mind. "Wait a minute—"

"You haven't got a minute. Time's up."

"How do I know you won't kill me anyway?"

Mask leaned down with the drill bit on Tanner's thigh. The metal tooth broke the skin and tore toward Tanner's scar.

"NOOO!" The chair moaned and the tape crackled under him, but neither gave.

The Mask eased back. With one hand, he dipped into a pocket of his gray slacks, pulled out a flip phone, and snapped it open. He faced the screen of the phone toward Tanner, showing him a digital photo of a man with dark skin and traditional Arab dress—a long brown robe and turban.

"Your friend, no?"

"What—"

The Mask advanced one photo. There was Tanner's brother Jimmy—with his giddy, dopey-eyed smile—sitting next to St. James, who was not smiling.

Jimmy.

The Mask closed the phone. "What happens to you is probably the least of your concerns."

Tanner's rage bubbled over the top. Veins stretched across his skull. His next words slithered between his clenched jaws. "Until you show me you've released my brother, I am done talking."

The Mask straightened, and the drill screamed in his hand. He threw the cell phone aside and surged forward with the drill.

This isn't happening! Being incapacitated won't help Jimmy.

"Okay! Okay! There are six points of the river where the water drains from a high point to a lower point, points, each of which would most likely have been in existence four hundred years ago. For some unknown reason, Bacon chose the fifth stop. Don't ask me why, but he did."

The Mask put the convulsing drill on the hole in Tanner's jeans. "How did you come upon this fifth point?"

"I tried each. Nothing sophisticated. I dove with ordinary foul-weather riding goggles. Mine are Speedos, just like swimming goggles. All I did was find the faceplate of Bacon's chamber. I couldn't open it."

"I need the GPS points of the site."

Tanner's eyes dropped to the drill. *This is not fucking happening.*

"I don't—I don't use GPS. I did, but I had to sell it recently."

The Mask bent to focus on drilling Tanner's thigh.

"For Christsake! I needed money for my brother's medicine! Check it out!"

The Mask straightened. "Bullshit."

"Listen to me! I marked my trail the same way I do a race course in practice rounds, with landmarks. In Dreavor's case, it involves tall trees, two twin rocks within the forest, and an outcrop in the river."

"I need you to identify it on a map."

"I didn't use a map to find it. B-but, but I can retrace my steps for sure."

The Mask shook his head. "The faceplate, what does it look like?"

Tanner's mind whirled through possibilities. "Circular. One foot diameter. Chiseled across its face it reads, Rex Verulam, 1627."

The hood cocked questioningly.

"When appointed chief justice, Bacon chose the name Lord Verulam, Viscount St. Alban. St. Alban was the first Christian saint of England. Verulam was a town of Roman ruins near his childhood home of Gorhambury. Rex, Latin, was just a take on his supposed kingship. The year 1627 was the year after his reported death. A man of mystery until the end."

The Mask stared at Tanner for a full, silent twenty seconds. The drill slowed and then stopped in his hand. He placed it atop the table.

Tanner dropped his head. For what seemed like minutes, he hung against the tape and watched as sweat dripped from his head onto his groin and his already wet jeans. The image of Jimmy in his chariot pounded in his head.

The door opened. Tanner heard the Mask leave, and through the top of his eyes he saw Kyle's boots strut in. He slumped back down, eyes closed. He heard Kyle approach.

She bent down toward him. "Why didn't you tell me? I had your confidence."

Tanner shook away the sweat again. "I need as much money as I can get for Jimmy's care. Until I knew what, if anything, I was dealing with, I wasn't inclined to share. Obviously, it was going to take me a lot of time to open that chamber." He could only hope she was buying this. "I still haven't figured out how to remove the plate without flooding the inside. I thought if we ran up against enough dead ends, you would get discouraged and give up and lose interest. I think we were probably close to that point."

Kyle smiled. "Not quite."

"Can I stretch my legs?"

Kyle shook her head and slid the cart to the side. She strode to the door. For a moment, she paused. Tanner thought she shifted her weight and was going to turn back to him and say something. But in the next instant, she left and closed the door behind her.

Tanner looked at the cart; the first shelf held the drill, a small circular saw, a beaker, the scalpel, the duct tape, and an empty glass dish. The lower shelf had an extension cord and what looked like a miniature rake with sharp, glinting razors. An old crust that looked like dried ketchup covered the saw blade. The drill mount had a hair of Levis fibers and blood.

Christ. He probably had only minutes before they figured out he was bullshitting. He first started thinking about what detail was the weakest. Then he sobered himself and focused on his options for escape.

He tried a full-body shimmy, throwing his hips up to inch the chair over to the cart, but the chair was too heavy. He tried to put all his might against the back of the chair. With his legs pushing down as if to flatten the earthen floor, he pushed his entire body against the seat back.

The seat creaked. Tanner rammed his frame backward.

The door opened, and Kyle briskly walked past him. He glimpsed a hypodermic needle in her hand. Tanner's eyes freaked, and his heart spasmed. He heard her heels on the ground behind him. He raged under the tape. "NOOOO!"

And then he felt a sharp prick in his shoulder. Before Kyle could cross back around in front of him, he lost consciousness.

Chapter 38

Seventeen repeated pictures of a window, with blue on the outside. The sound of a human engine. Not an engine—the hum of a voice box, a voice.

"Saaaaaa its," it said.

Tanner shook his head slowly, trying to find focus. A female face crystallized, like the horizontal and vertical chaos of a TV righting itself. A familiar face ... Kyle. She was busy with something in her lap.

"Save it," was what she had said. She was speaking condescendingly. "Need your strength later."

They sat across from each other on bench seats inside a van. Tanner's hands were connected with metal handcuffs, and he was laced around a pole connected to the ceiling and floor. A bump jolted the van and told Tanner he was eyes-open sleeping, watching his hands. His legs ... Tanner's eyes broke from their pasty sockets ... his legs were free. His most powerful engine.

The driver's section of the van was blocked by a divider, and the sliding portal was closed. Tanner licked his crusted lips. He had to try twice before he could correctly form words. "Where are we going?"

Kyle was busy with the project in her lap. "Where do you think?"

Tanner focused on her hands. She was fixing a syringe. Christ. Now what? If he slammed her, those up front would hear. At a new anger high, there was no telling what she would do with that syringe. And God knew what fucking shit they had up front. The image of the stained circular saw was still fresh in his muggy mind. "You don't need that."

Her head tilted to the side, her manner saying she was truly weighing what he said.

"I'm an athlete," he added. "You've probably fucked me from competition for a year already with whatever I'm riding on right now. I'll be good. Don't give me any more."

As his vision crystallized, he began inspecting himself. His fingers pinched his pants. He was now wearing blue surgeon's pants.

"You soiled your others," she said.

"Ah. How do your other boyfriends react to the needles and circular saws?"

"Cardiac arrest, mostly." She laughed. "This is sodium pentothal. It won't hurt you physically or ruin your chances at a gold."

Tanner sloppily wiped his soggy face with listless hands. "I've told you what I know."

"This isn't 100 percent foolproof, but it helps verify." She flicked her index finger against the syringe.

Tanner watched a drop of the solution fall to the floor of the van. "What did you do to Dreavor?"

She shook her head slightly. "I'm asking the questions here."

That did it. He knew he wasn't thinking clearly, but he concluded that he would take his chances—

The tires erupted in a hysterical scream on the concrete. The van lurched forward with a *whom!*—the sound of an iron garbage dumpster dropped from five stories. The van flipped ass over appetite and started sliding on its side. Kyle's entire body flew two full feet and collided with the divider. Tanner's cuffed wrists anchored him to the vertical pole.

When the mess stopped, Tanner's wrists and shoulders ached, but he was conscious and vertical. Kyle was slumped in a heap near Tanner's feet. Even though his world spun, he tore at the pole behind him. It had been bent in the collision. The pole popped out of its connection to the ceiling. Because he was standing on the side of the flipped van, it was simple to slip his cuffed hands off the tip of the pole.

Kyle had one hand on her head. She stirred and slowly rose up on her hands and knees. "H-h-help. You don't know ... uhh." She squeezed her head. "It's ... a ... pla—"

Tanner buried his Nike in her rib cage, launching her against the divider again. She slumped, eyes closed.

"Fair is foul," Tanner said as he madly rummaged through Kyle's suede jacket pockets. The only sound he heard from up front was a hiss—a steam hiss. One rear door lay open on the ground. The other swung on a broken hinge. Faint light from the cracked, yet still-lit taillight showed they were on a two-lane highway with no activity behind them. He pocketed her cell phone and then found a small ringlet of two short keys and jammed one into the handcuff lock.

Come on, goddamnit! One cuff clicked open, and then the next. He tightly cuffed one of Kyle's ankles and then brought her opposite wrist over her shoulder and connected the two. She looked like a Flamenco dancer caught in some strange position.

He noticed a tackle box lying in a corner of the upset van. He flipped it open. Inside, he found bottles, gauze pads, Band-Aids, syringes, empty plastic test tubes, and a flashlight. He grabbed the flashlight, shuffled to the rear door, and slipped out. The van lay across both lanes. The driver was slumped over the steering wheel, an imprint of his skull in the fractured windshield. A seatbelt restrained a passenger whose neck was bent at an unnatural angle. The front of the van was an accordion mess. Although it was nighttime dark, with the flashlight Tanner caught a prone moose flat on the pavement. Its moist nostrils dripped, and its eye was rolled back in its head. Pieces of one of its antlers lay separated.

227

He thought about pitching the handcuff keys into the woods, but instead he dropped them on the far side of the van.

Headlights broke over a ridge maybe a half of a mile behind them. Tanner was taking no chances. He crossed the road and launched himself into the woods. He popped open the phone as he bounced off tree trunks, hopped over roots, and ducked under branches. It was dark inside the woods. He checked his Swiss Army watch and the watchband compass.

North, keep going north.

Chapter 39

Kyle pushed herself upright. She sat on the side of the van and rested against the ceiling. Droplets of glass tinkled from her shoulders and her hair. She started to move her hand up to comb her hair, but it was caught on the cuff linked to her ankle. She looked across to the rear of the van.

Empty.

The pole from ceiling to floor lay bent and broken two-thirds of the way down. She turned slowly toward the front of the van. Through the divider window, open now, she saw the crooked neck of Jeff, the passenger. A navy blue bruise spread from underneath the skin at a ninety-degree bend in his neck. Michael the driver's head was frozen in the middle of the cracked, yet still together, windshield. One of them would have a set of keys for the cuffs.

The world seemed to move in slow motion. Someone or something pounded underneath her hair, and the van hadn't stopped spinning completely. She wasn't sure from exactly where the point of pain had initiated.

Between the thumpings in her head, her thoughts tried to assemble. He was gone—where would he go? What would he say to people? He must be rip-shit angry about Jimmy, how could he not be? And taking the old man … what had she been reduced to? She thought about her own parents. Why, why had they come here? She could not fail. She had to be the first to find it.

Chapter 40

He didn't know what to believe. It was one of the craziest phone calls he had ever received or even heard about. He had only met the caller once, and while he seemed rational, there was no lengthy context upon which to make any judgment. Nonetheless, he could hear the honest desperation. He had heard it several times over the years and had been burned by it on a couple of occasions.

His Jaguar cut through the night. The Dunkin' Donuts coffee cup was still steaming—he rarely went into battle on any important matter without caffeine. He checked over at the charged cell phone on the driver's seat. It had been ten minutes, maybe more since he had last seen headlights behind him. Was that strange? Worse case, state police were ten digits away. It wouldn't be long now.

He passed the billboard for The Alpine Race Track. Landmark number one. He reduced his speed to fifty mph. Desperation was fine, but he knew that this was the season of the wandering moose and deer. A collision with one of those brutes would ruin his night.

His headlights flashed momentarily on the "Scenic View One Mile" sign. His palms were wet and slippery on the steering wheel. The thought hit him to drive past the turnoff and eye it for trouble. He could always double back.

He did just that. His headlights showed barely anything of the turnoff, however, even when passing at a reduced speed. He didn't see any sign of another vehicle.

You're afraid of shadows now, is that it? One phone call and that's that? He spun the car in a U-turn and aimed for the turnoff.

He could hear the rattle and popping of gravel under his tires as he eased the car down the entrance path. He could smell his own coffee breath. The flat parking area, about eight cars worth, was deserted. As the Jaguar came to a stop, its front end pointed toward what amounted to a black gap, the valley, which during the day looked green and peaceful and treed for miles in three compass directions. At night, the space felt feathery and eerily quiet.

He cut his headlights and turned the car off. Slowly, as his eyes adjusted to the darkness, more of the valley's dimensions came into view. He sipped his now room-temperature coffee.

Tap tap tap.

He jumped within his seat. A hand slammed him down. He would've gurgled a cry, but his breath left him. No, there was no hand on him, just the seatbelt still locked in place.

Tap tap tap.

Professor Arbough let a load of tension fall from his chest; Tanner Cook smiled at him from the other side of the passenger window.

Chapter 41

Tanner asked Arbough to drive north, not tagging on a destination—just north.

"Mr. Cook, you don't look so good."

Why is he avoiding my first name? Tanner wondered.

Arbough nodded at a Dunkin Donuts bag at Tanner's feet. "There's a coffee and a French cruller in there for you."

Tanner attacked the bag like a raccoon.

"I can't tell for sure, but you look blue. Should we get you medical attention? I'm sure the university's clinic will have someone on call—"

"Thank you, but no." Tanner hoped his speed and certainty of answer communicated that Arbough's idea was a non-starter.

Over the next two minutes, Tanner gave Arbough a fuller picture of the night's events. As he did so, Tanner noticed Arbough looking in the rearview and side mirrors with increased frequency.

"I don't want to alarm you," Tanner said, "but even though I had the university transfer me to your home phone, I think I may have implicated you by virtue of using her cell phone. I'm sorry, but I didn't have anyone else to turn to. It would have taken too long to bring anybody else up to speed, and I'm not sure they would have believed me."

Arbough kept his eyes on the road. "Well, we can figure that out soon enough. When do we call the police?"

Tanner had been afraid of that question because he didn't know the answer. "Look, Professor, I know it'll take years for me to be able to repay you for coming all the way out here tonight. But I don't want to call the police yet."

"You think you're safer without their protection." It was more of a summation than a criticism.

"For now, yes. At least until I put some things together. I have to factor in that these lunatics have my brother somewhere."

"Okay. My assistant said he won't be heading out to his condo for another week."

Tanner nodded. The coffee cup jittered in his hand.

Arbough put his blinker on as they approached an exit for Morely. "I don't like to let the tank run past a quarter empty. Something my dad insisted on back home. I've kept up the tradition. We can probably find a washroom if you need it and some food."

"One more favor, Professor?"

"Yes?"

"Can I borrow your cell? I just have to make another phone call."

Arbough turned into a small town off the exit. The yellow sun of a Sunoco gas station sign half a mile ahead was the only source of light at that hour.

"Sure, I didn't use to carry one. Never felt that much urgency to call anybody. Of course, now, well, here you go." Arbough transferred his phone from his jacket pocket to Tanner and then popped out of the car to fuel it up.

Tanner had ditched Kyle's phone in the woods after his initial calls, one of which was to Rack. Right now, he needed to check back in with Rack. Tanner watched Arbough insert the fuel line. He heard Rack's voicemail kick in again. He left the same message: for Rack to meet him "where I chased down the VW with the Pamela Anderson look-alike." Only he and Rack knew where that was.

Tanner hung up and checked over his shoulder as the tank gauge blinked higher. Arbough worked the dispenser. Tanner fingered Arbough's cell. A Motorola. Who else could he call? He flipped it open. His thumb ran over the numbers. Unexplainably, he pushed the down arrow. A list of past calls. The most recent: Maine State Police ... one hour ago. That would have been just after Tanner called Arbough. He was trying to take Tanner to them.

Arbough angled the tip of the nozzle into its home in the fuel pump. The fuel cap still dangled against the side of his car. Suddenly, the Jaguar purred to life and then jumped forward. Arbough stood alone next to the fuel pump, too shocked to shout. He reached to his pants pocket for his cell phone ... which was speeding down the road inside his Jaguar.

Chapter 42

Rack walked into McDonald's wearing a Scotch-plaid bathrobe and moccasin slippers. "You weren't lying—you do look worse than me."

Tanner winced as he stood from his booth. He felt like meat that had been tenderized, and pain had started congealing in his bones. "We need to move." Tanner walked out the door through which Rack had just entered.

Rack followed. "You need a doctor?"

"I can't tell." Tanner moved to Rack's minivan in the parking lot. "We can worry about that later."

Rack started the minivan. "Not that I am, but are you hungry?"

Tanner looked over at him and then smiled. "You're not hungry?"

Rack turned onto the highway. "Nope."

"So, if I said, 'Let's use the drive-thru, I could use a Big Mac, you would sit quietly?"

"I would listen to the radio."

"Not even a pair of Happy Meals?"

"Not a fry. Well, maybe the Asian Fruit Salad."

"How much Scotch have you had?"

"T, what do you want to do?" Rack put his hands at ten and two o'clock on the wheel and looked over at Tanner. "My vote is a doctor, then the cops, in that order. What do you say?"

Tanner shook his head and let reality crawl back in.

"Dude, you look like hell."

Over the course of their relationship, Tanner could recall a few times when Rack had attempted severe sincerity. This was one. Tanner rubbed his face. "I feel like shit."

"Huh?"

"What?"

"You are shit."

Tanner rubbed his head. "Does that make you feel better?"

"It's a small start."

Tanner had taken back roads to get to the Ringsford McDonald's—roads he knew well from his training. Nonetheless, he kept an eye on the rearview mirror.

"What exactly did they say at Jimmy's home?" Rack asked.

"They said the men who came to take him had badges and said they were from the government."

"How fucking gullible are some people?"

"I slept with her."

Rack looked over at Tanner. "Yes, you did, didn't you."

"They also said they had a warrant. They offered to fax it to me. Not much help now, is it?" Tanner held his head in his hands. "Christ, what do we do now?"

"Go home. Enough's enou—"

"Are you drunk?"

"Probably."

"Haven't you heard anything I've told you?"

"Most of it."

"I can't go home! Those lunatics want to fucking kill me!"

"Okay, okay. I get it. So, let's go to the police."

"And where does that leave Jimmy?"

"With the police looking for him, which they aren't doing right now."

"I need sober Rack right now. Think you can dial him up for me?"

"Sober Rack hasn't been seen in these parts since his friend, selfish Tanner, stole his smokin' mamma from him and then didn't have the wherewithal to hold her down for long."

Tanner rubbed the sore spots on his wrists where the duct tape had torn away the hair. A map of Maine lay open across his lap. "I can't believe you."

"What do you want from me? I already suggested the cops. That's the right course, that's where everybody always goes wrong in these situations."

"What? Everybody?"

"You know, in movies."

"Are you comparing this to a movie?"

"They're always doing it on their own without the cops. And I'm always thinking how stupid they were to waltz into obvious danger."

Tanner closed his eyes. He always had to do the thinking for the two of them, and this time looked as though it would be no different. The countryside flew by. The side-view mirror was dark.

Rack upped the volume on the radio. "How about a little Tenacious D?"

Tanner shot up in his seat. "That's it!"

"Tenacious?"

"No, what you said. Going it alone. That's the only way out of this."

"Alone."

"Yes, yes."

"News flash, T. I don't do the thinking, remember? We don't listen to what I say."

"Look, the only way I can completely clear myself from this is to find the manuscripts and show them to the world. I don't know, donate half to a museum, show them I'm serious, and then use the remainder as an exchange for Jimmy and St. James."

Tanner was wondering what Rack thought of his plan. He checked over at him, and Rack had a content look on his face, watching the unfolding road and letting the music run its course.

When the song ended, Rack said, "Dreavor spent his whole life trying to find whatever it is, and we don't know that he ever found them. Now you're just going to walk out and then there they'll be. And you think that'll just stop everyone from pursuing you?"

"Yes."

"And maybe give you and Jimmy two tickets to Disneyland?"

"Maybe, if I ask nicely, I can get you into Sea World."

"Sherlock, you make me laugh."

"Look, we're already way ahead of where Dreavor started."

"I wouldn't want to get too far ahead. Remember, he finished dead."

In his head, Tanner couldn't think of any other way. He hadn't had the best experience trying to get the police to intervene with the Asian woman, and he truly did think that Kyle's network would find him if he engaged the sheriff's department.

Tanner slipped a pen out of the rubber bands that held it to the visor. "We know he was likely searching in a river at a depth that required scuba tanks. We've got a quote that I think ties him to the location."

"You mean the 'I came to bury Caesar' line?"

"Yep." Tanner fished a pad of paper out of the glove box.

"What else?" Rack appeared to be humoring Tanner, but Tanner didn't mind.

"Well. Hmm. Dreavor's body was found at the base of the Kennebec River, which skirts Heretsford Mountain."

"Okay, that's a nice coincidence, but it's a pretty big mountain. You're looking for some books buried in the dirt?"

Books. Tanner closed his eyes. He rested the pen on the pad, ready to jot down whatever came to him. His mind drifted to the collections of books he had seen recently. The library at the University of Maine. Mack's bookshelves. He envisioned Dreavor's house the first day he arrived there. Kyle's magnificent face and faded jeans were clear. Rack's drool from a slug of beer. The Spartan kitchen with the aged bubble refrigerator. The cabinets with their Campbell's soup cans. The dish rack with one spoon, one fork, and one knife. *One spoon, one fork, one knife.* The thin stairway to the second floor. The passionless bedroom. The covert study and its stacks of books. Like a python sneaking up on a mouse, his memory rose up and down those stacks, eyeing the titles, the thickness of each volume, the aged, yellow pages, and the nibbled corners. He slowed the image and began to count the books ... in each stack.

He began writing on the pad.

Still in his memory, he moved into the room to get an unobstructed view of each column of books. He continued counting ...

Rack leaned toward Tanner. "Don't flame out on me, buddy."

Tanner looked at the numbers he had written on the page. 13, 9, 12, 5, 19.

"What you got?" Rack tried to sneak a look from the road to Tanner's page.

"Numbers. Nothing much." Tanner looked at the numbers and thought about the quote, Dreavor, scuba tanks, the raw skin on his wrists ... a pain, like a door pushing out from inside his skull, pounded in his head.

Rack lifted an open beer from his cup holder and slugged it. "Feed it to me, brother,"

"Just a set of numbers. Not much repetition. Maybe I'm really lost here. Maybe you're right—we should go to the cops."

"Humor your buzzed driver. AAA recommends it."

"You mean AA."

"Both." Rack laughed deeply, like a dumpy hyena. "What are the numbers?"

Tanner read the list to Rack. For a moment, Tanner thought he smelled Kyle's perfume, or scent, whatever it was. Man, how quickly things had gone south.

His hands on the wheel, Rack shrugged his shoulders. "So, you could have a simple substitution series."

Tanner put the pad to the side and tilted his seat to the rear. "What are you talking about?"

"The first number, thirteen. 'M' is the thirteenth letter in the alphabet. Nine. 'I' is the ninth number in the alphabet. Get it?"

"So you think Dreavor not only arranged the columns of books in the shape of an 'F' and 'B,' but he stacked a specific number of books in each column, a number that corresponds to its place in the alphabet?" Tanner eased his eyes closed.

"Well, if you run through your numbers, biker-boy, you get m, i, l, e, s, w, e, s, and, let's see … t."

"Wonderfu …" Tanner started drifting into sleep.

Rack tossed his empty Molson can behind his seat. "'Miles west.' I mean, it's not perfect, but at least it spells something."

Tanner shoved his hands under his arms and scooched around in his seat to get more comfortable.

As Tanner faded into much-needed sleep, he heard Rack pop a fresh beer and talk aloud. "If only there were more stacks, we might know how many miles west, and from what."

Tanner's eyes sprang open. He shot forward as if his seat back was afire. "What did you say it translates to?"

The minivan jerked left as Rack ducked to avoid the blow he thought Tanner was going to deliver.

Tanner scrubbed his face with his hand. "Rack, you're a genius!"

He saluted himself with a fresh Molson. "Carbs."

"Sonofabitch. These are his breadcrumbs. I'll be damned."

"Earth to T. You *are* damned. We have no idea of how many miles west. Remember?"

Tanner sat back. "Okay, well, it's gotta be somewhere."

"Yes, well, maybe it's among the ashes of his former home."

Tanner closed his eyes and replayed his entire visit again.

Rack glanced over at Tanner and shook his head. "Man, you're gonna go into your trance again, aren't you?"

His eyes traced the stack of books up and down again. He announced without opening his eyes, "If you look down from the ceiling, the stacks outline the letters 'F' and 'B.'"

"Funny, I don't remember you on the ceiling."

"Two letters, two miles?"

"You're nuts." Rack shook his head.

With his eyes still closed, Tanner continued to replay his memory: Kyle's ass moving into the kitchen.

"Don't fall asleep on me, T. I don't want a repeat of Montreal." They had both fallen asleep on the trip home from a race, and the minivan had wound up as part of a yellow Crash Cushion water barrel safety barricade. No harm to them, but the minivan had seen better days.

Tanner opened his eyes. "You're right. I could use a cup of coffee."

"Yeah, okay, me too."

"Turn us around."

Rack lowered his beer. "What?"

Chapter 43

Rack fingered the saltshaker. "This isn't a good idea."

Tanner nodded and kept one eye on the front door. "We'll be quick. She'll cooperate." He wiped sweat from his upper lip. Tanner wasn't sure if he exactly knew what fear smelled like, but his three-day body odor couldn't be far off. If *they* came through the door, he would bolt through the rear exit. He could outrun them or die trying. Rack, on the other hand, he feared, was more in the "die trying" camp. He had given Rack the option of waiting in the van, but Rack wanted to see it all firsthand.

Rack ducked behind his menu. "Here she comes."

Betty Doyle crossed around the edge of their booth. "Help you—Oh, well, hello." Her face filled with recognition from sometime not too distant but then fell when she couldn't exactly place them.

Tanner spoke first. "Hiya, Betty. How've you been?"

Betty knuckled her hands on her hips and smiled deeply. "You know, pretty well, thanks for asking. Where's your friend, that little sweet potato?"

Rack smiled. "She dumped him for another skinny dude. Can you believe it?"

Betty laughed. "Shameful! What can I get you?"

"Actually, Betty, we're wondering about Frank Dreavor."

"That the dead man you chasin'?"

"He came here a lot, Betty. I'd guess at least every Friday for a number of years."

Betty shrugged her shoulders. "We get a lot of regular—"

Tanner held up a hand to stop her. "You waited on him, Betty."

Her smile leveled, wariness kicking in.

Tanner continued. "He didn't say much," Tanner said, "but little thoughts here and there added up over the years. In the end, you probably knew him better than anyone."

Her eyes faded, withdrawing to review something inside her.

"The last time you saw him. You remembered it the other night when we were here asking about him, didn't you?"

She didn't say anything.

"Did he give you anything, Betty?"

She shook her head.

"Betty, this entire … case …" Tanner sensed Rack's glance over at him. "This case has become much more serious in the past few days."

Betty's focus came back.

"He left something with you, Betty."

She checked across the other tables. Only one held a lone, round man, cutting away at his chicken dinner.

"Betty, please. For him."

"You're right," she said. "It was every Friday. I think he thought of it like his reward to himself, you know? Like the kid who saves his allowance for a new comic?"

Tanner watched her expectantly.

"He wouldn't ever say much. I'd always ask him how the week was. He always said fine. Maybe offer up something on the weather. Little stuff, you know?"

"Sure." Tanner nodded encouragement.

"He always seemed to me to be the loneliest guy. But he didn't mope. He just was alone."

"He was. There were no signs of anyone else in his house. And I haven't been able to turn up any link to family anywhere."

"The last few weeks, he was in less regular. He seemed tired, like he ... he was working hard or not sleeping or something." Betty took another look around the diner. "Then, the last night that I saw him, he put a fifty-dollar tip in my hand as he was shoving off for the night. He held my hand extra long and told me, 'Betty, you've always been here for me, you're the rock. No one has ever talked to me the way you do. I appreciate it. Take care.'"

"But you didn't ever really say anything out of the ordinary."

"Nothing 'cept 'How're you doing? How's work? How's the house?' I never saw him in the streets."

"You're the rock?" Rack asked.

"That's what he said," Betty answered and crossed her arms for punctuation.

"He never mailed you anything?" Tanner asked.

Betty shook her head.

"Ever call you or ask you to dinner?"

Betty smiled. "No. Never. Just a quiet customer."

"Why didn't you tell us this before?" Tanner asked.

Betty inserted her notepad in her apron. "I thought you were cops. Hell, I didn't know what the hell you wanted. Still don't."

"But now you're pretty convinced we're not cops?" Rack asked.

Betty answered in a tone imitating Tanner. "This case has become more serious. Nobody talks like that. Sorry. You guys clear now? You want to order?"

Tanner shook his head. "I really thought he left you something."

"Not a cocktail napkin?" Rack offered. "He scribble on a receipt or dollar bill?"

"Sorry, guys. He was just a good customer and a nice, quiet guy. I got to go." She pointed at Rack. "Fix the shakers, will ya."

Tanner looked over and saw that Rack had stacked the saltshaker on top of the pepper. They watched Betty pass into the kitchen.

Tanner's head swirled with ideas. Then a new one surfaced. "Shit." Tanner snapped his fingers.

Rack returned the shakers to their home. "I know, we should've ordered."

"Shit!" Tanner vaulted out of his seat, sped past the counter and through the kitchen's swinging door.

The chef was stirring freshly cracked eggs and a hunk of butter on a sizzling stovetop. Betty turned from stacking juice glasses in a cupboard. "Now what?"

"What is Betty short for?" Tanner asked.

"What—"

"Betty, your name—were you born Betty?"

Rack popped through the doors. "Jesus, T."

"No, I'm Elizabeth. My full name is Elizabeth. How does that—"

Tanner nodded and smiled. "Son of a bitch." He backed through the door. "Thanks, Betty. We'll be in touch."

Rack followed Tanner toward the rear entrance. "What was all that about?"

"Heretsford Mountain has a rock midway up." He pumped a fist. "It's called Elizabeth's Rock. If I had to guess, it was named by tourists some four hundred years ago. 'Betty, you're the rock.' How's about that for your starting point from which you go two miles west?"

Rack snagged Tanner's arm. "Wait, wait. How do you know there's a rock on Heretsford Mountain? And don't give me any of that horseshit of yours that this was all just a hunch."

Tanner tapped his forehead. "I studied a map of the area in the rest stop bathroom yesterday morning."

"You're an alien, is what you are. How did you know that Betty was worth talking to again?"

"Silverware."

"Silverware?"

Tanner stepped to the nearest table and picked up a spoon. "The silverware, the three pieces in Dreavor's kitchen. The same make as these. When we first sat down with Betty, she said he had never been in here before. She owns the place. It's a small town. I think she would remember him."

"You think she's lying now?"

Tanner shook his head. "There's only one way to find out."

Chapter 44

"How the hell did you know there would be no alarm?" Rack whispered in the dark. Then he fell forward, following his full weight over a low-rise bin of flippers.

"Now, why would he need one with you making all that noise?" Tanner asked. "I remembered noting there was no system when I was here two days ago."

They had chosen to leave the lights off even though Paul Knox's scuba shop had no immediate neighbors.

"What are you getting?"

"Just the basics. Tank, a regulator, a mask—Hey! Don't touch anything!"

Rack was trying to lift a harpoon rifle from its wall restraints, but the gun was additionally secured by fasteners attached to the rear of the gun. To Tanner, Rack's prying sounded like someone fishing through a tool box.

"All right, all right." Rack stepped away from the wall, navigating between two racks of life preservers.

Tanner clicked on his headlamp. "I can't see what these gauges say."

"This place remind you of my grandpa's store?"

"The Five & Dime? Not especially."

"I mean minus all of the sea stuff. You know, the haphazard approach to display, the challenge of walking from one end of the store to the next."

Tanner selected a tank from what looked like a long row of torpedoes. "I liked your grandad's store."

Rack squeezed the gloved hand of the *20,000 Leagues Under the Sea* underwater suit. "Me too. It served the family well." The faceplate squeaked when he opened it. "O-cah-Jesus!" Rack backed away, waving the air in front of his face. "Something sucks in there!"

Tanner walked over, and as he did, his headlamp fell on a patch of gray hair. Inching down, it lit the top of Knox's head inside the deep-sea suit.

"Oh, God."

Tanner covered his mouth and nose and peered inside the helmet. Knox's left eye socket resembled a scraped-out squash with its stringy flesh amidst globules of blood. Knox's skin had the pallor of blue cheese, which made the body look as though it had been emptied of blood and had been dead for some time—several hours at least.

Tanner tried to picture the final scene. Knox caught in duct tape, screaming like a motherfucker, thrashing and cursing at whoever was poking or torturing him. Who tore Knox's eye out? The Grocer? Kyle?

Tanner stared at Knox's various wounds. What kind of person delivered that? Who could stomach the pain, the cries that arose as blows were struck? How close had he come earlier to winding up like this? Who would grieve over him? What would become of Jimmy?

Jimmy. They had taken Jimmy. That thought sobered him.

Rack put up his hands as if to say, *enough.* "For Christ's sake, T! This shit is for the cops, okay! Shit! They really fucked this guy up."

"The term is 'killed,' genius."

"Don't get smart with me. I've been saying go to the police from the beginning."

Tanner hefted the scuba tank onto his shoulder. "Come on, we're outta here."

Rack wiped his shirt on the faceplate where he had touched it. "We've got to report this. You can't just leave him."

"Later."

"No, T. Now." Rack drew out his cell phone and punched 911.

Tanner snatched the phone and tore passed Rack. At this point, Tanner thought, the police would only slow him from finding Jimmy. Tanner himself would call the police soon enough, once he got to his next destination.

As he passed through the shop's exit, he heard Rack calling after him, "You can't leave the scene of a homicide, you stupid motherfucker!"

Tanner checked the bundle on his back, turned to Rack, and kept moving to the minivan. "Wait till you see where I'm heading next."

They sat parked in the minivan. Next to them on their right was a green 1971 Pontiac. Its left rear window was smashed, and glass was sprinkled across the back seat. Tanner and Rack thought it had been explored by desperate hikers or vandals … or worse.

Neither Rack nor Tanner had said anything meaningful to one another while leaving Knox's shop, during the entire trip to Heretsford Mountain, or while they searched Dreavor's car, which was empty except for a full door-handle ashtray in the rear seat, pistachio shells on the floor mat, and a tire iron, which Tanner took with him.

Rack threw his hands in the air. "So, what're you going to do, walk? With that sack on your back? And then just look under the Kennebec as if it's a mattress? It's a class five at points!"

"I don't need to excavate anything. I'm simply going to locate whatever crypt or cave I can find. St. James said there was a marker. I can trade the cavern's location for Jimmy. He's all I care about."

"What if you come across our friend with her saws and needles?"

"If I'm not back in two hours, call the cops. How many bars do you have?" Tanner nodded at Rack's cell phone resting in the minivan's cup holder.

"It works. I tested it while you were poking around the Pontiac. I've got the adapter for juice."

Tanner's mouth was dry. The pines outside were beginning to sway.

Was he really going to do this? Alone? The air and wind felt like a storm was arriving. It was close to one in the morning. Should he wait until sunup? Certainly this would be better in daylight. No, sitting around was not his nature. Plus, they had Jimmy, and St. James, for that matter. One thing was for certain—he would know more by daybreak.

"Why don't I come with you, at least part of the way."

Tanner knew Rack wouldn't get past the Pontiac without falling behind. He opened the van's door. "Thanks, but I need someone here to be ready to call in the cavalry."

"So, what, I'm Gunga Din now?"

"More Gunga than Din, I'd say."

"Don't shit on Gunga, he saved the day, man."

Tanner took a deep breath. "I trust your dad. He can execute my life insurance policy. If for some reason … do what you can to get Jimmy back."

Tanner shut the door and turned to the woods.

Chapter 45

Tuck. Tuck. Tanner heard the rain begin before he felt it. The labyrinth of branches above shielded him for the first minute of downpour, but once the storm gathered, even the pines' umbrella wasn't able to keep him dry. Within minutes, his pants felt as if they were pasted on his legs. The brim of his Red Sox cap dripped onto his watch as he verified he was heading northwest. It was close to 3:30 AM.

He kept himself on as direct a course as he could, which wasn't easy because there was no trail. He weaved in, around, and through the dense forest. The thirteenth time he wiped his face clean, he looked up to see the forest rise up to a tall shelf of rock. Elizabeth's Rock. The granite chunk stretched several car lengths in either direction. Trees grew up the sides, and a moss skin covered most of the lower face.

Right where you're supposed to be.

For a moment, the weight of his gear eased. Could this be happening? Tanner's arms lowered the bundle of equipment from his back. He needed light. Behind him through the downpour, the ghostly black shadows resembled nets and torn pantyhose. He hesitated with his finger on the power switch of the miner's light at his cap. The rain was too loud and the night too dark for him to be sure no one was following him. He felt so on edge, so tense, that a mere twig snap would have sent him sprinting. Yet, he'd match his foot speed against anyone.

He clicked on the light. Moss covered the rock like a rug—a lichen rug. The moss felt like crumb cake as it fell away from the rock face. At one time it may have attached itself to the rock, but someone had previously stripped it away and then taken care to place it back, like a throw blanket. Dreavor?

His fingers caught a crevice, and he traced the line with his index finger. The indentation bent into an arrowhead, an actual arrow chiseled into the rock.

Tanner hefted the tank bag onto his back and set off, his pace quickening. He had been hiking for an hour. His watch said 4:00 AM and that he was headed west. Two miles was all he needed to cover. Despite the darkness, the cold, the rain, and the rough terrain, he felt confident that he could cover two miles in thirty minutes. Had he been right to go it alone? Was he really alone out there? Where was Kyle? What about the Grocer? Was there any way they could be ahead of him? If not, were they close behind? God, if that were the case, he hoped Rack would see them coming.

As he stepped deeper into the woods, his energy soared. If his adrenaline was roaring and he'd only known about this gig for three days, what had the old man been thinking at this point? How the hell did Dreavor contain himself? The excitement alone must have nearly killed him.

He crunched over the pine needles and fallen leaves, and in twelve minutes he stopped at the river's edge. He shivered underneath his jacket. The current coughed up white water. The current was strong. Wasn't that what Dreavor had gone back to Knox's shop for help with? And Rack was right about that class-five roughness.

How the hell had Dreavor gotten down there? The drop was twice the distance from the swim club's diving board to the pool. Tanner lowered the tank and stripped off what he knew were sensible protectors of body warmth. He should've grabbed a wetsuit at Knox's.

"Just one more *should've*," Tanner said to himself to buoy his own morale. He cinched the tank harness up under his crotch and across his abdomen. When he was set, he slid on his side down the sharp incline to the river, digging the tire iron into the bank to secure himself on the way. He moved slowly to make sure he stayed vertical with the tank on his back. At the river's edge, he tested the water's temperature and thought he had singed his toes. But it wasn't heat that stung, it was the cold.

"Giddyup." He slipped himself in. Tanner's entire body shook as the cold slammed into him. The river was even colder than the pool in the lighthouse basement. *Christ! Christ! Christ, Bacon, what're you doing to me?*

Once underwater, Tanner stayed close to the edge, fearful of the strength of the current. He clenched the dog bone-sized regulator in his mouth, and the air *shushed*. Flippers would have been helpful too.

Tanner moved with speed in fear that the freezing water would quickly claim him. His hands scraped at the water's edge, prying through the sand and tugging at weeds. He jabbed the Pontiac's tire iron into the riverbed and its sloping walls. *It has to be there. Something has to be there!*

His tongue stuck to the regulator. He had the opportunity to scuba dive twice on a bike race trip to Greece about a year and a half ago. He knew the very basics. One of them said that the less you relax and the tenser you are, the quicker you use your oxygen supply. He knew he was drawing deeply on the air in his tank.

As he made his way along the riverbed, he thought about how the dimensions of the river had no doubt changed dramatically over four hundred years. Maybe the riverbed had grown thicker, with sediment piling up along its sides. Maybe it had worn in places from the river's friction. Regardless, his body was shaking like a cocktail mixer. Moving down the river was slow work. Tanner hugged the bed. He initially thought that he could easily handle the tank and the river, but the current nearly peeled him off the sidewalls and threw him into river's throat. Poking and scraping the riverbed was slow, arduous work. Twenty minutes felt like an hour.

He paused to check his regulator—seven minutes left. *Seven minutes!* His supply should've given him three times that. The current, the temperature, and his nerves were accelerating his breathing. Tanner tried to gauge how far he'd traveled, but the black jelly of the nighttime Kennebec had a visibility of two feet. He began to think about what he would need to do if he came up empty. Even if he found something, he would be near hypothermia once out of the water, with no dry clothes. He still needed to hike back to the car, which entailed somehow finding his path in the rainstorm without drawing attention to himself.

And then Jimmy popped into his mind. *Jimmy, God, how can I find Jimmy?*

His eyes were loaded down, his fingers felt like bloated sponges, and he told himself a short nap, a light snooze would refuel him. Wrapping his arms around himself and leaning against the riverbed, he settled into a nice, fuzzy, cozy blanket. *To sleep, perchance ...*

Pain! A needle hammer struck the back of his head. His gluey eyes opened, and he couldn't see. He was in water. He couldn't breathe. He thrashed, stripping his mask off, kicking in a rage, and thrusting himself up, but he was rolling, spinning as he shoved himself into the path of the current, into the teeth of the river. Tanner flagged his arms out to his sides and snagged a stick, a branch, a lifeline to shore. For a minute he caught his breath with his eyes closed, hanging onto what had to be the root system of a tree along the riverside. His entire body ached. It reminded him of a race he had ridden in Germany during an ice storm. Afterwards, in some condition resembling hypothermia, he had felt immobile and wrecked. This was much worse.

His hand still gripped his facemask. He put it on and dipped his face under to check the seal. Through the dark water, partially lit by his headlamp, he saw his scuba tank on the river bottom below his feet. *No*, he realized, and he blinked. He was still wearing his tank, still breathing from it. *What the …* Tanner trained his headlamp on the lone tank, and he saw the same bee-yellow, Yamaha-brand tank sitting on the riverbed. A small slope of silt rose up the tank. Tanner's frozen mind clicked into gear.

Dreavor! The missing tank!

Why here? Did he discard it? Tanner couldn't see attackers leaving behind such a large piece of evidence. Maybe like Tanner's, Dreavor's tank had run out. The old man didn't need to lug an empty can all the way back to his car. Tanner dove for the tank. He followed the gauge line and scraped the face of the gauge clear. It read … 400 PSI. A good ten minutes remaining—not quite unusable.

Maybe, like Tanner, the old man had just given up. The race had been run. His dreams unfulfilled. Had Dreavor simply unstrapped and let go the air, surrendered to the river? Like Tanner, he had little to return to, a future so uncertain, so …

But then Tanner thought about Dreavor and the images that filled his mental scrapbook of the man. The house, the lawn, a John Deere, the stacks of books … dozens of books with incalculable streams of calculations. Anyone who could withstand years of lonely drudgery, figuring, scribbling, recording, rejection, rinse and repeat—anyone with that stamina was not likely to pitch the whole effort, especially this close to the end. So how did the tank wind up here?

Tanner choked. His throat had turned to a dry cloth. His air was exhausted. He shoved upward, broke the surface, and spit out his regulator. The rain pricked the river faster and harder.

"Fuck you, Dreavor!"

He found his line of roots connected to the shore. Why did he leave the—wait, what if he left the tank here *on purpose*? Tanner fixed his mask and headlamp. He dropped into the water, swam down to the riverbed, and frantically poked and scraped the river's edge. *You left a marker, didn't you?*

His left hand clunked something. A rock. No, a brick. Up for air. Then, down again.

Tanner's light traced a flat masonry face, the bricks narrow and irregular. The rustled, sandy silt obscured clear visibility. He was looking through a brown dust storm, but Tanner could see engraved markings.

Christ! Oh, Christ!

On his next budget of air, Tanner dug around the bricks to try to uncover its dimensions. The frost in his fingers prevented him from easily distinguishing where the wall ended and the earth began. The brick face was long, wide, and deep. For the little reconnaissance he achieved, he needed to rise and dive several times. Soon, however, his adrenaline yielded to his low body temperature. The sensation in his hands was gone, his legs would barely respond, and his teeth rattled against one another. Time to get out ... way past time.

He tried to pull himself up using the tree's roots. His weight felt immense. Could scuba tanks weigh more empty? Was he that waterlogged? His shoulders were a knot, the muscles grinding on themselves. His breathing was labored, as if someone were sitting on his chest. He dropped in a heap back into the water, still holding the root rope.

Damn it! Uhloomp! His tank splashed as he dropped into the river. Tanner gathered his strength. *More legs, lower your center ...*

He cranked his frozen legs and tugged hand over hand, drawing himself up. He finally collapsed over the river's edge. In moments, Tanner awoke face down, rain pelting him. *Dreavor, you stupid shit, what've you done?*

He crawled on his hands and feet and rested against the rough trunk of a giant oak. The episode underwater came back to him. As he remembered it, the brick face was rectangular. Okay, what was behind it? Nothing? A possibility. A cave? Maybe. A grave? Maybe. How big could this thing be? The River Wrye expedition had uncovered a cavern the size of the oval office.

Thunder shook the sky and ground. Tanner was shivering, arms crisscrossed and hands tucked into his pits. He looked out at the river *slushing* downstream like a dangerous serpent.

If anything of any depth or dimension were behind the faceplate, then he was likely sitting on top of it. The faceplate was just below the tree, and the oak was ten feet from the water's edge. He crawled around to the far side of the tree. Tanner made his way over a ground covered with fat roots poking through the skin of the earth like the veins they truly were. He didn't know what he was trying to do. Somewhere in his mind he hoped that up there on shore there would be a connection to the faceplate in the riverbed.

This area of the forest was dense with trees, and with the slight visibility he had, Tanner could not detect any trace of a trail. He thought he saw a flash of light and looked over his shoulder. Was that an engine he heard … in the sky?

His frozen hands tilled the ground as he crawled. One good thing about the cold and his exhaustion was that he had grown numb to most sensation, including the pain in his injured thigh. He stayed in a straight line from the tree toward the forest. Rain spilled down his back and across his—

His hand fell into a hole and caught on something … something solid steel, an iron … long, thin "U" … a … handle. It was covered by a muddy puddle of slop, leaves, and pine needles. He tugged at it, but nothing gave.

He stood and wiped, scraped, and pushed, searching for a hinge or an indication of what he was holding. With the handle between his feet, he planted himself and lifted, pushing with his powerful legs, leaning backward, and pulling with every fiber in his quaking arms. His raw fingers burned against the rusted loop. A slab of stone lifted. Muck dripped from its edges.

Tanner stumbled backward as the hatch fell open and thudded on the wet ground. He felt the thud through his sneakers. For a few seconds, he just stared at the opening.

God, did I find this?

The hole was deep, whatever it was. A thick, red cord was tied around the hatch hinges. The red line dropped into the opening. Shivering and hunched over like the bell ringer at Notre Dame, Tanner pulled the rope all the way up, about thirty feet of it. *Thirty feet!*

The rope was knotted at intervals of four feet. Tanner looked all around him. Between the night and the density of trees, he saw no other life. The roar of the raging river and winds deafened him to anything else. He secured his miner's lamp and dropped the line. Exhaling whatever warmth he could into his hands, he started down.

When his body was fully in the shaft, the air grew quieter. He squeezed the rope tightly with both his hands and his feet, all of which were still partially numb. His light showed a sizable room, maybe twenty by twenty. On one end was a table, and on the other … a coffin. Tanner's blood chilled, an accomplishment given his body temperature. And from somewhere … maybe the howls of the storm, Shakespeare's Mark Antony spoke:

> *Friends, Romans, countrymen, lend me your ears;*
> *I come to bury Caesar, not praise him.*
> *The evil that men do lives after them;*
> *The good is oft interred with their bones!*

He looked up the line into the even darker hole in the ceiling. A scattering of raindrops and puddle spillage fell on him. He thought about going back up, but he doubted he had the strength. So, he continued climbing down the line.

When he dropped to the ground, his feet stung, and he rolled over on his side. The ground was a dirt floor. He rose to a squat to more closely inspect it.

The walls and ceiling were constructed of a laced series of thick wooden beams, and heavy, intricate brickwork peeked through between them. To his right, upright against the wall, stood the old coffin. To his left were three deteriorated chests, footlocker size, and an iron table of glass beakers fixed in specially designed holders. Some beakers were corked and others capped. One row contained a grayish-green liquid, another brown. An amorphous lump of goo floated inside each beaker. Standing in a row next to the beakers were six black deck cannons like the ones in the museum.

An iron stick, a lever perhaps, protruded from the earthen wall itself, the wall that braced against the river. The wooden chests had caved, and just the iron braces remained. Amidst the wreckage, leather bindings were cast about like corroded roast beef, rolled up on themselves. Only Triscuit-sized bits of parchment remained. On the wall next to the coffin, crude wooden shelves bore stacks of still-healthy papers.

The upright coffin was laced with rows and rows of iron plates, and then the same type of iron strips crisscrossed in vertical columns. A knee-high bin beside the coffin held molded walking sticks, some with decorative handles of horse heads, boar heads, and flowers.

Tanner continued to shiver, and he buried his hands under his arms. From the depth of the hole, Tanner figured he was below the river level. He squeezed himself so tightly he resembled a wet towel spun around itself to wring it out. Like a woman in tight, long dress, he took short steps over to the coffin. It was shorter than more recent models. As he was about to turn to the far side of the room, his lamplight caught a small fleck of paper, a card, wedged into one of the coffin's braces. Tanner's shivering hand snatched the card. In the headlamp's light, Tanner smiled as he read it. It was a Class-IV license to operate maintenance vehicles issued by the department of motor vehicles for the state of Maine. In the miniature photo in the lower left corner smiled Frank Dreavor.

You captured the flag, old man, didn't you?

The storm winds and rain formed a conch shell howl through the ceiling opening. Above all of that, he heard a human voice, small and very distant. Then, other tiny voices. Although small, he thought they were shouting. Through the drips coming down more steadily, he saw flashes of light beams, albeit faint, slashing in one direction, then another. He had not minutes but seconds before someone arrived.

Tanner snatched up a walking stick from the bin and began inspecting the chamber more closely. An object that looked like an accordion. What was once a series of stuffed birds now looked as if they'd collided with a plane engine. A violin, warped and cracked, hardly recognizable. An old coat rack with tatters and a collection of buttons sprinkled at its feet. The beakers on the iron table full of foul, filthy liquids.

Something made him turn around. The walking stick dropped from his hand. Except for his shivering, he stood motionless. Kyle Murray hung midway down the knotted rope.

Chapter 46

She wore a black vinyl suit with tape securing the suit to her gloves and boots. She looked up to the hole, held up her hand, and then made a fist. Then she turned back to Tanner.

"We don't want you, Tanner. You're free to go." She dismissed him with a wave of her chin.

"B-b-bullshit!" His jaw was nearly frozen. The circular saw revved in his mind. Now that they had the chamber, they didn't need him.

"Tanner, listen to me. Somewhere in this room is a strain of the plague."

The plague? *The plague!*

"We want to extract you safely," she said. "I work with the NSA."

Of fucking course! *That* would rustle international resources. *That* would command highly trained professionals. Dreavor didn't stand a fucking chance. Plague. It fit. Bacon, the scientist, the law student whose study at Oxford was postponed by an outbreak, the chancellor who ruled when a variety of outbreaks occurred throughout the kingdom. Tanner's mind cycled through tallies of plague victims during Bacon's lifetime: in the year 1563—20,000 dead from the plague; in 1578—6,000 dead; 1582—7,000 dead; 1593—18,000 dead; 1603—34,000 dead; 1625—50,000 dead.

The very pissed-off son of the queen who was rejected time and again, who had to struggle for every little accoutrement he ever got. The bankrupt and banished felon. It fit.

Kyle held her position on the rope. "We don't want you to get hurt."

Tanner shouted over the howling winds from above. "Y-y-you expect me to believe that shit?" *How to get out?* Tanner's mind was twisting and racing through turnstiles. He backed up, arms still wrapped around himself. *Clink, t-clink.* He had backed into the table with the beakers and tarred cannons. He checked Kyle, and she was fascinated. He snatched a beaker from the rack and held it over his head.

"Tanner!"

"That's enough." He held a stop-sign hand in front of him.

Her eyes popped. "What are you doing?"

His shivering heightened. "B-b-back. Y-y-your suit can't protect you against this."

"Don't be a fool, Tanner! Think it through—you know it makes sense. I'll help you up this rope and back to your van. We followed you. We know where you and Rack parked."

"F-f-fuck off." His eyes flicked left and right. Tanner saw the rain puddle on the floor. And the idea arrived. *The lever in the wall.* With his free hand he grabbed the lever, not sure what it would do.

"We were supposed to have scared you off long ago, but you're different. We found a collapsed cavern under the river a mile upstream. Our guys didn't know this alternate existed."

"Th-they spend t-t-too much time with chain saws."

"Forget that, will you!"

"Somehow I c-c-can't."

"Are you crazy? There are a series of towns along the lower reaches of this river. The DNA on the bones we found at the bottom of the harbor showed remnants of the plague. Is that what you want, to spread a plague throughout New England?"

"P-p-plague and madness! *Troilus and Cre-ssssida!*"

"You want to take Jimmy with you?"

"So th-th-this is why you were so s-s-shocked to learn your parents were over in New Hampshire."

That thought tripped her. Just for a moment. She soon shook clear. "That threatened torture was just a ruse to get you to talk. We wouldn't have done anything serious. We needed to know where this chamber was. You think we wouldn't try everything in the book to get you to tell us?"

Tanner shook. He felt as if he were standing on top of a train at high speed. "Go to hell."

Kyle softened. "Tanner, please put the beaker down and move away from the wall. I'll radio up there. Take whatever papers you want. Rack's out there somewhere. Jimmy is with us. He's safe. Let us secure this room."

Tanner's brain was rattling in his skull. Could he trust her? Even in her suit, she was still a vision, honey poured into vinyl.

The minivan. A short hike. Then he could be inside with the heat cranked, driving back home to the thick, plaid comforter in his bedroom. He counted: five knots to climb to the opening in the roof.

"Wh-wh-why—"

"We can't have a plague outbreak in the US, Tanner. It's that simple."

"Wh-wh-why didn't y-you tell me?"

Kyle tightened her hands on the rope and she glanced up to the opening.

"You won't believe me if—"

He shook his head. "N-n-not good enough." His arm waved unsteadily, holding the beaker.

"Tanner, you traveled extensively over the past two years. We placed extremists in each of the foreign cities where you raced at the same time you were in those cities."

Tanner's heart sunk. Could they know? Tanner's mind flashed visions from his most recent race across Spain. Photos of men he befriended, twisted men and memories of the favors they asked of him. "Ku-kuh-coincidence." Tanner's vision was fading, and his eyes narrowed.

"Tanner, give me the glass."

He snapped backward, stiff but shaking. Kyle froze. Bracing herself with the rope around her forearm and her feet on a knot, she thrust her hands out disarmingly.

"It seems ludicrous now, I know, I know. But it's a colder world now, Tanner."

"C-c-cold, alright." He forced a smile. "Give me your g-g-gun and get up the rope."

Kyle's expression dropped; she hadn't expected that one. She checked up the rope, as if she were expecting something.

"For all I know, Jimmy is dead. You think I give a shit about this world without him? I should take you out with me right now!" His hand squeezed the beaker, and the veins on his forearm stood up.

She shouted from the rope. "Jimmy's fine! That was just another bluff to get you to talk! We had to protect him from the Koreans!"

Tanner blinked.

"That's right. You were right. They were trailing you and Dreavor. His death was no accident. They were on to Bacon before we were."

Popping noises like bursting balloons sounded from above outside the hole.

Kyle looked up at the hole and then quickly back to the beaker in Tanner's hand. "Tanner, please—trust me."

He shook his head and leaned back into the wall for support. "When ... I-I mean, you ..." he began. He wiped his forearm across his forehead. "Back away. I'll leave, I'll walk away."

Distant shouts were only partly drowned by roaring winds. Kyle swiped a hand behind her back and produced a black pistol. She tossed it toward Tanner's feet. "The safety's on."

He slid down the wall to his butt. He picked up the pistol. "Up." He waved his chin at the rope.

She reached over her head at the next knot. Her tone dropped somberly. "Can you do it?"

Tanner nodded and waved the sealed beaker at the ceiling. She gave him a final look and then rose into her own strength and began shimmying up the line.

Choom! Choom!

Gunshots exploded just outside the entrance. Tanner bolted upright. Kyle was two knots from the opening. Suddenly, a female face wearing goggles popped into the opening; gunshots lit the sky behind her head. She thrust a fat handgun into the hole. When Kyle looked up, her headlamp flashed into the woman's long goggle lenses. The woman grunted and her gun roared.

Kyle's shoulder tore backward as if she were yanked from behind. She dropped ten feet, and, leading with her left arm, crashed through the remains of a sea chest, blacking out her headlight. Goggles turned her pistol at Tanner and fired. Tanner spun to the side, collapsing on the lever, which clanked down.

A square block of the earthen wall fell inward. In the scant ray of his headlamp, Tanner watched as a battering ram of foaming river slammed into the room. The hole in the wall quickly expanded. A colossal wave tore into the chamber, upending the workbench and the cabinet, launching Tanner and Kyle, and even tossing the coffin.

Tanner's vision spun. The cold glaze swallowed him. He felt his body bounce and roll off of larger, stronger masses, but he couldn't see anything. He felt … fast. He tried to stop, to control, but nothing responded. He couldn't tell which direction he could go to open his mouth safely. His lungs pinched.

Granite crashed into his side. The last teaspoon of air burped from his lips. His eyes strained in their sockets. He allowed his body to drift up with the bubbles that vanished quickly in the ray of his headlamp, which was now gripped in his hand.

Tanner surrendered, and water rushed into his mouth. But fresh air filled his nose. He had broken the river's surface just as he caved. A subway train of water pinned him against a collapsed tree. A wave formed a hollow over his head and deafened him. The torrent jammed the space around his head. He was too exhausted to hold himself above water on the moss-covered trunk. He couldn't spit the water out fast enough.

He inched out across the log with his elbows and pushed himself into the main stream. His limbs sank. He rolled on to his back, and monster raindrops pelted him. *Is this how it ends?* He let his body succumb, and the water rose over his ears and face.

Then a claw tore at him. A rake of five fingers scraped across his chin and nose and dug into his hair. The grip snapped his head up out of the water. Another pinch under his armpit, and he rose up out of the water. Tanner felt a hot scrape from his right ribs to his lap as he rose up onto a rock.

A low voice with a forced southern accent greeted him. "Mmm, you gonna ... squeal like a pig ... for me?"

Tanner rested face down across the rock. Rain slapped at him. The river roared on both sides, but he was still. In the blur of his lamplight, rain dripped from a familiar face.

Rack. "Sure do have a purty mouth."

Tanner coughed. "T-t-toss ... me back."

"Yeah, missed you too." Rack resembled an antelope fresh from a bath. He scanned the forest. "I'm freezing my nuts off."

"Not m-m-m-me."

"This place is whacked tonight."

"Oh, I d-d-don't know." Tanner had gone fetal, shivering like a stripped homeless man on a sidewalk in the winter.

Rack pulled Tanner up by his arms. "Can you stand?"

"I can swim."

"Dude, you're dead if we don't get you warm."

Tanner coughed as if allergic to oxygen. He put a quivering hand up behind him to tell Rack to wait.

Rack wiped his soaked face. "What?"

Suddenly, Tanner lurched headfirst off the rock and plunged into the river.

267

Chapter 47

Rack leaped and snagged Tanner's right ankle, gripping it with both hands. "You miserable fuck."

Tanner was submerged to his waist in the black snake, whitewater slamming against his trunk. Rack angled his entire weight backward, and his body shook, a contestant in the strongman competition—the Mack Truck pull.

Tanner's body jerked like a fishing line. Rack's front foot slipped on the slick rock face, and his fall to a knee saved him from crashing into the river. "Ahhh!" Adrenaline from the fright of falling injected a surge in Rack's thick arms, and he fell back, bringing Tanner up and onto the rock. A bucket of black water rocketed out of Tanner's mouth. His left hand was locked around another arm, an arm in a wetsuit. Rack backpedaled, his sneaker squeaking on the rock. More of the wetsuit became revealed ... a female wetsuit.

Kyle.

When her face cleared the water, Tanner collapsed flat. Rack sat on his haunches like a dog too exercised in the park. He managed a commentary between heaving breaths. "Throw ... that ... fucking trash ... back."

In seconds, Tanner was bent over Kyle, feeding her mouth-to-mouth.

"Let me have a shot," Rack said over Tanner's shoulder.

A child's cough, then deeper and ... then a gurgle and vomit. Kyle's body rolled onto her chest. Tanner flopped onto his back, coughing along with Kyle.

Rack threw his hands at Tanner. "Great, you're the big hero again. Let's go—I'm out of here." On his back, Tanner coughed. Rack snagged Kyle's wrists and dragged her off the rock toward shore. She was still coughing spit. The rain's shower blasted them.

Rack mumbled, "Fucking place sucks," as he crossed a series of scattered rocks to put himself back on shore. In a minute, he was back for Tanner. As he got Tanner vertical and wrapped across his shoulder, Rack asked if they should leave Kyle there and go on to the car.

"Yeah," Tanner added, "fuck her."

Rack led him over the rocks. "You were blind, but you're coming round."

Chapter 48

White snot sputtered out of Rack's nose. His labored breathing almost drowned out the rain. Tanner's eyes rolled back and then dropped shut. His left arm was draped over Rack's neck. Tanner's legs jellied, and his bodyweight yanked Rack down.

"Get up, you stupid shit!" Rack hissed. "They're coming."

"Go ..." Tanner's hands sunk into a salad of pine needles and leaves. "Find Jimmy."

Rack hauled Tanner to his feet and then pried open Tanner's hand and removed the headlamp. The skinny ray seemed like a candle flicker in the forest's hood of darkness. Tanner's eye's fluttered. Through the grunts of the winds, through his own hacking breaths and hissing rain, he heard them again.

"Dogs!" Rack said. "Jesus Christ!"

Tanner froze. The growls were getting closer.

A step ahead, Rack parted a web of branches. Tanner held two weak arms up in front of him as he ducked and twisted through the swipes of the pines, maples, and rogue vines.

Rack narrated as he led the way. "We are lost in some thick shit."

Tanner paused to navigate using the luminescence of his compass watch. "R-r-read this f-f-for me."

"Stop shivering, and maybe I can."

Then they heard it more clearly—a collection of spastic barking. Tanner squinted into the forest behind them. "Oh, hell. They let slip the d-d-dogs."

"Any chance they're puppies?"

Tanner's head was spinning. "I got nothing left." A distant, angry bark cut through the rain. *Something wicked this way comes.* Tanner laughed and winced. "Maybe they'll prefer juicy steak to bony meat."

Rack put his foot through a five-foot tree branch. He handed a split piece to Tanner and kept the other section. The splintered ends were sharp. "I don't suppose you can conjure a detailed map in your memory bank."

Tanner shook his saturated head. "How f-f-far downriver … was I?"

"Half a mile, tops." Rack slid his shoulder under Tanner's armpit.

"Let's m-m-move."

Growls were growing louder, but they were no more directionally distinguishable. "This is like walking in a dark closet."

"Y-y-you do that a lot?" Tanner asked.

"Fuck you."

"Oh, we're f-f-fucked all r-r-right."

Tanner thought he could feel the growls. "Sounds like there's more than one." They parted, and Tanner shifted so his back was to Rack. Then each cocked his tree limb as if they were stepping up to the plate.

Rack tensed. "What do you think the odds are that they're just wild coyotes?"

Tanner didn't answer.

"Maybe we should scale a tree?" Rack suggested.

"B-b-behind us." Tanner shifted to swing at anything that would attack from the rear.

"Who am I kidding? Not like I've got the body for climbing—"

A soaked hound broke into their path ten feet from Rack.

"Rack!"

The hound leaped—an explosion of teeth and muscle.

Rack swung. His tree limb connected with the side of the dog's head and spun it into the dirt.

Another hound leaped from the woods beside them. Tanner stepped up and met the hound with the jagged point of his branch, spearing the dog in midair. Tanner drove with his legs, finally flipping the raging dog backward into the tree line.

Rack stepped up and brought his limb down on the dazed first hound. Tanner's dog scrambled to its feet and backed into the forest. It barked so fast and furiously, it resembled a fast-rewind version of itself. Rack smashed his stick down again on the first dog, now rolling slowly in the dirt.

Klapchow!

A gunshot! Rack and Tanner spun to face it.

Kyle dropped to all fours in a mist of her own heavy breathing and the smoke of a small pistol. Another large dog lay on its side near her. She coughed. "You have to find her."

Tanner bent over to catch his breath. "What? Who?"

"The ... Korean. Don't let her get a ... get a sample."

Rack stepped closer. "Sample? Sample what?"

Kyle folded. Her chest and face slapped the ground. The top tip of her shoulder was ripped and bleeding. Tanner knelt down and checked her pulse. Definitely one there. He grabbed her gun.

"Korean?" Rack cinched up his pants. "Let's get out of here."

Tanner looked toward the direction of the river. Maybe Kyle was for real. What if she were? The plague? Running through Maine? Jimmy ... Tanner felt a new surge. "I c-c-can't explain." Tanner ran back the way they had come.

"Wait! Wait! You dumb—"

Tanner's legs felt like frozen plastic. Behind him, he could hear Rack's labored breathing and tree-branch swatting. In minutes, Tanner was back at the riverside. He scampered along the embankment, upriver, moving as fast as he could with his arms intermittently wrapped around himself for warmth. He pulled farther and farther away from Rack.

He recognized the slope and slowed. He tiptoed forward, but it was getting harder for him to control the shivering in his limbs. He stepped from between two trees.

A man knelt over the open entrance to the crypt. To Tanner it looked as though he were adjusting the red cord into the hole.

Tanner leveled Kyle's pistol at the man. "Step away." The man spun, fast like a squirrel, and in a flash his arm was extended with a gun aimed at Tanner.

Suddenly, an object flipped over the crypt entrance and thumped on the ground next to the man—a sealed deck cannon. Then two hands flapped on the side of the hole, followed by forearms, and then the Grocer popped her head out of the flooded crypt. She unstrapped a snorkel and mask from her head and let them flop to the ground. As she wiped dripping hair from her eyes, she digested the fifteen-yard standoff between Tanner and her associate.

"Good evening, Mr. Cook."

She pushed herself up and flipped out of the entrance like a gymnast, tumbling. Tanner tensed and stiffened his arm, edging his barrel's focus between the two. She was nude. Older, yet fit—chiseled, in fact.

"Relax, Mr. Cook," the man said with an accent that was similar to the woman's.

Tanner nodded at the cannon. "Leave that, and g-g-get out of here. C-c-cross into Canada. You can disappear there."

"We will not do that," the man said. "I will shoot you if you do not lower your weapon."

He said it as if he has rank here. "Too many people live in this area for me to let you go anywhere with that."

"I will dress." The Grocer bent down to the duffel bag, unzipped it, and withdrew several items, focused on her clothing.

Tanner's gun quivered with his frozen arm. He found it hard to put words between his chattering teeth. "I-I-I have a brother."

"We know," the man said.

"Then you know he can't take care of himself."

The man smiled. "The state will do that."

"The state will s-s-store him, n-n-not care for him."

"You don't give the state enough credit."

The Grocer had slipped on pants and a top.

"This ends n-n-now. I d-d-don't care about you."

"As we saw in Spain, your ambivalence is not trustworthy."

"*My ambivalence?*" *How the hell does he know about Spain?*

The man stood. He did so quickly, as if he had levitated to his feet. "Feigned innocence does not suit you, Mr. Cook."

Tanner's gun jiggled in his hand as if he were balancing on a vibrating high wire. "I can't stand much longer. But I'll shoot before I drop."

The Grocer was dressed and folded her arms across her chest.

"Let me think about it," the man said. His arm was arrow straight.

The Grocer bent again to her duffel. A painful cramp shot down Tanner's arm as if someone had inserted a long slice of cracked glass from his shoulder to his elbow. "W-w-what will you do w-w-with—"

"Study it."

Tanner didn't believe him. "Is it still active?"

"This we will examine."

"I don't think so."

"Do not think so much, Mr. Coo—"

The Grocer swung the cannon down on the man's skull. It connected with the sound a broom clapping a rug. He fell forward, unnaturally failing to brace himself for a collision between the ground and his face.

Tanner gasped. He swung his gun toward the woman. He had never heard a skull crushed before and hoped he never heard it again.

She looked him in the eyes. "I have a sister. For years they've threatened to harm her if I fail. Perhaps if they think I'm dead, this all ends." She bent over and picked up an object next to her duffel. A book. She tossed it to the ground next to Tanner: *Romeo and Juliet.*

"Good night 'til it be morrow," she said with her characteristic Korean trill. Then she sprinted to the embankment edge and leaped into the roaring river, her arms spinning, splashing in a ball of foam whose sound was drowned by the river's roar.

Tanner's eyes closed, and he collapsed.

Chapter 49

Tanner's world shook. He needed to concentrate to keep his eyes open. Rack had a hand on his shoulder, shaking him awake.

"Dude, you look bad. I think you're purple. It's too dark to tell for sure." Tanner scrunched in a fetal curl against a tree. Rack crouched next to him. "T, I've still got some go left in me. You're gonna die if we don't get some warmth soon."

"N-n-not gonna m-m-make out with you."

"No, I'm going to find us a ride."

Tanner nodded. "M-m-my k-k-kingdom for a h-h-horse."

"If I'm not back in a couple of hours, turn the light off."

Tanner passed out.

Chapter 50

Tanner opened his eyes. His vision vibrated, and not solely from his shivering. His head ached, his skin burned, and he was sweating all over. But he was inside ... somewhere. The ground shook.

"You having a good night, sweet prince?"

It was Rack. Tanner rotated his view. From his back, he watched an orange and blue logo shake. He was in the back of a delivery truck, sprawled on top of a heap of large packages.

"When you absolutely, positively need a ride in the middle of the night," Rack cackled from the passenger seat.

FedEx. Tanner stared at the stacks of FedEx packages in the space near him. He was covered in ratty moving blankets. It wasn't hard to imagine how Rack flagged down this ride, but it was easier to close his eyes.

Chapter 51

The pines clicked by. He was in the hollow of his zone and had the road to himself. He eyed his heart monitor, and a comfortable heart rate smiled back at him.

He was crushing his average time, and he felt it from his toes through his shoulders and in the handlebars. Seven months ago, he had lain with his sweaty back stuck to hospital sheets for two weeks after that night on Heretsford Mountain. Hypothermia, exhaustion, dehydration—all the "shuns," as his doctor referred to them. But Tanner bounced. Over the course of five weeks, they had pumped the hospital's supply of IVs into him, including antibiotics, vitamins, sugars, liquids, and a Thanksgiving-night meal. Soon afterwards, Tanner was discharged, and within hours of getting home, he was watching CNN from his stationary bike.

Now, he was pushing strong times around the back roads of Maine. Along the way, he had decided to make a bid for a national team. Rack and Tanner worked together again. They didn't have much of an opportunity to dwell on that night on the mountain, though Tanner knew he owed Rack his life, and Rack knew he knew it. In what was a similar move toward long-term progress, Rack was taking an accounting class at UMaine at night. He sped off every weeknight, racing to zip through the McDonald's drive-thru with a large coffee and a Big Mac ... or two.

Just after Tanner emerged from the hospital, a room opened in St. Pius X, a Catholic Church-supported institution situated in an old monastery one hour north of Tanner's apartment. Tanner jumped at the opportunity for Jimmy to be closer to him.

Two days a week, he and Rack took Jimmy along for Tanner's run. Jimmy sat in the passenger seat with the window rolled down, Neil Diamond blasting, and a quarter pounder with cheese on his lap. Jimmy never stopped smiling.

On one such spring morning, Rack's familiar observations came through Tanner's helmet. "Watch your beats, T."

"Yeah, watch your beats," Jimmy echoed.

"I'm watching ... but I feel good." Tanner grouped his words in short bursts. He knew he had a fairly flat stretch for another mile or so, and much of the road was shaded by tall pine cover. In many ways, the next two miles felt like riding through an old covered bridge, those for which only New England was famous. The wind felt sensational, like a nice, cool massage, bathing his muscles and keeping them from fatigue. He leaned left and dipped into a hard curve.

He didn't see the car until it was almost too late. An SUV. Gray. Parked across the road, blocking his path, anyone's path. He squeezed the brakes. The tires sizzled against the road, the crushed rubber smoked, and the rear wheel swung out perpendicular.

Toke! The rear tire burst under the pressure. Tanner stopped within a foot of broadsiding the car.

"Shit!"

His earphones crackled. "What is it? Your heart rate—"

"Someone broke down and is spread across the road!"

"Jesus, are you okay?"

"Popped the rear in the skid."

"Shit."

Tanner dismounted, letting his bike fall and unsnapping his helmet. He marched around the front of the car. And froze.

She leaned against a tree, hands in the pockets of her jeans.

"You trying to kill me?" Tanner shouted. *"Again?"*

"Relax, I knew you could handle it," Kyle Murray said.

"You owe me a tire!"

"Uh huh." She stepped from the tree and pointed at his Jack Daniels T-shirt. "They your latest sponsor?"

She slid behind the wheel and started her Explorer. The driver's window came down. "Put your bike in the back."

"Fuck off."

"Relax. Your times are good. You're in fine shape." She threw a thumb over her shoulder. "Put your bike in the back, already."

Tanner slammed his heel into the front-right signal light, cracking the cover. "Drop dead."

"Tanner!" She jacked open her door.

He removed his spare tire from under his seat. She slammed her door and spun around the front of her car. "Look, I'm sorry you got caught up in all of that." Her hair was much shorter. "I have a job."

"I used to."

"That wasn't a job—you were a janitor for the dead."

"Yeah, well, all the liar and deceiver jobs were taken."

"Can't you see yet that the role is all part of it? Do you see how close we came to losing something so serious?"

"Imagine how much easier things would have been if you had only told the truth."

Kyle smiled and laughed.

"I'm glad you think this is so fucking funny."

"I'm not laughing at you. But don't pretend to be mad at the fact that I wasn't telling you the truth. You didn't mind the role-play when we were together late-night. You didn't seem to mind when I was feeding you bits of the puzzle."

"Oh, yeah, you're right. How could I be upset at all?" Tanner unclipped his tire pump. "We're square. Carry on."

Kyle jabbed her finger at the space near him. "Okay, rewind. I tell you off the bat who I am. How quickly do you think you would've deferred looking for an answer? If I told you that the plague was involved, how many seconds do you think it would've taken for you to drop it?"

Despite himself, Tanner thought about her words.

"Accept it, Cook, what did I have to go on? You took one blow to the thigh, and you pouted your way out of competition permanently."

"She's got you there, buddy," Rack needled him over the ear set.

Tanner clicked off his transmission and whipped his helmet off. "Ah, yeah, sure. Nice tactic. Where the plague and highly communicable diseases are involved, hide the truth to force participation." Tanner hooked up the pump to his tire. "You're right, I respect that."

"Look, I needed your help."

The tire was taking shape. "How old are you? Really?"

"I'm twenty-six."

"Another lie."

"They put me on that case as a proving ground."

"I hope you get the promotion. What kind of self-respecting person sleeps her way through her case?"

"The horny kind."

Tanner stopped pumping, nonplussed. Californians.

"I don't regret any of that." Kyle smiled. "For God and country."

Tanner shook his head and pumped harder. "Okay, apology *acknowledged*. You're free to go ruin someone else's life." Tanner began remounting his rear wheel.

"Look, Tanner, I was hoping we might go have a cup of coffee and talk—"

"Talk!"

"Calm down! Your life isn't ruined. Just the opposite."

"What?"

"Your life was enriched by the experience, not ruined."

Tanner tossed his old tire on top of the Explorer. "Enriched, huh? Nice try."

"I'm sick and tired of watching you every time I get a free moment. Why the hell did you think I stopped you today?"

Tanner had felt something lurking every so often over the past several weeks. Beyond her eyes and body, Tanner felt a ghost of warmth from her. "Just go."

"What do you have to lose?"

"We're done. Get it?"

"Look, what's the harm? A cup of coffee."

"Good-bye, whoever you are."

Tanner fastened his pump on the frame and moved to take off, but Kyle caught his arm. "For Christsake! Can't you see I need to talk with you?"

Tanner looked at her grip on his arm as if it were dog shit.

Her eyes glassed up. "You think Jimmy's room just opened up at St. Pius on its own?"

Tanner had already done the math. He half expected that there was intervention. He sighed. "You shouldn't hang around me, Kyle." He looked down and made sure his audio connection was off. "I—I'm not who you think I am."

Her grip loosened, and he walked the bike around her car and targeted it on the road. "I deserved it."

"Wait, what the hell are you talking—"

He turned to face her. He started to speak and then stopped himself. Then, it came out. "Your buddy, the one with the circular saw."

Kyle nodded.

"He was right."

Kyle face pinched, confused.

"I knew the Iranian. Rholeni. The one in the picture on his phone."

"You don't have to make shit up—"

"Think! You never told me he was Iranian!"

Kyle froze mid-word. She aged in a split second.

Tanner dropped his head between his toned shoulders. "When I was in Spain, I received word that Jimmy's condition had set in. The critical time was at the onset. I didn't have insurance. I didn't have the money, no relatives to lean on …"

"This isn't happening." Kyle steadied herself with a hand on the car's side.

"They approached me to transport a tube's worth of whatever it was. They wanted me to carry it between two legs of the tour, hidden in the handle of my air pump. I thought no one would ever know. I doubt they would've."

Kyle turned away from him. Her eyes were locked in a dead stare on her right front tire. "Who'd you deliver—wait! *Would've?*"

"Although it didn't weigh anything and I was cranking in the race, that pump felt like a Volkswagen strapped to my frame. I didn't really know who these guys were, but I knew they weren't good. Around a turn in Valencia, I unstrapped that thing and chucked it off the peak into the depths of the Atlantic. Deep water, rough surf. Even if they saw me do it, they may not have been able to retrieve it."

"And?"

"And I've never seen them again."

"What was that?" She pointed at him.

"What?"

"You. You just looked at your leg."

"Is that against the law?"

A sad look came on her again. "They took out your leg, didn't they?"

Tanner looked at her and thought about trying to avoid it. "I awoke on my back at the bottom of a ravine. Riders were zipping by. Made no difference whether they saw me or not. I remember the blow to my side knocking me clear over the edge. I've never seen a bike break apart and spear a man, but there I was."

"Savage."

"Probably fair." Tanner began to walk his bike down the road.

"So that's what took you so long to re-engage. You didn't want to get back to riding. Who knows whether they would come back or not? Better to stay down, stay hidden."

Tanner kept walking. The wind ruffled his T-shirt.

She walked quickly to keep pace. "Rack never knew. And all along, that's why you stayed away from the sport. What changed your mind?"

He remained silent. Then, he stopped and turned to her. "I'm meeting Rack and Jimmy at the next town, Winters. You can have the authorities waiting. I'm sure Lieutenant Clay will take some sort of twisted pleasure in seeing me behind bars."

"This changes nothing."

Tanner mounted his bike and moved away, down the road.

Kerchow! A gunshot froze him stiff. Slowly, he turned.

Kyle stood with her pistol pointed straight up. "I need a cup of coffee. You're buying."

The birds had grown silent. Tanner wasn't sure what to do. "That way lies madness."

She smiled, and her shoulders eased. "It'll be my job to convince you otherwise." In the lowering sun, her smile shattered Tanner's cold front.

Tanner pinched his audio back to life. "Winters is six miles from here. This road'll take you."

She nodded, smiling deeper.

He clipped on his helmet. "If you can catch me, we'll see about that coffee."

She stood watching him. "I should warn you that there could be something communicable about this."

"Go!" Tanner leaped into gear. In his rearview, he watched Kyle sprint around the front of her car. Tanner felt a soaring roar in his body as he dipped into a turn around a patch of sugar maples.

"Watch your beats, T."

"Yeah, your beats, T!" Jimmy echoed.

Tanner drummed his pedals with fury.

"The ... hell with ... it. You watch ... the clock. I got ... my heart."

Chapter 52

Tanner's watch said 2:46 AM. He could hear the old inn creak in the stillness of night. Lucius slept at the foot of the barstool next to him. The dog's arms cradled its head. Mack limped across the large room. A fire flickered in the stone fireplace, lighting then darkening a pair of scotch glasses full of homemade banana rum. Tanner finished chewing his final bite of a Bunk sandwich, and Mack set the glasses down.

"Good sandwich." Tanner's mouth was half full.

"Haven't met the complainer yet."

"No?"

"Well, one." Mack grinned. "We let him out of the basement for a leashed walk every Friday morning."

Tanner sipped and swallowed the rum, savoring its sweet burn and cleansing rush. "Mmm. Hot ... and rebellious liquors."

Lucius licked his lips in his sleep.

Tanner set his glass down. "So."

"So."

"I saw the crypt."

Mack's wrinkled face held its place. "Which crypt would that be?"

"You know."

Mack slid off his stool. He shook his head, stepped over Lucius, and limped over to his favorite bookcase. "I'm afraid I don't."

"In the river. Bacon's crypt. I was there, eight months ago."

Mack massaged the cork out of its position. "Good for you, lad. But I'm not sure what in the devil you're talking about."

Tanner locked on Mack's eyes before he opened his mouth again. *Let's try this again.* "You were there." *The eyes, the eyes, do they give him away?*

Mack sipped his fat glass, and he sipped until it was empty. He stared at it for a moment after he was done as if it would talk to him to let him know how he did.

Tanner let out his line a little more. "The walls and ceiling were made of timber, big trunks. But the floor ... the floor was just dirt."

Mack focused on his next pour.

Tanner watched Mack's eyes for a reaction to his next statement. "You leave an unmistakable footprint."

Mack limped back over to the bar and topped off Tanner's glass. "Did you ever read *As You Like It?*"

Tanner looked down at Lucius. The fire hissed. Winds blew in from the ocean and encircled the inn. He studied his glass. "Yeah."

Mack corked the bottle. "I've lost count how many times I've read it."

"So, you like it." Tanner smiled at the turn.

"It's one of my favorites. Thing is, the first time was my favorite." He married the bottle with Tanner's glass. One of the candles on the far side of the bar puffed out.

"What's that have to do with the crypt? Why didn't you tell the world what you'd found? You'd be rich! No more Bunk sandwiches, no more pouring drinks. Maybe get a new hot water heater. The shower upstairs doesn't—"

"Can you imagine the thrill?" Renegade white hairs of his unkempt eyebrows infiltrated his eyes. He didn't elaborate on the question—he didn't need to.

Tanner wondered as he looked at the old man. He envisioned a living Dreavor, hunched over, his thin chest ballooning in and out as he recovered from his descent down the knotted rope, slowly rising to full height with his flashlight, a methodical inspection of the coffin, the dry walking sticks, the stripped, taxidermied birds, clouded beakers, his heart racing with fulfillment that perhaps lovers feel on their wedding day, that he, Tanner, felt winning the Hampton 500, his first national competition. Tanner realized he was smiling.

"They'll be others," Mack said. "And for them, it will be just as sweet."

And then Tanner's heart cracked. He sipped his rum. "It's gone."

The nests of Mack's eyebrows rose.

Tanner sighed. "There was a battle for his potions."

"His potions?"

"Some believe he was harboring the plague for eventual hometown revenge."

Mack sat on his stool to bear the news.

Tanner felt overwhelmingly guilty. "I was there, but they came with guns. The wall caved, and water washed the room into the river. I never even touched a thing. Well, maybe a walking stick."

Mack nodded. He stared at his empty glass. After what seemed like minutes, he spoke. "Such a shame. Truly."

Tanner's belly felt warm with rum. He took the bottle and topped off their glasses.

Mack raised his glass. "The king is dead."

Tanner clinked his with Mack's. "Long live the king." They rested on their stools a moment and let the caramel burn play with their taste buds. Tanner broke the silence. "What did his writings look like? Were they any different from today's versions?"

"What writings?" Mack pushed himself up from the stool and clapped his hands. Lucius sprang awake and followed at

Mack's heels as he walked to the door that led to his first-floor bedroom.

"The books. You know, the plays, Shakespeare's plays. His original drafts. Those stacks of papers on the shelves."

Mack turned at the entrance to the kitchen. "Oh, there weren't any plays in that crypt."

Tanner watched as Mack left. Lucius trailed, his tail waving goodnight.

'Til it be morrow.

The End

CPSIA information can be obtained at www.ICGtesting.com
Printed in the USA
LVOW080911061211

257985LV00005B/40/P